Also by Sue Lawrence:

The Green Lady
Down to the Sea
The Last Train
Fields of Blue Flax

The Unreliable
Death of
Lady
Grange

SUE LAWRENCE

CONTRABAND

Published by Contraband,
an imprint of Saraband,
3 Clairmont Gardens
Glasgow, G3 7LW
www.saraband.net

ISBN: 9781913393694

1 3 5 7 9 8 6 4 2

Printed and bound in Great Britain by Clays Ltd, Elcograf S.p.A.

For Jess, with love
It all started with a trip to the Hebrides...

SCOTLAND
1732

SHETLAND
ISLANDS

FAIR
ISLE

ORKNEY
ISLANDS

LEWIS

ST KILDA

*SOUND OF
HARRIS*

NORTH
UIST

MONACH
ISLES

SKYE

*LOCH
HOURN*

KINTORE

ABERDEEN

STIRLING-
SHIRE

EDINBURGH

"Forgive me father, for I have sinned."

Prologue

1732

"Mother is not in that coffin, you know."

"Don't be foolish, Mary; it's your mother's funeral. Of course she's in there. And a rather fine polished oak your father chose for the cask, too, I must say."

"Aunt Jean, Mama is not dead. She can't be. She wasn't ill; she never was."

"Keep your voice down, child."

"I am not a child," Mary hissed. "I am…"

There was a loud bang as the door flew open and four pall-bearers entered the room, heading for the coffin. They took up their places at each corner and turned towards the minister, who approached and rested a bony hand upon the wood, rubbing his long fingers up and down it, as if enhancing the sheen. He raised his head and surveyed the room.

There was Lord Grange, whose wife's burial was about to take place. Beside him stood Aunt Jean's husband, Lord Paterson, and the five surviving Grange children, all dressed in black, arrayed in descending order of age. Mary, the eldest daughter, stood beside her father's sister.

"I repeat, Aunt Jean, she was not ill. I can't remember a single time when she was ailing; she was always as strong as an ox. Besides, how is it possible that her waiting woman has also disappeared, vanished into the night?"

"She never was a reliable servant."

"Fannie and Aunt Margaret agree with me; Mother is not dead."

"Fannie is but a child. And really, Mary, as if your mother's sister would say otherwise," Lady Paterson harrumphed. "Hush now, the minister is about to speak."

The Reverend Elibank began, in his reedy, high-pitched voice, speaking to the family and the assembled great and good of Edinburgh, including several from the bench. There must have been some thirty people packed into Aunt Jean's parlour and they all turned to hear something of the remarkable life of Rachel, Lady Grange, who had sadly passed away so unexpectedly three days earlier. In a solemn tone, he told them how she was mourned by her beloved husband and her seven children, two of them from beyond the grave.

Lord Grange's face remained still, unfathomable. Yet as his eldest daughter peered under her bonnet at him, she thought she saw a flicker of something, a twitching around the lips on the otherwise impassive features.

The minister droned on about Rachel Grange's journey to heaven, guided by the angels and archangels on her ascent. His voice became louder as he described her arrival at the crystal-clear river of the water of life and how she then came before the throne of God. The crescendo continued as he intoned the lines from scriptures: "I am Alpha and Omega, the beginning and the end."

Mary nudged her sister, who had put her hands over her ears as the minister's voice peaked. He was exclaiming to the mourners – but particularly to the women and children, who of course would not be attending the burial at Greyfriars Kirk – "I am the first and the last". There was a sudden hush in the room as, finally, he closed his eyes as though in silent prayer to end his homily. Slowly, as if for dramatic effect, he opened his eyes and bent over in a deep bow towards Lord Grange. He then nodded to the pall-bearers, who raised the coffin upon their shoulders, as he squeezed his willowy body through the throng of people, heading for the door.

Everyone watched the coffin shudder a little as it settled on the four pairs of shoulders; it tilted over at the head end, where the shortest bearer raised one shoulder high to try to regain his balance. He turned and nodded to the assembled men and they trudged towards the door.

Lord Grange lifted the hat that he had been holding at his side and leant over to his sister. "We shall return within the hour, Jean. Be sure the table is laden – and be especially generous with the wine and brandy."

"We've discussed this, James. Cook has excelled herself. As well as the roast meats, there are plum cakes and sweetmeats in abundance. The stoups are already filled to the brim with claret, brandy and ale; there's also tobacco aplenty. Now, be off and don't upset yourself further, dear brother."

The man kissed his sister's cheek, patted his youngest children on their heads then glanced over at his friend Simon, whose ruddy cheeks and bulbous nose were already flushed with claret.

Mary stared at her father as the two men exchanged glances, hoping for some token of sympathy from the bereaved man to her, his eldest daughter; but she saw only the glimmer of a smile around his lips as he acknowledged his fellow mourners then turned away, striding towards the door, where he placed his hat firmly on his head as he prepared to face the January chill.

Part One

7

Part One

Chapter 1

Rachel

I have at last managed to secure some rudimentary writing paper, a quill and ink. And so I write down my account to dispatch with a kindly envoy, in the vain hope that my husband, Lord Grange, once advised of my pitiful circumstances, might set about arranging my repatriation to civilised society. If not, perhaps one of his eminent colleagues on the bench in Edinburgh might concern themselves, but that is unlikely. Or my adoring children? Admittedly, some are too young, but Charles is now twenty-three and surely able to plead on his mother's behalf once he hears news of me, although he is of course busy with his new position at the Court of Session. And so, my only hope is that Mary, though a mere girl, might be permitted to intercede on my behalf through her husband the Earl. My Angel must be so distraught.

I am ill and weary and exceedingly disquieted living here in this godforsaken place, with no one for company but a glaikit serving wench. The only sound, apart from the roaring of the wind and the crashing of the waves, is the squawk of the seabirds: the purring puffins, the screeching guillemots, the harsh, croaking solan geese.

The inhabitants speak in their still largely indecipherable tongue and I can expend only so much energy using signs and gestures. It is tiresome and monotonous, but not as cruel as the means by which I arrived in this barbaric place. And now

I abide here, the only Lady so far from civilisation and my beloved family.

But I am jumping ahead. I ought to begin this tale in 1708 when I was but eighteen years old. I had travelled from Edinburgh down the coast into East Lothian one unusually warm day in early May. I was with my mother and sister and we were to visit the splendid grounds of Preston House, which were open to the public every Saturday afternoon. The three of us strolled along the shaded alleys between the tall hedges of elder and briar to the high stone walls that had obviously been built to protect the estate from the fierce winds of the River Forth; that day there was nothing but a balmy breeze. From there we entered the maze and, as I stopped to admire some trailing ivy, I let my mother and sister continue on. I was drawn towards a glorious aroma emanating from the hedgerow and I leant in to inhale the scent of honeysuckle, shutting my eyes as I did so. On opening them, I noticed a tall young gentleman at my side. I looked around but we were completely alone. The man inclined his head and addressed me in a courteous manner, asking if I should like to take a walk with him.

"Sir, I can't possible agree to your request, it would be unseemly. I don't know who you are."

With this, a smile flickered on his full red lips and he inclined his head.

"I am James Erskine, proprietor of Preston House."

I was taken aback at how young he looked, as I recalled some talk about this very man in the coach earlier. Mama and my sister Margaret had been arguing over the gossip that was currently rife throughout Edinburgh, about the degeneracy and carousing of James Erskine, also known as Lord Grange.

Margaret had been told about it by her friends, the Dalrymple sisters; Mama hushed this talk as nonsense and insisted he was a good man, intelligent and, most importantly, of noble stock.

As I studied his face, I realised that Mama had been correct and Margaret's claims must be untrue: his blue-grey eyes looked so innocent, those boy-like freckles on his full cheeks suggested naivety, something childlike.

"I should like that very much, Sir," I said, smiling, and he gave me his arm.

We emerged from the maze and he led me along a stone wall with a bower in it. We sat down there and he turned to point over towards the wide river.

"That island in the Forth over there is the Isle of May. It has been a place of pilgrimage for centuries; people used to come from far and wide to drink the water of the well. Many poor folk with terrible ailments were cured. God works in wonderful ways, don't you agree?"

I nodded.

"If I hadn't decided to study law and become a judge, I should like to have trained as a minister of religion," he told me as he continued to gaze over at the island.

I swallowed. My handsome companion not only owned this whole estate, he was a man of high intellect who was about to become a judge, as well as being a devout, religious person.

"I don't yet know your name," he said, taking my hand from my lap.

This was untoward and I found my heart begin to beat faster. As I turned to face him, the plaid around my shoulder slipped a little and I saw him glance down at the lace around my bodice. Thankfully I was wearing my family's fine Belgian lace.

"I am Rachel Chiesley, Sir," I whispered, awaiting the usual reaction from anyone acquainted with both Edinburgh and the law on hearing my family's name. But there was no such response. Instead, he smiled and touched my face with his other hand. He was leaning in towards me and my eyes were opening wide when I heard them.

"Rachel, Rachel, where are you?"

I leapt up and pulled my plaid tight around my shoulders.

"Here, Mama," I cried and glanced at the young man, who had also arisen.

They rushed towards me and James Erskine bowed deeply then introduced himself.

"Ladies," he said, smiling, "I hope you are enjoying the grounds of my estate. Perhaps you will permit me to show you the hothouse and the walled garden?"

Mama looked taken aback but managed to stutter a reply. "Thank you, we should like that very much."

As he took Mama's arm and guided her back along the terraced wall, past the doocot and towards the back of the house, Margaret and I followed on behind. My sister tugged at my elbow and leant in close. "Does he know who we are?" she hissed.

I found myself beaming from ear to ear. "I told him who I was, Margaret, and he didn't look troubled at all."

⌒ ⌒

There followed the most ardent, albeit swift courtship. James took me to two grand parties, the first of which I shall never forget, at Corstorphine House, where we danced our first minuet. I had always adored dancing, but this was different. We had partaken of supper and punch and as the music struck up once again, he took my hand and guided me to the dance floor. I believe this was the moment we both fell madly in love.

Mama could not, obviously, be there, since Edinburgh society was slow to forgive and forget, so James' sister Jean was my companion that evening. I must admit I found her rather haughty and unfriendly, not the kindly soulmate I had hoped to spend the soiree with. It was as if she knew perfectly well about the Chiesley family history, even if her brother seemed oblivious to the facts, and she was making it all too apparent that she thought me unworthy of her noble brother. She seemed to know many other ladies and they too shunned me; I noticed two lean behind their fans and nod in my direction. I took a deep breath, raised my head high and ignored them; I had had six years of rejection and I would not give up on happiness now.

But then, when we danced, everything was put to rights. He gazed into my eyes with such fiery passion that I was thankful the beat of the music meant I had to swing away from him, as I found my face redden with delight. Holding his hand was also an unexpected joy; I had been used to either my brothers' grimy, fidgety hands or the sweaty hands of my uncles. And the man Jean had forced me to dance with before James had hands so greasy, it was as if he had washed them in a basin of fatty mutton broth. But James' hands were silky, soft and cool; I will never forget his touch. I quivered all over when, at the end of the dance, he held both my hands and raised them to his lips. His eyes burned with fervour and mine opened wide as I stood transfixed. Returning to my seat, trembling, I ignored Jean's scornful scowl and took a long draught of punch, which made my fluttering heart steady once more.

Our second outing was to a gathering at the Assembly Rooms in the West Bow and thankfully his sister was not in attendance. We danced and talked to other grand people of the city as if we were already a married couple.

This time I noticed no one appeared to be in any way disdainful when he introduced me; but I did detect a difference in the way he pronounced my surname. He uttered it as if it were spelt Chessle, not Chiesley. Perhaps that was the reason I was addressed as an equal at all times; but no matter, it suited me well.

On the way home, he leant over to me in his carriage as we left the Assembly Rooms and headed up over the cobbles towards my home. His hand lifted the plaid a little off my shoulder and he peered through the dark to admire my gown once more. His breath smelt sweetly of claret and punch as he whispered to me that he wished he could have spoken to my father, but instead he would speak to my uncle, Aunt Margaret's husband John, for my hand in marriage. It was all so romantic and when he touched the silk around my neckline, brushing a finger over my bosom, I felt that this was not improper, for I would soon be betrothed to James Erskine, Lord Grange, and without delay. And to think it all began at Preston House among the hedges of elder and the mazes and labyrinths of one of the finest gardens in Scotland. And soon it would all be mine.

Chapter 2

Rachel

The preparations for our wedding were swift. I had only met James on that auspicious day early in May, but a mere five months later, I was upstairs at Preston House with Mama, who was attempting to force my voluptuous body into the pale blue, silk gown my cousin Marie had worn a few months earlier. She did not care that the stomacher – something she admitted was more often worn by older women like herself – was causing me agony. The stiff panel dug into my stomach and I found it difficult to breathe. But, as she and Margaret kept reminding me, it was essential for a bride to look radiant on her wedding day; and radiance seemed to somehow include a slim waist, which I had never owned.

The sacrament was held at Prestonpans kirk and led by the Reverend Elibank, a pious man who was already a confidant to James, with whom he discussed many spiritual matters. As I walked up the aisle towards the communion table in the kirk that glorious day in early October, I saw a shaft of sunlight fall upon James, resplendent in his stockings, silk shirt and breeches adorned with silver buttons. I looked down at his feet and noticed his shoes had wonderfully shiny buckles that sparkled in the sunlight. And I felt such love for this man who would soon be my husband; I was blessed to be marrying such a handsome, noble creature. Our eyes met and I could not help but smile at the sight of a face – and body – I now knew so well. His expression, though, was not one of undying ardour that I had become used to. Indeed, it was difficult to read what he was thinking, for he did not smile; as a religious man he probably thought that to do so would be improper in the church. But as the ceremony proceeded, I also became aware of a spiritual presence and felt that our relationship, which seemed to be already blessed, was reaching new peaks. As the Reverend Doctor continued and James closed his eyes tight while mumbling in prayer, I was reminded that I was marrying not only a law lord, but also a devout person.

The wedding breakfast at Preston House was splendid and Mama was thrilled with the buffet tables, laden with potted pigeons, boiled beef, roast hens, salmon, hare, fricassees and ragouts. The fine sauces to accompany the meats and fish were French style, enriched with butter. James' brother, the Earl, had brought his cook to Preston House kitchen to oversee the preparations, and his fancy accompaniments were the talk of all the guests; he had trained not only in Paris but also at the royal court. There were so many fine sweet things too – flummeries and fools flavoured with sack and mace, and trifles infused with rosewater, all strewn with dainty French comfits.

We were so happy that day and indeed every day and night thereafter for the first glorious couple of months, especially when it became common knowledge that I was with child; the joy spread throughout the entire household. According to James' sister Jean, this boy – for surely I was carrying a boy – would be the first to be born at Preston House for over two decades. She pressed upon me how great this honour was.

Then one misty, grey morning, I awoke to find blood on the sheets. And the pain that ensued was horrific. My maid Annie rushed off to fetch James, who bellowed at Old Peter to send the carriage to Edinburgh for the physician. Even through my anguish, I was able to shout to my husband that I did not need the family doctor from the city, but a local medical man from nearby; time was surely not on my side. But he insisted and, as the pains continued and still no doctor arrived, I fell into some sort of stupor. When I awoke, both Annie and my mother were at my bedside, anxious looks on their faces. I did not even have to ask them what had happened.

When James eventually strode into the room, he did not even look at me; all he demanded to know was if it had been a male. I stared at my husband in disbelief and bellowed out some profanity, but Mama put her finger to my lips and swept my hair up over my sweaty brow, muttering some niceties to James as if excusing me. This after what I had just been through? I yanked my hand away from hers and turned instead to Annie who, as ever, knew just what I required to steady my nerves. She handed me my glass.

For some time my feelings for him were altered; he seemed dispassionate and cold. But as Mama kept insisting, I had made such a good match, I was lucky he wanted me and I must make the best of things.

And so, with him so eager to produce an heir, thankfully I gave birth to our first son, Charlie, on the twenty-seventh of October the following year. Our family would grow even more over the next few years. And what a family we were to become, well loved and respected throughout the county. I admit, I was at my happiest in those early days when Lord and Lady Grange were the talk of the town – and for once, given what my family had suffered, being spoken about in public for all the right reasons.

Chapter 3

Annie

I had never heard a lady use language like that before. Her mother looked horrified, but said nothing, always eager as she was to placate His Lordship. He too looked shocked, but instead of comforting his wife – she who had just been through such an ordeal – he swore back at her. I scraped back my chair to leave the room, thinking I should not be there, when My Lady turned to me and gestured towards the claret, so I refilled her glass and she began to regain her composure as he trudged towards the door.

As I watched her sip, I noticed her expression change from ghastly to calm, just like those mornings when she awakes gasping for air, so distraught. But then I pour her morning draught and she begins to breathe normally as she tells me of her nightmares. The bad dreams are always about her father. There was a heavy silence in the room as I kept thinking about what Lord Grange had just said – or rather, not said. He had not spoken to his wife at all; he had not even looked at her. He had merely asked her mother if it had been a boy or a girl. When she told him she had no idea, perhaps the doctor was the one to ask, he harrumphed and motioned to me to tidy up the mess of old blood-stained bedclothes that still lay in a pile on the floor.

He then moved the frame of a portrait on the wall a fraction to make it straight; he was always a perjink, but he was getting worse. He flung open the door and slammed it behind him.

He had not even asked how My Lady was feeling. She looked terrible, so pale and wan, but he seemed to care only about the lost baby. When she started sobbing, her mother tried to comfort her, but she was having none of it.

"I despair, Mama. You saw what just happened. He is no longer interested in me."

"Dear child, what you have just been through is horrid. But these things happen. You will be with child again very soon and that will make him happy. Remember, you must keep him satisfied, that is your role as a wife. And when he has his heir, he will be glad once more."

"I am not just his wife, Mama. What about me? Rachel Chiesley?"

"Sssh, remember only I and your brothers now bear the burden of our shameful family name. You and your sister thankfully take your husbands' names. Now lie back down on the pillow and get some rest."

My Lady turned away from her towards me and nodded at the bedside table. I lifted the decanter and poured her another glass of claret, which she took in trembling hands. She downed it in one then reached out her glass for more.

I had heard talk in the kitchen before the wedding about the Chiesley family scandal, but did not choose to believe the gossip about her father's madness and how she might have inherited it. Admittedly, she sometimes flew into rages, but only if provoked.

There was that time the week before the incident when she was taking breakfast in her bedroom and he knocked on the door then entered. After his usual straightening of items on her dressing table and checking the pictures were exactly in place on the walls, he went towards the bed, took her hand and raised it to his lips. I shuffled a little on my feet, uncomfortable to be witnessing such an unexpected display of affection.

"My dear Rachel, I must be off to London for a few days.

I do hope you have all you might need during my absence? I have asked your mother to come and stay. Be sure she does not go to the village in case the name Chiesley is heard."

He kissed her fingertips once more then lowered her arm gently. His smile disappeared at once as he stared at her other pale white hand lying on the bedclothes.

"I have told you before about wearing this ring!" he shouted. "Take it off. At once!"

She tucked her hand under her other arm. "I cannot, James, my fingers have swollen."

This was true; I had helped her try to pull off the ring the night before, without success. He yanked her hand out and tried to pull the ring off, but it was indeed stuck. The finger looked red and sore.

"You're hurting me, James, please stop."

He stomped his foot then turned on his heel. "I'll have Old Peter make up an oily solution so it can slide off your finger. I will not have that man's ring in my house. Do you hear me?"

"That man, as you call him, was my father," she yelled, then breathed heavily. She began to sniffle, then wiped her nose, hissing, "I am not your servant, James. I am my own woman, you know." She thrust her chin forward and glowered at him as her voice grew louder. "And always will be." She was yelling even louder now. "Don't you forget it!"

I sneaked a sideways glance at her; she had a rather unhinged look about her. I crouched down as she picked up the book on her bedside table and flung it at him.

He ducked then shook his head. "I think not, My Lady. This is my house and you are mine. For ever, God help me."

And, I am sure, as he turned around to head for the door, that I saw him crossing himself, something I had not seen since my granny converted. But it must have been the dim light; no devout man of the kirk like him would make such a papist token, surely?

Chapter 4

James

She held a pistol to my head. I had no choice; I repeat, no choice but to marry her. I had no inkling before I agreed to this marriage that she was deranged. I had simply fallen desperately in love; or rather, let me be frank, in lust. But the madness soon became evident; well, look at her family, for God's sake. Her father brought shame and dishonour to the Chiesley name, not only in Edinburgh, but all over Scotland, as word spread. Everyone knew the family was tainted, but I had elected, in my besotted, prenuptial state, to ignore all the talk. However, as I realised more fully what a disgrace he had been and the attendant implications for his daughter, who was obviously marred by it, my feelings for her began to cool. As a religious man, I became aware of how evil he had been, how he could surely never be forgiven for his transgressions. And it soon became obvious that the daughter had also inherited his madness and his temper.

Admittedly she was only twelve years old at the time of the scandal, but she remembered it well and still had never denounced him. Can you imagine? Ah, but you do not yet know the crime; allow me to explain what evil act he committed.

John Chiesley of Dalry and his wife, Rachel's mother Margaret, did not enjoy a happy marriage and so, during a legal separation, when Margaret insisted on alimony for herself and their children, it went to court. The Lord President in the

Court of Session, Sir George Lockhart of Carnwath, found against the husband and awarded the wife some ninety-five Scots pounds per annum. Chiesley was enraged and threatened the judge in that very court of law and before the jury that he would not let matters lie.

This was not, of course, the first time the Lord President had been intimidated in this way and so he dismissed the ravings of a thwarted man and continued life as normal. This turned out to be a grave error as on Easter Sunday 1702, he was murdered in cold blood in front of witnesses in the High Street, the busiest street in the city. They say Chiesley had followed Sir George the day before to ascertain where his house was; the crime was planned to the minute.

After leaving the kirk service that day at St Giles, Sir George headed towards Hope's Close, which led to the stair up to his townhouse. He was accompanied by his two brothers and, as they continued to discuss the sermon, they turned off the High Street into the entrance to the close. Here they encountered a gentleman and, once they realised who it was standing there, they greeted each other cordially. Chiesley saluted Sir George and his brothers as if all was well. The three men bade him farewell then, as they turned, Chiesley removed the pistol he had hidden within the wide cuffs of his coat and fired straight into the Lord President's back. Sir George collapsed and died immediately in his brothers' arms.

Indeed, I know, such an egregious act he committed, such cold-heartedness. To murder someone is evil enough, but in broad daylight and having just passed the time of day with him. And, worst of all, this was on the Sabbath. He was immediately apprehended and his trial followed within days. The jury consisted of ten landed gentlemen and five city merchants. Chiesley confessed to the murder, yet he repeated his claim to the court that the deceased had handed him an unjust ruling. This of course had no bearing on the verdict, which meant that a mere four days after he had committed the act, he was punished.

Taken from the prison at the Tolbooth, he was dragged on a wooden sled along the High Street. On the way he was jeered by the many city dwellers who had come out from their homes to taunt the prisoner in the usual boisterous manner of braying crowds.

Once at Mercat Cross, he was pulled from the sled, brought to kneel, and his right arm placed on a chair. As the crowds jostled and elbowed past their neighbours to see, the right hand was cut off. Then he was raised up onto a gibbet, the severed wrist dripping profusely with blood, and hanged for all to see. The crowds were silent for the short time it took his body to stop quivering, then a jubilant roar was heard. The pistol he had used to fire the fatal shot was then hooked around his broken neck on a chain and the body was put on display, first in Edinburgh, before being taken to Leith in the north. His right hand, the one that had fired the pistol, was thrust onto one of the spikes of the railings of the gate at the West Port. It is said the Chiesley family collected the body as soon as they were allowed and buried him. My mother-in-law apparently took her children, including her two daughters aged just twelve and fourteen, with her when they removed a handless bloodied corpse in the middle of the night, with the assistance of her brother. They were permitted to bury him – reunited with his hand – in hallowed ground; God knows why. But what became of the pistol was never discovered.

I know, I am sorry, it is all so vile and ungodly, but what he underwent was surely right and proper retribution for his sins. So, can you understand why I had no choice but to marry his deranged daughter? When she put a pistol to my head and demanded that I marry her for some specious reason, what could I do but agree; she had me swear on my Bible and so I had no choice. It was the start of my marriage to Rachel Chiesley, youngest daughter of that notorious family of vengeful, deranged sinners.

Chapter 5

Rachel

He brought the news to me himself at Preston House. As I lay in bed nursing My Angel, little Mary, he bounded into the room.

"It's official, Rachel. I am now Lord Justice Clerk of Scotland. They announced it in the Court of Session yesterday evening." He beamed and stood there, head tilted to one side, waiting. Even though his smug expression did not become him, I knew some fulsome praise was required.

"Why, that's worthy of a celebration, James. What excellent news on this miserable, dreich day." I looked up from my daughter, who was sucking noisily at my breast, and stared at him. His pallor was dreadful; he was as grey as the haar outside the bedroom window.

"But I see from your haggard looks that you've already celebrated in style with your Edinburgh cronies."

"There was perhaps an ale or two consumed at Clerihugh's Tavern."

"And many a flagon of claret too, I'll wager." I could not help myself.

"Nonsense. I consume no more claret than you do."

I plucked the baby off my nipple and jerked myself up onto my elbow. "How dare you, James! You know the doctor says it is good for my milk."

He drew nearer and looked down at Mary, who was beginning to girn.

"Three glasses at dinner then the same at supper? I am not convinced he means that amount."

"That is a…"

"Silence! Sometimes you forget your place, Rachel. You are living in all this splendour solely because of your husband."

"Splendour? Stuck down here in this draughty house with ancient furnishings and incompetent servants; any spare money you insist on spending on some folly for your famous garden. And while the children and I suffer here in this frigid place, you meanwhile live the gay life of a wealthy bachelor up in Edinburgh and, all too often, London."

"You must remember your duty as a wife is to obey, not to argue incessantly."

He strode to my dressing table and rearranged the disarray on there as usual. "Ensure your girl organises your belongings better. Your untidiness appalls me!"

As my sister is always telling me, he is such a fusser and fiddler; it is beginning to get on my nerves.

He coughed, a sign he wanted to change the subject. "I've been thinking about this child." He waved his hand over Mary's head. "I have decided you will acquire a wet nurse as we did before. I've had enough of pandering to your peccadilloes. No other wife of your standing feeds her own child like this. It's barbaric – only the peasants in the field or the poor of the city suckle their own young. You are to desist at once. I am about to charge Peter with rehiring that woman in the village." He turned to go just as I lifted the baby to nuzzle at my other breast.

"I won't have it, James. I am the baby's mother, I am the one who…"

He strode back with that swagger I had come to know. He leant over me, his breath heavy with stale claret.

"You will do as I command." He straightened up and gazed at my exposed breast. "Besides, we have now but two children.

I need more sons and with you insisting on feeding, another confinement is unlikely to happen."

"You forget Little John and the two I lost before they even emerged from the womb, James; how can you be so heartless? They are all my beloved babies."

"You can hardly count miscarriages as babies, Rachel. Death is another thing." He leant over and stroked the nape of Mary's neck and I remembered his mother's letters of condolences addressed to James, saying how sorry she was that "poor Rachel has miscarried again". She was so sorry for his loss. His loss? Aye, well that summed up his entire family. To them, all of them, I was but a womb, ripe to produce heirs for James, Lord Grange, as my primary duty in life.

I watched him smile at My Angel then turn and saunter over towards the door.

"I do hope Cook has some of that goat's whey to hand. I feel its medicinal qualities will settle the stomach before my morning draught of ale. For breakfast, I fancy Cook's fine barley cakes and some of the meat from last night." He licked his lips. "What roast did you have yesterday?"

"Hens, we had roast hen."

He nodded. "That will have to do then."

He pulled the door open before turning round and inclining his head at me as if taking leave of a fellow judge, not his wife.

As he turned back round, I stared at the back of his head; something about his coiffure had been troubling me. On realising what it was, I burst out laughing and pointed at his head. "James, your wig's on back to front; I thought it looked odd. You look more like a court jester than Lord Justice Clerk."

He slammed the door so hard the carafe of claret on my bedside table, which was full to the brim, shuddered. Some droplets of red spilled over the top of my beaker, so I lifted it to my lips and drank deep. I replaced the cup on the side and bent over my baby's head, placing a kiss on her soft, downy forehead. He would not get away with this hare-brained notion of his that a mother should not suckle her child. I'd agreed to it before, but it had never felt right – and it had had dire consequences. I reached once more for my wine, sank back against the pillow and shut my eyes as I listened to the peaceful sounds of sucking and snuffling.

Chapter 6

Rachel

I could not bear to see the sunlight. I wanted everything to be grey and gloomy that winter's day some three years later. For that is how I felt when another of my dear children died; my grief was insurmountable. The first tragedy was when my second-born, John, passed away of a fever that had tormented him for his short little life; he never fully recovered from spending his first six months in that hovel where the wet nurse lived. I was not allowed to visit him there, although one day I had felt so passionately that I simply must see my baby that I stole down there when James was in the city. I had to bribe the maid with those sweetmeats she was addicted to – the rose-water tablets in particular – in order to extract from her the details of where the wet nurse lived in the village.

I shall never forget the damp, the dark and the foul smell in that tiny cottage. Since I arrived unannounced, the woman opened the door scowling. My eyes were drawn from her glowering face down to her bulbous breasts hanging out over her grubby smock. She looked as shocked as I did and, as she tried to curtsey, I looked over her dwarf-like figure to see where my John was, for I could hear a baby crying and it was surely mine. She ran over to grab him from a rickety wooden cradle by the fire and wrapped him in a filthy blanket. He was soiled and his face was red. I found I had to sit down to recover from the shock. The woman pressed his little face to her sweaty, grimy breast and sat down beside me on a low stool. Her stench was so overpowering, I had to suppress the urge to gag as I gazed at his little red face, sucking away, milk dribbling down his chin.

"I was just away to get him washed, My Lady. If I'd known you were coming, I'd have cleaned him up a bit. He's doing fine, just fine. Growing well. Good for a six-month-old. Bigger than my own wee one over there."

I looked over the fug from the smoking fire to where she pointed and saw another baby lying on the floor, wrapped in a scant blanket.

Eventually the power of speech returned to me.

"The minute my child is able to be weaned, he shall be leaving here. You will be paid as agreed, but you shall not, I repeat, not, be suckling my next one." I placed both hands over my belly. "When can he start on the arrowroot?"

"Well, My Lady, he could start soon, but he'll be needing mother's milk too for a while so…"

"Nonsense. I shall have him collected tomorrow and that will be the end of it."

I stroked his grubby little cheeks and felt tears stream down my own.

And so, was it surprising that, given that vile start to his life, poor little John died of a feverish cough and the ague before he was two years old? He kept trying to battle on, with his rattling little chest, but he never recovered from his early months in that damp, smoky hovel.

And how was my husband at that time? Full of sympathy and remorse at insisting on sending our babies out to nurse? Not at all. He simply told me to get on with it and stop making a fuss. There were plenty more children to be had, he would say.

Our first son Charlie was so strong and robust, he could have been left outside in a field of snow all night and he would have survived. And so, I never doubted the woman's word when she told me of her living circumstances, how warm and clean they were. Charlie was fine after his first year there, why not my next babe? I had had no opportunity to see exactly where the wet nurse lived. I was always told that the baby was being reared in a cosy, comfortable cottage and that the woman did her job for the love of the babies, not just for the money, which was of course not inconsiderable from people of our standing.

When Mary was due, I began to petition James. I tried to insist I suckle her myself, which I knew would be such a joy and a pleasure. At first he refused, of course. But, with the horrid picture etched forever in my mind's eye of that dank hovel, I managed to persuade him. Though I admit it meant I had to undergo a night of passion that, God forgive me for ignoring my wifely obligations, I really could have done without, since I was so close to my confinement. But he gave me a chance, provided none of our acquaintances knew. And this of course worked well until that morning when he stormed into my bedroom with his risible back-to-front wig. Fortunately, Mary too was a strong little cherub and so survived the wet nurse she was sent to at two months.

And so, to the second death of one of my precious little ones, which I can hardly bear to write about. I have to shut my eyes tight as I recall that dear little Meggie, born but fourteen months after My Angel Mary, lived until she was barely six months old before being taken by smallpox. And all because he had insisted once more on her going to that same wet nurse who had, unbeknown to me, taken in babies from the village whose houses were rife with the pox. As ever, his reasoning was simply that she was cheap. Unimaginable. I could not bear to think of the sight of the little mite, all red and covered with hideous blisters, even after the physician had prescribed everything from his special tinctures to leeches. She died, again a result of a filthy start to life.

Fortunately, James at last saw sense, although I failed to understand or forgive him for the fact it had to take two of our babies dying first. And so, when Jamie came along, followed soon afterwards by Fannie, then William, a different wet nurse was brought at each confinement from the city to live in Preston House. Each had a bed in the nursery, so it was always clean and warm and was not too far from the kitchen and the servants' quarters, but thankfully, as far as James was concerned, nowhere near our chambers.

James, of course, complained every single time he saw the babies – which was only once a week on the Sabbath, when he remembered his previous calling to the Church and the attendant charity embedded within his faith. He moaned about how much money it was costing him to have these wet nurses stay with us. Of course, he understood by then how essential it was for our children, but he would never admit it. All of the last children born were healthy, the women just getting on and doing the job without poisoning them with filth and disease.

Having the wet nurses live with us meant that my nursing duties with the babies were relinquished, which of course made me sad, but there were inevitably unexpected benefits. Even though he insisted I be confined to the country and not permitted to venture into Edinburgh, I would occasionally be required to accompany His Lordship for some grand occasion. Then I did my utmost to play the beautiful, loyal wife, dressed in my finest blue silk gown with lemon-coloured, Persian lining and my best Glasgow chequered plaid, walking by his side.

Little did he know that when he was away on one of his many jaunts down to London, he was unable to prevent me doing the things he could not see. The servants knew only that I was visiting my critically ill mother or my sister's new baby. My God, how dim they were; my mother must have nearly died several times and Margaret must have been delivered of at least fifteen babies. Only my loyal Annie knew the truth. And so, I had secret outings to the city, where I felt able to breathe, even though admittedly the air in Edinburgh was often foul. The country did little for me and living there was a constant reminder of my "duty" as a wife, which was to reproduce. Aye well, I too was entitled to a life, especially after all I had suffered; all those years since I was twelve years old, the nightmares about my father and the memory of that hideous night when we had to witness his limp, dead body and now the memories of my dead babies. Sometimes it was all a little too much to bear.

Chapter 7

Rachel

I turned around to gaze at the sea on this fine summer's morning and smiled. Would that every dawn in the country were this magnificent. The sun was already glinting on the water, which reflected the azure blue of the cloudless sky. The colour reminded me of the lapis lazuli stone in my mourning ring.

This was the ring that remained hidden at the bottom of my jewellery box most days, for I was not permitted to wear this legacy from my father's family; we were never allowed to mention him.

I remember one day at tea, Fannie asking my mother where Grandfather was and before she even had a chance to finish the scone in her mouth to start on the lie she'd been taught to pronounce, James quipped, "Dead. And you children will not mention his name again, ever."

Poor little Fannie was only eight at the time and so alarmed was she by the severity of her father's tone, she burst into tears and ran from the table to the nursery at once. She was always such a sensitive little soul. I think that is why she turned so much to religion and studying her Bible all day as she does now.

"I told you she was too young to join us at tea," James had harrumphed as he reached for the jug of wine. He'd proceeded to fill his glass to the brim, even though he could clearly see mine was already empty.

Now, as Annie handed my bags to the coachman, I stepped into the carriage and pulled my worsted gown down over my twilted petticoat. She sat down with a thump beside me and pulled the blind downwards.

"Open the blind, will you? I want to see daylight. I've had enough gloom already." She raised the screen and sat staring out, in silence. She knew better than to engage me in conversation early in the morning.

I was therefore able to mull over the news freshly arrived from the Earl of Kintore the day before. This was surely the most auspicious of days; the date of the twenty-first of August 1729 will remain with me forever. The envoy from Inverness-shire arrived to meet James, who then relayed the joyful news that Mary would wed in a year's time, on her sixteenth birthday. So, of course I had to discuss new ensembles with my dressmaker in the city, both for her and of course for me. A countess' mother had to be dressed in finery at all times. Mary was at first not enamoured of the prospect of marrying someone over twice her age, but I managed to placate her so much that she is now happy as a bird. I felt I should also dispense some maternal advice.

"Mary, there are certain duties you must assume as a wife, but then, once your wifely obligations in bed have taken place and you've produced heirs for the Earl, you can simply enjoy being a countess with all of its trappings and leave him and his urges to mistresses or courtesans."

Mary's eyes opened wide, but I continued, "And think of the wealth you will have and that splendid castle at your command. You will be so unlike your poor mama, My Angel, who is always having to scrimp and save, even though ours is a substantial enough house."

I could hardly believe I was repeating the trope that a wife must look away when a husband took a mistress, but I said only what my mother had said to me and hers before her.

But even as I uttered the words, I reminded myself that if my James ever went elsewhere for his needs, I would not let the matter rest. Not at all. The ire of the Chiesleys would see to it.

Eventually, we came to Edinburgh and stopped halfway down the High Street, where I alighted and waited for Annie to fetch my bags. As I watched her, it occurred to me once more how much taller she was than our other servants, certainly the cook and that maid she shared a room with, both of whom were half her size.

She was as tall as I was and indeed if her auburn hair were ever coiffed, it could be almost as lustrous as mine. Her nose too was quite comely, though of course, as James used to tell me years ago, in those heady days of our courtship, not even Helen of Troy could have had such a pretty nose as mine.

I hobbled along, over the uneven cobbles, trying to avoid the filth that was strewn all around. My silk slippers were perhaps not the most suitable footwear, but I most certainly was not going to look like a peasant with those clogs some ladies chose to don when outside, to protect their shoes.

I turned around at the cry of a street-seller pushing a barrow; by the smell of her, she was selling cockles and whelks, things I have always loved, but James constantly repeated how unseemly it was for a lady to eat in the street. He, of course, can buy oysters or hot pies from street vendors and eat them with relish, standing outside or indeed anywhere he likes, for he is a gentleman.

I looked up the High Street towards the magnificent kirk of St Giles. As usual, there were many groups of beggars around it. I decided I must get Annie to fetch some of my old clothes – and the children's – from Preston House on our next visit and give them to the poor in the city. I continued on down over the cobbles, taking in the bustle of the street and the smell of those wonderful, hot mutton pies and wondering what treat Mistress Wilson might serve for luncheon.

Finally, she caught up with me with the bags and we turned down into the entrance to Niddry's Wynd. We passed the filthy urchins playing on the stone steps in bare feet and I looked up to see the women hanging out their washing on the lines swung across the narrow close. It was a fact of Edinburgh life that the poor lived cheek by jowl with the wealthy, down the closes and wynds of the city. They had the hovels on the top floors, we had the fine first-floor residences with our servants. That is a reason many of our acquaintances preferred to remain in the country, since within their estates they did not have to come across the malodorous poor, apart from in the kirk on the Sabbath.

For me, it was different; I tried to instill it into my children that this "social intimacy", as I called it, was a reminder that it was God-given good fortune that we led the privileged lives we did and that one should be as decent to the poor as possible – though sometimes the stench of them was a little too much to bear.

I had decided not to send word ahead of our arrival, so I stopped on the doorstep to pull out the solid brass key to the house. There were one or two things I needed to check out and had determined that an unexpected visit would be best. The servants always had beds ready, often for any of James' cronies who happened to require lodgings late at night after one of his many long days at the bench. I did not mind at all; how could I when I was stuck in the country with his children?

But there was one man to whom I objected fervently. Simon Fraser, not a law lord like the others, was a vile and conniving Highland chief, also known as Lord Lovat; he was a bad influence on my husband. He was one of the reasons I wanted to make this unanticipated call at our Edinburgh residence; I had begun to fear what control Fraser was having on James, given his family's unfortunate political leanings and loyalty to the old papist ways.

There had been much whispering among the ladies when we withdrew after supper one night at the Morays' that he, like his brother, was a Jacobite. I was unable to find out anything further but hoped I might ascertain snippets from the servants at some stage.

The main reason to arrive unannounced, however, was to check my husband's study. During my last visit, I had discovered that the lock on this door had been changed for no apparent reason and so I was barred from entry. When I asked the housekeeper about it, she looked abashed and mumbled something about the locksmith making a mistake. I knew this was a lie and so I had to discover what, if anything, he was hiding from me.

I turned the key in the front door lock and entered, inhaling deeply the clean air after the stale smell of squalor outside. Annie dragged in the bags and set them down in the vestibule. There was a rush of footsteps and Mistress Wilson appeared, hair escaping from her cap, flour on her smock. She stood panting at the door to the kitchen.

"We didn't expect you today, My Lady. His Lordship didn't alert me to the…"

"No, I thought I would surprise you." I turned to Annie, who stood at the door, unsure of our welcome. "Run along and fetch Bobbie, lass. He can take the bags to my bedroom."

"And now, Mistress Wilson, I think I could manage a glass of claret to calm my nerves after that bumpy ride in from the country."

I headed for the drawing room. "And some of your fine plum cake, if you please."

The stout cook bobbed her head, scowling, then scuttled off, while the servants fussed over the bags and began to haul them up the winding staircase. I turned and tiptoed towards the study and put my hand on the handle. I turned it gently and the door eased open. I smiled, removed the key, slipped it into my pocket, then sauntered into the drawing room in anticipation of my restorative wine.

Chapter 8

James

"Meddling, that's what she's been doing, Lovat. Meddling."

I was in Clerihugh's Tavern with my friend late one Friday night. I had been conducting business there all day long with my fellow lawyers and enjoying a few glasses of finest claret. My local tavern might be clarty and noisy, but they had a fine cellar. Just when my fellow advocates and judges were set to wind their ways home, I had spied Simon Fraser across the dingy gloom. He had hurried over to join me, his voluminous red plaid swirling behind him.

"Who? That deranged shrew you continue to call your good wife?"

He beckoned over Young Hugh for more wine, which he poured until our glasses were overflowing.

As we raised our goblets in a toast, I took in Lovat's red bulbous nose and bloodshot eyes; it was obvious he had been in his cups for some time.

"I'll tell you about My Lady once we have eaten." I needed something to restore my spirits before I told my old friend about her conniving and interfering over the past year.

"I had a fine powsowdie at The Sheep Heid earlier, but I do believe I could eat again."

Once more, he summoned Hugh and demanded to know what meats Mrs Brodie had left. On being told there was still some fine roast hare and turnips, Simon enquired if there was any fricassee; so many friends of his political persuasion were devotees of French cuisine. Hugh said he thought that might be possible and so Simon ordered all three.

"Oh, and bring us some Newhaven oysters, too, I have an inexplicable hunger."

He licked his fat, red lips; he was always a man with an appetite.

"What were you doing in Duddingston today? That was hardly on your way down from the north?"

"Grange, you know perfectly well why that was my first port of call." He raised an eyebrow and took a large gulp of claret.

I drew towards him and became aware of the vinous odours around his corpulent being.

"Were they meeting there again?"

Lovat drew out his bonnet from under the folds of his vast plaid; the hat was festooned with the white cockade.

"You shouldn't be wearing that in the city; people will talk. Put it away."

"You've changed your tune since last time we spoke, Grange."

I leant over and whispered in his ear. "You know perfectly well my allegiance is as yours, Lovat, with the Jacobites, but I can't be seen to support them. Don't forget my position on the bench. And within the kirk too. It's all very well for you Highland papists, but for me it's double treachery."

I jerked my head back on seeing Young Hugh approach with the platter. Nothing was said as he laid out the food and topped up our pitcher of claret.

"I think some of your home-brewed ale would be in order, my man," said Lovat, belching, as the servant ran back towards the kitchen. "And now, let me eat, then you can tell me all about your troublesome wife."

He stretched over and grabbed an oyster from the platter then proceeded to lean his head back and tip the mollusc down, the glistening juices running down his chin.

Once the chieftain had swallowed his last mouthful, he sat back in the chair and beamed, his black teeth crooked in his twisted mouth. I pushed my plate away and filled our glasses to the full.

"She's been interfering with my affairs. I believe she's found things in my private study that could easily incriminate me."

"What right does she – a mere woman – have to meddle in your business?"

I sighed. "I know, but it is done. I discovered only last night that over the past year she must have rifled through my letters and documents and found information that could incriminate me."

"Good God man, what sort of evidence?"

"My papers swearing allegiance to the cause." I shook my head then downed my wine, followed by my beer. "I have an organised desk, which is how I know she has been in it; certain papers are not in place."

"I repeat, she is but a woman, who would believe her? She is powerless. You worry too much, Grange."

"Do you know what she is capable of? Do not forget her father and the inherent madness. Any indiscretion would ruin my career."

Simon Fraser sat up in his seat, lifted his wig to one side and scratched his scalp. He then played the tip of his tongue around his mouth before drawing near.

"Then she must be dealt with."

"Have you seen her temper?"

He flicked his hand away. "No matter, she must be silenced. But first of all, why not instigate some sort of legal separation? In your position, you can draw up some basic document to prove she's guilty of something or other. Then she must live either in the country or in other lodgings when in the city."

"But what of the children?"

"They will be fine. Does your sister not have a big enough townhouse to accommodate them all? Is it seven you have now?"

I took a deep breath. "Five; remember I told you two had died as infants."

He shrugged. "So, they can stay with your sister and you can find lodgings for your wife when she's in town."

"It must wait until after our daughter's marriage to the Earl of Kintore. Any scandal must be deferred."

He shrugged. "Very well. Then, once the separation has been finalised, we can devise a plan."

"What sort of plan?"

"We will consider what would suit a mad, hot-tempered woman best. Since we have no madhouse in Edinburgh, the options are limited and I suppose you would not contemplate something more, how shall I say, final?"

I gasped. "No, no, remember my position as a respected man of the kirk. I could not break one of the Commandments." I shook my head.

But Lovat, instead of agreeing, began to chuckle and, as he did, his blubbery body shook with mirth. Tears streamed down his pockmarked cheeks. When he eventually opened his eyes, he drew in close and said, "And what about the other Commandment?"

I shrugged. "You think the chambering and whoring is frowned upon by the kirk? Do not be so absurd. A man has to follow his natural desires. I often meet the Reverend Elibank with some of his fellow ministers down at Jeannie Wilkie's."

"So, a separation plan is devised – by you and your colleagues – and in the meantime, I shall think of a plan that is more final, but that is not fatal. Do we understand each other, my old friend?"

I nodded, attempted to tidy the mess he had made on the table, got to my feet with some difficulty and staggered out of

the dark room into the close, to relieve myself. As I stood there
in the wynd, the douce Edinburgh rain falling down upon me,
I thought of you, my darling. You are the one thing she will
never find out about.

Chapter 9

Rachel

My sweet nature has been challenged. Over the past year or so, I have felt victimised. First of all, as I discovered, James had had the study locks changed and the servants would not even engage in conversation with me about it. But once I had managed to get my hands on the key, I found out some terrible things. That day I arrived unannounced at Niddry's Wynd was the start. I had always thought he was hiding something from me, but to discover that my beloved husband was keeping devastating secrets from me was simply too much for someone as blameless as me.

I had just returned from my appointments with the seamstress and the milliner, and Mistress Wilson had brought me a restorative glass of brandy. The woman is a scowling busybody, but she knows my every need.

"Did you get everything ordered then, My Lady?"

As if it were any of her business.

"I did, Mistress Wilson."

"Nice frocks and ribbons ordered for Mary?"

"Indeed, and please don't forget, soon you will be addressing her as Lady Kintore. In fact, I shall have to defer to her too. A countess is a noble title to hold." I took a sip of the brandy and stared at the woman, who refused to budge. "That will be all."

"Can I get you anything else before I go out, My Lady? I have to go to the grocer as I have run out of currants."

Again, why would she think such domestic trivia interested me? But no, she sallied forth.

"You wanted me to do my chicken pye today when your sister and mother dine with you. I've got all the spices and even the sugar to strew over the top, but I'm right out of currants since Master Charlie entertained his friends last week."

"Did he? Who was with him?"

"His fellow students, I believe, My Lady. It's not for me to ask who the young master's guests are. I just get the dinner on the table." She smiled, a rare sight. "It was my very fine mutton pye, the one with winter savory and marjoram I asked Master Charlie's man to bring from Preston House Garden."

I sighed at her persistence in providing me with domestic detail, then downed my drink. "Fill up my brandy and bring me some of your fine seed cake before you go."

She turned and headed for the door.

"Wait. Is Bobbie in, should I require anything further?"

"No, My Lady, he's down at the cobblers with your slippers, seeing if they can be fixed. They took a bit of a beating in the rain yesterday."

She peered over at my empty glass and I looked up at her; I detected a sneer. "I'll bring over the decanter and leave it by your side, shall I? Then you won't have to get out of your seat."

She bustled out of the door before I could admonish her for her impertinence. Truly, she was an excellent cook, but she did have a problem with the fact that she sometimes forgot she was a mere servant. However, today she was going to be useful by her very absence. She was always so slow when on shopping errands, chatting to every fishwife and pie-man she met on the High Street; she would be out for hours. I fingered the key in my pocket and sat back in my chair; it was time for me to do a little investigating.

That was the first day I found some letters from the Highland ogre, Lord Lovat. I was always suspicious of the vile creature who smelt of mould and damp. This I attributed to the fact that his castle, according to James, was so big it was always cold and humid as he had little in the way of funds to attempt to heat it.

The letters mentioned the fact that he was joining 'others of the same persuasion' at Duddingston to discuss matters that were surely of interest to James. It was only when I was taking tea one day with Lady Forsyth and she mentioned that an inn in that very village was the meeting place of certain anti-government people, that I began to unravel the web of deceit my husband had woven around himself.

Then, on a subsequent visit to Niddry's Wynd some months later with Mary, to attend to her bridal vestments, I sent her off with Mistress Wilson to purchase the correct spices to cook her lobster soup. She had insisted that only mace and perhaps a little hint of clove should be added, but on this occasion the finer details of a receipt interested me and I consulted with James' brother's cook, who was familiar with French cuisine, and he disagreed.

I persuaded her therefore that a fine lobster bisque cooked "à la française" also required some thyme and bay leaf, whatever that was. The dinner was for Mary's future family and so the lobster soup had to be perfect in every way. We had heard that the Earl was a man of great taste and was keen to hire a French chef once he and My Angel were wed. I was determined not to let my daughter down in any way at all, certainly not through a minor culinary faux pas.

So, while the irksome servant went off with Mary, and Bobbie was out at the cobbler's, once again I headed for James' study and took out my key. It was remarkable that the servants still had no idea that I'd had the deaf old devil at the locksmith's shop down on Bakehouse Close fashion me a duplicate of the study key whenever it was changed. And I kept it in my snuff box, for fear of an interfering servant finding it in any of my clothes. I sat down, opened the drawer of his escritoire and discovered some new papers since I had last been here. I removed the top paper carefully and saw that it was in fact a document, not just a letter from his vile Highland Lordship. It had a wax seal of authority on it, so I took it out very carefully.

As I read down the flowery script, sentence by sentence, my mouth opened wide in incredulity. For here was written evidence of what I had come to suspect ever since I knew of his dealings with Lovat – who, by his papist loyalty and also his Highland affiliations, was undeniably a Jacobite. Not that he would ever admit it; there was history in his family of outright affiliation to the cause and that had not ended well. He cannot have been that old when his elder brother Alexander was killed at the Battle of Killiecrankie, the first Jacobite rising against the government. And now of course, since 1707, we Scots have been tied in with the English, who want the Jacobite cause crushed forever.

So, as I read, I became aware of the implications. My husband, a man of the kirk, a Lord revered by all those with him on the bench, whose loyalty to the government was part and parcel of the job, was not all he seemed. This document was proof that James Erskine, Lord Grange, was in fact a Jacobite. Loyalty to the Jacobite cause meant that he was not in fact a government supporter, but someone who supported the restoration of the Stuarts, the papist royals.

Good God, was he also a closet papist? His signature at the foot of the document showed he had sworn allegiance to the Jacobite cause. He and the Highland Lord had been together at The Sheep Heid in Duddingston with several others – most of them papists; I recognised the other signatures as such – welcoming my husband to the fold and plotting another uprising against the great House of Hanover.

I tidied away the other letters, removed the document, shut the study door and went back into the parlour, where I emptied the dregs of the decanter into my glass. As I drank deep, I leant my head back against the chair and thought of the implications. Not only would he be disgraced if the truth was ever out, my entire family and I would be snubbed. He would be hanged; but we would be shunned. And, given my family background, I had known antipathy, I had known shame. There was no way I was going to put my beloved children through that. Something must be done, I mused, while tipping the last of the maroon-red liquid down my throat.

Chapter 10

Rachel

However, before I had the opportunity to bring up this matter with James, something else even more catastrophic occurred. It was something no wife should have to bear, even one of my placid and accommodating nature.

Charlie had gone down to London with James on one of his father's frequent trips. James had told me it was important for our son and heir to become acquainted with London ways, since Edinburgh was but a village compared to the capital. I had assisted in the preparation of Charlie's things and finally, as I stood by the carriage at Preston House to say farewell, he promised to write to me soon after their arrival at their London lodgings.

"You won't forget, Charlie? Your mother will be desperate to hear news of her bairn in the big city."

"Stop speaking like one of the servants, Rachel," James snapped. "He'll write when he has time. I have many appointments for him for the first few days."

I kissed my son goodbye and awaited a salutation from my husband, but none was forthcoming.

"When will you return, James?"

"When I'm ready. I shall send word," he said before commanding the driver to drive on.

I had much to do that day as two of the children required new petticoats and it was impossible in the country to find decent local dressmakers. And so, I had asked the housekeeper and one of the maids, who was good with a needle, to spend a morning with me making them ourselves. I was keen to supervise as they had no experience in sewing such fine fabric; coarse wool was more the norm for servants, not fine silk serge. We gathered around the table in the parlour, fabrics stretched out, and began the work. There was no talk at all at first, so keen were they presumably not to offend my sometimes irascible mood after my husband has left on a long trip.

But soon Muriel, the housekeeper, spoke. "I do hope young Master Charlie will enjoy his first visit to London. I should so love to visit England. Have you been, My Lady?"

"No," I replied. "And why would I? There is nothing for me to do there apart from look at the wonderful shops. And you know perfectly well His Lordship forbids any extravagance."

They both nodded.

"Besides, where should I stay? Lord Grange resides in lodgings that are only for men. Some sort of gentlemen's club, I believe. Better for associations and meetings than the coffee houses, he tells me."

The two women looked up, glanced at each other, then bent their heads back down over their work.

"Is Master Charlie to stay at the club too, My Lady?"

"Obviously, where else would he stay other than with his father?"

They both mumbled and carried on sewing.

"Unless of course you know differently?"

They both shook their heads and Muriel got up.

"Shall I bring in your morning claret, My Lady? It is nearly the hour."

"Yes, and some of your seed cake. I prefer yours to Mistress Wilson's in the city. What do you do differently?"

"I can't say I know, My Lady. I use caraway seeds of course, everyone does, but – oh, I did add a little rosewater the last time. Did you like it?"

"Yes, that's it, the same as you put in your sweetmeats, those rosewater tablets. Good. I like that flavour."

She stood there at the door.

"Hurry up then, woman!"

I thought nothing more of the conversation that morning until some ten days later when a letter arrived from London.

Old Peter brought it to me in the afternoon and for once, he appeared to smile. Usually, for me he frowned and his speech was more of a growl.

"A letter from London, My Lady. It will no doubt be from Master Charlie."

He stood back, the salver at his side.

"Well give it here, man, and hand me that lamp. The nights are beginning to draw in early."

He sauntered over and handed me the letter with a nod then went for the lamp. If he ambled like that when serving his master, he would be admonished severely.

"Do hurry up, Peter."

Once he had left the room, I rubbed my hand over the thick parchment, enjoying the textured feel of its ridges under my fingers. I was going to savour this news from my dear boy. I opened the letter and skimmed to the foot. What a joy to see my eldest son's name.

Dearest Mama, he began. First, he told me of meeting many of James' acquaintances and of the society he met when at his cousin's house in Richmond for tea one day. Then at the end, he wrote:

> *I am writing this at the Gentlemen's Club here in Haymarket,*
> *where we want for nothing, while Father is out at Mrs*
> *Lindsay's. At her coffee house, which is but two buildings*
> *away, there are people he says I would not like as much, for*
> *they are perhaps of a lower social standing than us and there-*
> *fore their discourse would be without the intelligence of the*

*other acquaintances of his we have met thus far. But I am
very happy to have some solitude and to have time to write to
you, dear Mama. Do please give my brothers and sisters my
fondest. Papa hopes we shall be ready to return in a week or
so when his business affairs would permit him to leave the city.
Your loving son, Charlie.*

I leant back on the chair and screwed up my eyes. Mrs
Lindsay? Who was she and why does some woman who runs a
coffee house even warrant a mention in my son's letter?

Chapter 11

Rachel

Some fortnight later, after my husband and son had returned home from London and James was in Edinburgh attending to business, all was quiet at home. The children had all gone with James to the city to visit his sister Jean. It was delightful not to have the noise of children bickering or servants clanging pots in the kitchen. Preston House was big, but noise travelled everywhere, unfortunately. I took my time sipping my morning wine then rang for Annie to help me with my toilette.

After the final curl was perfectly in place, I dismissed her, then headed out of my room. I looked along the corridor towards James' bed chamber and noticed his door was shut. I stole along there and turned the handle, but it was locked. At once I felt the ire rise in me again. He used not only to visit my bedroom at night but often stay. He has not done that for quite some time. And now he locks his door from me, his loyal, dutiful wife?

I went downstairs, trying to decide whether I might take a stroll outside, for the weather looked fine. There was still frost on the ground, but the sun was beginning to break through the early-morning mist. Perhaps a walk down to the beach might be pleasant; the sea buckthorn would be in bloom and what a fine sight the golden orange berries were; they would lift my spirits.

At the foot of the stairs, I paused and listened. There were voices in the drawing room. Did we have visitors that the maid had forgotten to tell me about?

I approached the room, where the door was ajar and soon realised the voices were those of my two elder sons. I was about to push the door open when I heard the word "whore".

"So, Papa left you every night to go whoring, Charlie?"

"No, I told you, Jamie, he wasn't after any old whore, it was one particular woman, a Mrs Fanny Lindsay. She runs the coffee house just along from the club in Haymarket."

"So, what's the difference? He still goes whoring every night?"

"No, no, I met her with Papa on a couple of occasions outside the coffee house. She looked like a lady, with a fancy gown and jewels, the type Mama would wear."

"But I don't understand. I thought you said it was all right for a husband to go to another woman if she was a whore and even the minister said that was allowed."

I clasped my hands tight together in an attempt to stop the trembling that had taken over my entire body.

"Papa would not discuss it with me, but I talked to my friend Archie about it and he said if it's the same woman a gentleman goes to, then she's a mistress and that must be what Mrs Lindsay is. But it doesn't mean Mama need know because…"

"Because what?" I bellowed, flinging the door wide open.

My two sons swivelled round from the fire they were huddling over. Charlie leapt to his feet as I strode towards them.

"What are you talking about, Charlie? Who is this Mrs Lindsay? If she is only a coffee house owner, I find it extremely unlikely that your father has taken her for a mistress."

I threw myself onto the day bed and took a deep breath.

I glowered at the boys, who were staring at me speechless. Jamie was bright red and his lower lip started to tremble. Dear God, he is only sixteen; he should not be discussing whores with his elder brother.

"Sorry, Mama," Jamie snivelled, backing away.

"Come right over here, Jamie, and stop that whimpering." I sat up straight, recovering my senses. "Why are you boys here anyway? You were all meant to be away at Aunt Jean's."

"Jamie was unwell, so I offered to stay with him at the last minute. Papa said that was a good idea."

"Oh did he? Well, you look perfectly well to me, Jamie. Come over here!"

The gangly boy tiptoed over to me, twitching as if I were about to hit him. Admittedly I had smacked him last week when I'd seen him deliberately trip Fannie up outside on the path and she'd cut her chin on a stone wall. Her looks are challenging enough, I'd told him, if she is ever to get a husband; don't jeopardise that further.

He burst into tears. "I don't like going to Aunt Jean's, those boys there are horrid."

"Dear God, you are sixteen, don't be such a baby. Here you are discussing whoring and you're still nervous your big cousins might bully you." I shook my head.

"Tell me everything you know about this Mrs Lindsay, Charlie."

He kept his head down as he mumbled, "Papa says you should not take the Lord's name in vain."

I harrumphed and gestured to the drinks table. "Fetch me a glass of claret. And Jamie, stop snivelling like a baby."

Once I had downed my wine, I felt slightly calmer and forced myself to try to suppress the rage; I even managed to smile sweetly. "Come over here, my darling boys. Charlie, tell Mama all about London. What is the club like?" Inside I was in turmoil, but I had to remain calm in order to make my son talk.

After another glass, I felt able to ask the only question I wanted to ask.

"And is the club very near the coffee house?"

Charlie swallowed and looked at his feet. "It's only two houses away. They serve very good coffee. Papa says Mrs

Lindsay makes the best coffee in London."

"I see. And what is Mrs Lindsay like? Is she a fine lady like me?" I could feel the furies grow inside until I could keep them in no longer. I leant towards them and growled, "Or a common slut like the whores you visit with your friends down the Grassmarket, Charlie?"

I exhaled slowly and rubbed my hands together, trying to stop them from skelping my sons, even though none of this was their fault.

They drew away, possibly reminded of my occasional rages and how those invariably ended.

"She seemed like a lady, Mama," he muttered. "But not as fine or beautiful as you."

"So, why do you think your father goes there?"

There was a knock at the door, then Muriel bobbed her head. "Sorry to disturb you, My Lady, I did not realise the young masters were here. I just wanted to ask if you were ready for your morning tea?"

"Tea? Do I look like I need tea? Fetch me brandy. Now!" The woman ran out the door and the boys continued to gape, their eyes wide.

"Go!" I shouted at them. "Go and keep out of my sight. Wait till your father hears about these falsehoods you have been telling. Lies, all lies." I watched them head towards the door, Jamie cowering into Charlie as they slunk out.

Then all at once I felt a sense of despair. These were my sons, my darling boys; dear God, what kind of harridan had I become, what manner of mother lambasts her children for the sins of another? None of this was their doing, it was their feeble, duplicitous father's fault. I screwed my eyes tight shut, slumped back into my seat and waited for my brandy.

Chapter 12

James

It was the morning after Mary's marriage to the Earl of Kintore that she chose to make a spectacle of herself; and unfortunately, this occurred in front of my old manservant, Peter. Because my wife and I had to share chambers at the castle during the festivities, she chose the moment when Peter was serving me my morning draught and Her Ladyship her claret; that was when she elected to explode. We had not had the opportunity to be alone since my return from my last excursion to London. Before I departed on that trip, I had left her the official letter requiring that she continue to live in Preston House with the younger children, Fannie and William. The two elder boys would lodge with my sister Jean in her Edinburgh apartment and, as each child came of age, they too would leave Preston House and lodge with Jean. It seemed perfectly fair to me. Then, after they had all gone, she could live in lodgings somewhere in the city, preferably at the other end of the High Street, far from Niddry's Wynd, and I would resume living at Preston House. This was the beginning of the separation that I had discussed with Lovat and which made so much sense. I did not understand her reaction to my plan.

Her behaviour had been increasingly erratic and uncivil and her rages had become more and more frequent. The servants and children alike were wary of her. The minister agreed with the terms, so that was that. Or so I had hoped. The day of

Mary's wedding she had managed to remain civil and obedient and when we fell into bed after the festivities we were both too inebriated and drowsy to attempt any communication and sleep descended fast. And so, revived by her first sip of morning claret around midday, it was then that she hollered like a common Newhaven fishwife.

"How do you think you can take my children away from me? They are as much mine as yours, James."

"Do not be ridiculous, woman. Custody of the children in law is mine. You are lucky I have felt lenient enough to leave you two of them for the time being."

"But within five years I shall be alone. And then what shall I do? How am I to live?"

"The allowance I have set down in the document is sufficient."

"Sufficient?" she bellowed once more. "You truly think a hundred pounds a year could feed a family, never mind clothe them and pay the servants and look after the crumbling house in which I am to be prisoner? That amount would scarcely even afford me carriages to the city."

"You will not be going to the city, Rachel. There is no need, now that Mary is married. And you will not be a prisoner." I sighed. She really made me so weary these days.

I gestured to Peter to leave us. He bowed and began to walk backwards towards the door.

"Bring me some more wine, man!" she shouted and he hobbled over to the table to fill her glass from the decanter. I nodded at him to leave.

The argument continued awhile, unpleasantly; several times I had to insist she lower her voice for fear our hosts could hear.

"Don't be ridiculous, James, this castle is ancient. The walls must be ten foot thick, which is why it is so icy cold everywhere. And I now wonder if Mary will indeed be happy here, so many days' travel away from the city. I thought it was but a few hours. Why did you not tell me?"

"I did, Rachel, but…"

She was not listening and so I simply let her rant on, a thing I had become used to over the years. At last, as invariably happens, she quietened down.

She began to snivel. "James, is this separation for ever?"

"For the time being, Rachel, until your behaviour becomes rather more stable. The Reverend thought it would be a good idea for us all."

I did not say that, had Moorfields in London been nearer, she would have been sent there, to Bethlem Hospital. I was being both lenient and kind. She was a danger to herself, and to the good name of the family.

She downed yet another glass then sat up straight. I could almost see her mind ticking over.

"Is Lord Lovat behind this?"

"No, he is not." If only she knew what Lovat was planning next. "This is my decision and the minister is in total agreement."

"That scoundrel Elibank is no more God-fearing than those ministers along the coast from us at North Berwick. You know they denounced their own parishioners, left them to be burned at the stake?"

I sighed. I should not have given her permission to read the books in my library.

"They were found guilty of witchcraft, Rachel. The ministers simply did their duty."

"Duty? They let them be tortured hideously. Their fingernails were pulled out slowly," she said, screwing up her face like a child. "Or they pricked them with pins, needles and bodkins to check if they possessed the Devil's Mark and felt no pain. And then, after all that, they were burned alive…" She shook her head and her eyes glared like a madwoman.

I had had enough of her incoherent ravings. I held up my

hand to silence her then rang the bell. "It is time for me to dress. Go and fetch your waiting woman and I shall expect to see you down at dinner in a suitably contrite manner."

I walked towards the antechamber and looked back. Rachel's raven hair was now flecked with grey and silver. Her skin, which used to be so fresh and clear, was puffy and mottled. Her bloodshot eyes were slits in her face; her excessive drinking had taken its toll on her former beauty. There was no doubt about it, I was most definitely making the correct decision. And just in time, before she did any more meddling.

~~~

Over the next few months, I found the trial separation seemed to work rather well. I was so busy with my work in Edinburgh and my journeys to London that I managed to avoid her completely. Then, one winter's day, I found I had to journey down to Preston House. There was no choice; I had been summoned by the minister on an important parish matter for which he needed legal advice. She would have been alerted to my arrival by the servants bustling about as usual before my carriage arrived at the door.

I stepped into the hall and was greeted by Peter, who was frowning.

"My Lady is in the dining room, still at her breakfast, My Lord. She requires your presence. At once."

I sighed. "What time is the Reverend Elibank coming here?"

"In an hour, Your Lordship." He gestured in the direction of the dining room. "Shall I bring you your morning draught? And some cold roast beef?"

"That might help ease the pain."

I strode into the room and saw her there at the far end of the table, two empty decanters at her elbow.

"Good morning, My Lady. I see you have dined well."

She smiled and clasped her hands on her ample bosom. I peered more closely; a deep blue gem was glinting in the morning sun.

"Is that the Chiesley family mourning ring upon your finger, Rachel? You know I have forbidden you from ever wearing it."

She rubbed the stone with the tip of her finger then jiggled her fingers; the gem looked more violet than blue now in the sunlight.

"James, James, I believe you have forgotten. I am now mistress here of all I survey, including my jewels and my two remaining children. I can do whatever I like."

"I think not, Lady." I sat down at the far end. "And they are not your children, they are not even our children, they are mine."

She gestured with her hand as if swatting away a fly then stretched her head up. She looked around the walls, pointing at the many family portraits. Among my predecessors were austere statesmen in periwigs and rigid-faced dowagers in starched ruffs. Along at the far end was Rachel's portrait, painted just the year after our marriage. In it she looks so beautiful and young, her glorious dark hair cascading down her long white neck, her fine nose as pretty as Helen of Troy's. And her most perfect bosom, which lured me in all those years before. You would not take her as the same woman now, with her blotchy, red-veined skin and tired, red-rimmed eyes.

Peter came over to pull out my chair along the table from her and poured my morning ale; she continued to smile. She waited for Peter to vacate the room before she leant over in my direction.

"I was just wondering what your strict Presbyterian ancestors might have thought of your political and religious persuasions nowadays."

I started. "What do you mean?"

She rang the bell and her maid appeared.

"Annie, go and fetch the things by my bed. At once!"

The girl sped off and I bent down to sip my beer. What was she scheming?

She continued to look around the walls at the various portraits, while silence ensued. She had a wry smile at the corner of her dry, cracked lips.

Presently Annie returned and handed her mistress some papers. Rachel removed one of the documents and even before she held it up, I knew what it was. I felt a sense of jeopardy flood over me. Dear God, if she exposed me – or indeed any of us – our lives were over. I looked around to check that the serving woman had shut the door behind her, then waited, taking in her jubilant features with dread.

"You may recognise this, my love. It is a document in which you swear your allegiance to the Jacobite cause," she smirked. "I believe the Reverend Elibank is coming round here very soon. I am not sure how he would take this news since I believe, even though I am but a feeble-minded woman, that the Jacobites stand for two things he might take against. First of all, it is a papist cause and secondly it is anti-government. Blasphemy and treason, quite a pretty package."

She ran her fingers up and down the thick parchment in front of her, teasing.

"Also, I wonder how it would look for an eminent judge to be denounced while sitting in judgement at the bench."

I downed my beer then walked over to her seat. I leant down over her and had to wave the claret fumes away. When had she started to drink so much?

"Rachel, should you mention one word to the Reverend Elibank, do you know what will happen? The two remaining children will be removed from you and put in Jean's care with the others; you will never see any of them again. Furthermore, you will no longer be chatelaine here at Preston House. And as for your idle threat to, as you call it, 'denounce me at the bench', no lady is allowed near the courts. Besides, I would see to it that you were barred from ever crossing the threshold."

I shook my head. She had no business meddling in my affairs; I would not tolerate such interference. "Idle threats, my dear, idle."

"Well, I still feel that the minister will be interested to see this." She held the document above her head and smiled.

I tried to grab it but could not. I rang the bell and Old Peter entered at once.

"Peter, Her Ladyship has become unwell. Please could you escort her to her chambers. And ask Will to assist?"

I grabbed at Rachel's arm and dragged her to the door. She began to shout and bawl like a common fisherwoman but soon Peter and Will had managed to manoeuvre her upstairs to her chambers. I followed and, once at her door, they stepped back as I pushed her in and pulled the door to.

I turned the large key in the lock and pocketed it. I bent down to the keyhole and shouted to her, "I will be going back to the city after my appointment with the minister. I do not expect to see you anywhere else but here at Preston House. Goodbye, Rachel."

I turned towards the stairs, intent on going down to finish my ale and beef in the dining room, then stopped on the top step. There was a howl, long and low, like a wolf. I shivered; it was true what Lovat had said, she was deranged. She was wild; she needed taming.

Chapter 13

Rachel

I sat in my lodgings in Edinburgh, Annie at my side, contemplating the successes of the day. It had been difficult leaving Preston House that morning; the servants tried to insist I was not allowed to go, with threats of "What would the Master say?". How dare they! Eventually they had no choice but to order me a carriage.

On arrival in the city, we headed straight down to the Canongate and to the stagecoach inn, Annie lugging my bags down the cobbles. After a restorative glass of sack at the inn, I managed to secure a place in the coach to London the following morning. I had business to attend to down there and, who knows, I might perhaps take a refreshment in a particular Haymarket coffee house.

Back at the lodgings, Annie had asked my permission to meet a friend in the High Street. While she was out, I started to plan what I would do in London. When she returned, she was flushed and her eyes shone bright. I smiled and asked if it was a male or female friend she was meeting, but her cheeks reddened and she turned away. I do hope Annie has a male friend, she deserves happiness.

That evening, we sat in silence in the rather mediocre lodgings my sister had found me on Anchor Close; these were the only lodgings Margaret could secure for me at such short notice. I insisted I would not stay with her since she had just given birth to yet another baby; and this time the story of my fecund sister was true.

And so, after a light supper of mutton broth and eggs, brought up to our room, I sat with the last of the claret by my side, admiring the sparkle of my lapis lazuli ring as it glimmered in the firelight. Annie knew better than to speak to me late in the evening and so, having unpacked my night clothes, she waited for my command.

I must have been sitting for quite some time, watching the embers on the fire as they glowed then faded away, one by one; it was quite mesmerising. I shivered, aware that the room had become cold, and pulled the shawl round my neck. Eventually Annie gave a little cough.

"My Lady, it is already very late. Shall I fetch water for your evening toilette then you can retire to your bed closet?"

I aroused myself from my reveries, dismissed her to go about her duties and out she went.

The next thing I heard was a loud knock, as if someone was striking the door downstairs with force. I sat up straight and looked around. I had no idea what time it was, but I imagined possibly near midnight as all was quiet in the street outside. Surely it was too late for a social call? I then heard some men's deep voices coming up the stairs. Where was Annie? I could not possibly open the door to strangers. The thud of their boots reverberated on each step.

"Annie?" I cried as I heard the door handle turn.

It was not the girl, but two tall Highland gentlemen, swathed in their plaids.

The sturdy men entered the room and shut the door behind them.

When they spoke, it was obvious they were not from these parts.

"My Lady, we beg your pardon, but we have been instructed to remove you from here and if you come quietly, you will…"

"What? Who has instructed you? Where is my waiting woman?"

They moved towards me and as I stared at them, I realised where I had seen the red colours of their plaid before.

"You are sent from Lord Lovat, aren't you? What is that fat, lying scoundrel after?"

One of them removed a dirk from his sheath and I drew back.

"If you come quietly, My Lady, it will be easier," he said. Now both of them stood, massive and imposing in front of me.

"Annie! Annie!" I hollered. "Murder, Murder!"

One smiled, a rueful grin, as he brought out a large, filthy-looking handkerchief. "No one can hear you, My Lady. Now if you just…"

I leapt forward, trying to squeeze between them, but they grabbed me. I felt rude hands upon my arms and as I twisted and struggled to get free; they also grabbed my hair and pulled so hard a clump was torn from my scalp. I shouted and yelled; I was a Chiesley, I would not be taken advantage of. But no one heard.

One man rammed his malodorous handkerchief into my mouth, ripped the shawl off my shoulders and tied it roughly around my mouth, knotting it at the back of my neck. He then threw me over his shoulder as if I were a suckling pig, not a fine lady. They bounded down the stairs as I kept trying to bite him, but the handkerchief was making me gag. All I could do was wrench the loose plaid down off his back and scratch and scratch until I drew blood from the Highlander's skin.

At the foot of the stairs in the hallway, where yesterday there had been at least three servants waiting to attend upon me, there was darkness and silence. Where was my serving woman? My eyes darted around, in case she too had been taken by ruffians. They opened the door into the close and I saw there was a sedan chair with a thin man sitting there.

They bundled me in, on top of this man, who grasped both of my arms with quite some strength; he might be scrawny, but he was evidently strong.

The Highlanders tied my feet to the man's with rope and wrapped a large cloth tight around my mouth to cover my own shawl, which had become loose; I was now completely mute. The man pulled down the curtains on both sides, but one stuck so I could still see out a little. I made out one of the Highlanders adjusting his plaid, presumably to cover the long scratch marks on his back from my nails. They positioned themselves at either end and picked up the chair with me sitting strapped to the thin man's lap. The chair swayed and wobbled as they scrambled up to the top of the close to the High Street, where they turned right then left then right.

I peered under the curtain and soon saw two figures under a lamp on the wall; I could hear coarse words and realised they were whores just starting to ply their trade. We were entering the Grassmarket; the castle must be up on our right.

All this time, I attempted to flail my arms to try to catch any passer-by's attention, even the strumpets' would do; but the man in the chair held my arms so tight, I knew I would be bruised black and blue. As we bounced along the cobbles, I saw there was no one else around. It must have been well after midnight, when even the street-sellers were abed.

After what seemed like hours of agony, but was obviously only some minutes, I realised we were about to leave the city; I recognised the arch of the West Port and, as I peered ahead, I saw the spiked railings on the huge opened gate. I trembled as I recalled the childhood trauma of having to watch my father's bloodied hand being removed from the spike it was rammed onto after he was so unceremoniously and unfairly hanged.

I took a deep breath as we went under the arch and then I saw a huddle of men and horses. As we approached, I noticed that the men were all dressed in the same plaid as the brutish

Highlanders who had abducted me from my lodgings. So, Simon Fraser, that ignoble Lord Lovat, was behind all this. Dear God, where was I being taken?

They spoke in another tongue – Gaelic, I presumed – so I could not understand anything they were saying as they untied me roughly from the discomfort of the chair and held me upright. I rubbed my arms, which were tender and sore. The thin man jumped up and straddled one of the horses then held out his arms. One man ripped away the cloth from my mouth and another lifted me roughly in front of the rider.

I was then tied once more to him, with the cloth and a piece of rope, while three – or perhaps four – more men mounted the other horses. With one command, all of the horses and their riders cantered off into the dark, icy-cold night. I shivered; I could not even pull my woollen shawl around me, I was rigid under the bonds. I wanted to sob, I wanted to yell, but I was weak with exhaustion. I set my head against the coarse wool of the rider, whose body was shuddering in time with the gallop of his steed and I shut my eyes. I hoped that very soon I might die.

Part Two

Chapter 14

Annie

I had been at Preston House for several years when his letter arrived. It unsettled me; all those feelings from the past returned, those urges I'd forced myself to suppress over these past few years. I read the letter once more and trembled as I recalled the past. Ours had been love at first sight. We were both still children when he moved to Dirleton Castle with his mother. I'd been working there since I was ten when my mother had died, so I was tasked with showing him around the estate. He was tall for his age, just like me, but that was where the similarities ended. He was dark-haired and swarthy, whereas I was fair-skinned and ginger-haired; my mistress called my hair auburn, which sounded nice, but it was just coarse and red. Our friendship grew and flourished with time, in an innocent way at first, then, after a couple of years, it developed into something deeper.

I will never forget that evening in the autumn when it was early dark and I had to go into the walled garden to see if there were still any turnips or cabbages left for Cook to make her broth for the next day.

He followed me, took hold of my hand and led me around the garden to the back of the house where he pressed me against the wall. That original kiss, so soft and longing, made me crave love for the first time. After my mother had died, my father had returned to his home up north, so I could hardly even remember much affection, until Johnnie came into my life. For most of the time we worked together there, we were lovers. It was all so perfect; he was my reason for living.

And then, as suddenly as Johnnie had arrived, he left again with his mother. I had no idea where he had gone and nor did anyone at the castle; obviously I could not ask my mistress or master, even though they must have known. And now, all those years later, Muriel the housekeeper had come to the back door of Preston House where I sat cleaning My Lady's slippers on the step, and thrust his letter at me.

"This is for you, Annie. Who on earth would write a note to the likes of you?"

She stood over me as I opened it carefully, but I didn't even try to hide it from her, for she couldn't read. None of the servants, apart from me and Old Peter, knew their letters. The mistress at Dirleton Castle had insisted all of her servants could read; she was kind, but strict. I was often skelped if I was ever late or spilt the milk when I brought her morning tea tray into her chamber.

She was so different from my Lady Grange, who is both kind and lenient; well, she is with me anyway. Before she goes out to a soiree or a ball, she has me wear her silver and diamond necklace to warm it up so it's not too cold when placed upon her beautiful white neck.

She explained to me one evening, as I removed it from my neck and fastened the clasp on hers, that ladies wore their diamonds and pearls only at night, since candlelight enhanced the sparkle and sheen. In the daytime she tended to wear her brightly coloured gems, as daylight showed off the colours better. She sometimes allowed me to wear her special blue ring, the one she called lapis lazuli. But since the master had forbidden her wearing it at all, I could do that only when he was not at home, which nowadays was often. He had an important position as a law lord and so was frequently in Edinburgh, where he stayed at their town house in Niddry's Wynd. He also went to London rather often. I could not imagine ever going on such a long journey; I've only ever been in Dirleton then Preston House and sometimes, if I am lucky, I travel to Edinburgh.

I used to wonder if Johnnie had gone to London, too; perhaps his mother and he had jobs down there. She was a mysterious woman, with her tanned skin, inky-black hair and funny accent. She always wore dark clothes, adorned sometimes with a crucifix, until the day the Cook bellowed at her to remove it.

"If the master sees you with that papist pendant, he'll have you sent away. The minister's coming for his dinner today. Take it off at once."

And the very next day, she and Johnnie left. Johnnie, the love that made my life worth living, the lad I was to spend the rest of my days with, was gone.

The letter I received that day at Preston House said that he was now working in Edinburgh and could I manage to travel there one day so that we could meet up. He made no mention of his mother, or who he was working for. But I was so overjoyed, I didn't care, nor did I wonder how he knew where to find me. The following week I was due to go up to the city from Preston House and so I rushed to see my mistress to ask for some paper and ink to practise my letters. She smiled at me and handed me them both, with a quill.

"It's wonderful that you can read and write, Annie. I really ought to teach the other servants, but I have no energy for it now, after all the babies."

I wrote Johnnie a note to be delivered to the address he had told me to, and sent it there with the boy who helps Old Peter when the master is in the city. And for the next five days I was nearly sick with trepidation – and excitement.

My Lady Grange and I had just left for her sister's house and I was trying to look calm and normal as I carried her embroidered silk purse down over the cobbles of the High Street towards their close. Inside, however, my stomach was churning and I was hot all over, even though there was a chill in the air.

At the entrance to her sister's house, I handed over her purse and curtsied. She smiled and stroked my cheek then I turned and headed back up to the High Street, thinking that she's sometimes nicer to me than to her own children; she seldom even touches the boys, unless it's with a wallop. She was only ever truly affectionate towards Mary, who is, admittedly, the prettier of the two girls. Poor Fannie is never going to be a beauty and, besides, she always has her nose stuck in the Bible.

So, I headed for St Giles Kirk and went inside, looking around in case I should bump into someone I knew, though that was hardly likely. I walked towards the King's Pillar, where I stood and waited; I was nervous; no, more than that – terrified. What if he had changed; what if he no longer loved me. What if he was married and could no longer be mine; what if he didn't turn up at all?

I was just trying to breathe normally, practising taking a long breath in and out with my eyes shut, when I felt a tap on my shoulder. I turned around and gasped. It was Johnnie, still so handsome and perhaps even taller. His dark hazel eyes crinkled up and he smiled so broadly I wanted to fall into his arms and kiss him all over but we were in the kirk.

He leant his head towards my ear and I remembered the smell of him. It was still the intoxicating woody smell of the grass round the back of the castle and the bluebells in the woodland where we used to walk, and the fresh, salty tang of the sea by the sand dunes where we met. He swept back my hair and whispered, "We should leave here, let's go to one of the taverns down the street to talk."

He took my hand, lifted it to his lips and kissed the ends of my fingers. I let him keep hold of my hand as we walked out of the shadowy church into the bright autumn sunshine. As we passed the beggars and street-sellers I wanted to cry out that my lover had returned for me.

I glanced round to look at his swarthy face and the dark wavy hair, longer than before, and saw that he was beaming still. He looked back at me and I remembered the mole on his forehead and how his teeth were so straight; how I longed to fall into his arms. Hand in hand, we headed east then down the cobbles of the High Street as if nothing between us had changed.

He stopped and looked up. Above us was a battered old sign that said "Luckie Dreghorn".

"This is it, let's go in here."

I bit my lip. "Johnnie, I've never been in a tavern before. Is it all right?"

He grinned. "Of course, it's fine. I know someone who works here, he'll get us a quiet table."

I followed him into the dark, dingy tavern and screwed up my nose. It smelt awful, of stale bodies and rancid meat. I watched as he tapped a man about his age on the shoulder and soon we were guided to a quiet nook in the corner, where we sat side by side, our shoulders and legs touching. I turned to him and asked, "Johnnie, my Johnnie, where on earth have you been these past four years?"

Chapter 15

Annie

"Never mind me, Annie. First tell me about yourself. You look fine; no, better than fine. You look beautiful. Your hair's lovely up like that."

I blushed. "I'm so much older now, Johnnie, no longer the wee girl you knew."

I kept staring at him. There was something different about him, but I couldn't quite pin down what it was. He was obviously not the boy I had known; he was now a man in his thirties. But there was something about his manner that was perhaps a little less shy; yes, that was it, he was more confident.

"You're not taking a drink, lass?"

I looked up as the lad Johnnie had spoken to earlier arrived with a tankard of ale.

"No. Thank you." I leant my head down and cowered down into the seat. I really wasn't sure I should be in a tavern, especially one as noisy and rowdy as this. What would My Lady think?

"So, tell me about where you work now, Annie?" Johnnie took a gulp from the mug in front of him.

"Preston House. Well, you know that of, course. How did you find out where to send the letter?"

"I know a lot of folk here now, I asked around."

Who on earth would know that I worked down the coast at Preston House was a mystery to me.

"I work for Lord and Lady Grange; they're better to work for than our mistress and master at Dirleton. Not that I see His Lordship much these days, mind you."

"What are they like, then?"

"Well, he's a godly man; in fact, he used to sometimes be a lay preacher at the local kirk. He's very right and proper about everything; and strict too about how their children are brought up, their manners and so on. When the children were younger, and they all used to go to church on the Sabbath, the minister'd bow to him and all the congregation lowered their heads as he passed. They'd all sit in the front row and it'd be as if the minister was addressing just them. Well, why would he speak to us all packed into the back? We aren't important at all."

"Oh, I wouldn't say that, Annie. Though we're servants, we can still be heard."

I stared at him.

"How?"

He shrugged. "I don't know, but we can. Anyway, carry on."

"I don't know what he does up here in Edinburgh, but it's obviously really important as he's the Lord Justice Clerk for the whole of Scotland."

Johnnie nodded. "And what about her, your mistress?"

"Oh, she's a fine lady. She is very beautiful, even though she must be well into her middle age by now. And she has a dainty nose and a long white neck."

"So, a bit like you then, Annie." Johnnie reached over to the back of my neck and stroked it; I shivered at his touch.

"Not like me at all, with my dull, ginger hair. She has this lovely shiny black hair that cascades down her back. Oh, actually, it's a bit like your mother's, Johnnie. How is she?"

He looked down at his beer. "She's no longer with us."

"Oh, I'm sorry, Johnnie; so, she's … d'you mean she's dead?"

He was very still for a moment, obviously gathering himself together, then he mumbled, "Yes, she died."

He took a gulp of beer and I glanced at him. As a lady's maid I was well versed in when to speak and when not. So, I decided to leave the subject of his mother alone.

"Anyway, Lady Grange is good to work for, kind to me, doesn't skelp me like my last mistress did. She's a good lady, though she's had her problems with her children; the boys don't seem to appreciate her. Well, they take after their father. And…"

He raised an eyebrow. "And what?"

"I just don't think her husband values her highly enough. I know he's a religious man and that is maybe why he sometimes, well, disapproves of her."

"Why?"

"Well, she can shout a lot, sometimes. Though never at me. She's got a temper on her. The other servants say the reason he no longer stays at Preston House is to punish her for it, but I think it's maybe just because he's so busy here in Edinburgh."

I watched two gentlemen nearby down the last of their jug of claret and bellow for more. "And she does have a fondness for the wine, but after all the illnesses and deaths and horrible things she's witnessed since she was only a bairn, it's hardly surprising." I felt disloyal saying this, so I changed the subject.

"But please, Johnnie, tell me what you've been up to for the past four years? Why did you not tell me you were going? Why did you not contact me from wherever you were?"

Instead of answering, Johnnie leant in to kiss me and I was under his spell once more. I felt transported back to the woods at the back of the castle and the dunes leading down to the sea. I shut my eyes and could almost hear the lapping of the waves on the shore and feel the itch of sand on my bare back. I pulled away and looked around.

"Johnnie, we're in a public place. We must not…"

He smiled and shook his head. "Annie, I've missed your funny ways, and your pretty face. Will you do something for me?"

"Anything, Johnnie."

"At the place I work now there're many eminent men who come to discuss things that are really important. And one of them has asked if you can help."

"Me? What on earth can I do?"

He swirled the last of the ale round in his tankard.

"I work at a tavern called The Sheep Heid in a place called Duddingston."

"Is that far from here? How long have you worked there?"

"Not too far away, it's to the east of the city. I've been working there a few months, but it's taken me this long to find you, Annie. Anyway, at the tavern these men who meet often wear the white cockade." He stared at me as if waiting for me to respond. "Do you know what that means?"

I shook my head.

He bent towards my ear. "Wearing a white cockade in your hat means you're a supporter of the return to the throne of the Stuarts. It's an emblem of the Jacobites. Have you heard of them?"

"Yes." I bit my lip. "Are they not the men who want to get rid of the king?" I was whispering now. "Were they planning some sort of invasion by the French?"

"Not really. It's all a bit more complicated than that, but yes, they do want the rightful king on the throne."

I leant in further towards him. "But are they not all papists?"

Johnnie smiled. "Most followers are Roman Catholics, that's true. But you're hardly one to judge, Annie. I remember you told me one time that your grandmother had been a papist."

"Yes, before she married into my Presbyterian family and forgot all about it." I sat back and shrugged my shoulders. "But I still don't understand what on earth I can do to help; and besides, why would I?"

"You could do it for me, Annie, for old times' sake."

I frowned.

"And for what we'll have when we make a life together, now I've found you again."

I smiled. He still loved me, old though I must seem to him now. I hadn't waited all these years in vain; I knew he would come back for me.

"It's really simple and I'll you tell what the plan is. Then, once it's all done, you and I can escape from this place, go far away and marry." His eyes twinkled. "And you can have those bairns you always wanted. How does that sound?"

How did that sound? Like birdsong on a sun-kissed morning.

"Tell me what I have to do, Johnnie, but quickly please. I have to be back at the house before the mistress returns from her sister's."

Chapter 16

Annie

The day of the "enlèvement", as Johnnie kept calling it, was stressful. When Lady Grange had insisted on going to the stagecoach inn to book tickets for the next day's coach, I panicked. But then realised that Johnnie would be with me that very evening and so whatever happened the next day was of no importance. I could hardly wait to see him again. I had seen him only once since that first meeting in St Giles and Luckie Dreghorn's and most of the talk was about what would happen tonight. He also explained that the French word "enlèvement" meant removal and that My Lady was being taken somewhere for her safekeeping.

When I asked Johnnie why she needed to be safe, he told me that some things had to be secret, but that I must trust him; of course I trust him. I also asked why he would use a French word when there were plenty of good words in English and Scots. He laughed.

"Sometimes a French word is just perfect, though."

"How do you know French? That's what the young masters at Preston House are taught by their tutor, but you're hardly going to be a gentleman, are you, so how come?"

"I've learnt many things since we were bairns, Annie."

"We were hardly bairns, Johnnie, the things we got up to." I giggled, then glanced at his serious face; I hoped there was no one else he'd found true love with.

On the allotted day, I found it difficult trying to conceal my excitement that I would soon be married to the love of my life, my Johnnie. So, when My Lady and I got to the lodgings in Anchor Close, I made sure she had everything she needed and was comfortable.

All the cook had to offer was mutton broth and eggs, but she seemed perfectly happy with that; for a lady, she was really not particular about her food, and always ate with such gusto. And of course, I ensured there was plenty of claret at her side.

I was beside myself with nerves for the couple of hours after she'd finished her supper, waiting and waiting for the bells to chime from St Giles up the street. I sat by the tiny window, not saying a word, for fear I would miss the sound. Luckily, she looked as if she was already dozing, a half-smile on her face; perhaps she was imagining a pleasant journey the following day to London. Then, when I heard it strike midnight, I said to my mistress I was going to fetch the water for her toilette. She smiled at me and I felt a pang of conscience; I wondered, once again, if I was betraying her. I did not think I possibly could be, for as Johnnie had explained when I voiced my concerns, I was simply helping her be removed from a potentially dangerous situation and into a place of safety. Those papers she had commanded me to fetch during her husband's rare visit that day could possibly put her life in peril if they got into the wrong hands.

I ran downstairs and tiptoed to the door. I unlocked it and saw through the gloom that the men were already there, waiting. Two of them, both sturdy and tall, rushed past me.

"Which room?" one of them hissed at me.

I pointed upstairs. "Second floor, on the right."

As they bounded upstairs and my eyes adjusted to the darkness, I peered out. There was a man sitting upright in a sedan chair, the curtains pulled back a fraction. There was no sign of Johnnie.

"Where's Johnnie?" I asked, trying to keep my voice down.

"Who?"

"Johnnie, my friend from The Sheep Heid. He said he'd be here."

He pulled the curtain back further and I could see his face, gaunt and pale in the faint light. He was swathed in a Highland plaid. He leant forward, towards me.

"Ah, that Johnnie. Don't worry, he'll be here soon, probably just after we've left." He was mumbling, so I had to lean towards him. "You need to stay here after we've taken your mistress; remain here by the door."

"Why isn't he here now?"

"He got waylaid; he won't be long, though. So, you run along inside now, then once we've taken her, stay right here by the door and wait. I'm sure he won't be long."

I heard a noise and looked up to see My Lady being carried downstairs in an undignified manner by one of the men. She was slung over his shoulders, her legs writhing behind his back. I hid behind the parlour door so she could not see me and peeked out to see them thrust her onto the man's lap in the sedan chair.

He yanked her arms back so the two men could tie her to him and then they bound her mouth tight so she could not shout out or even speak. Her eyes were full of tears and her cheeks were red and livid.

I was shocked; it was not meant to happen like this. Johnnie had said she would be escorted by coach to a safe haven; he did not mention the fact that ruffians would forcibly carry her from her rooms and bundle her into a chair as if she were a criminal. I felt sick as I watched the chair wobble when the men swung the poles onto their shoulders.

They staggered on up the close to the High Street, where I thought I could just make them out turning to the right, but perhaps not; it was difficult to see anything through the tears that were now streaming down my cheeks.

I wiped my face with my sleeve and went inside, pulled the door over a little and sat down on the cold stone floor. I could feel my heart race as I continued to cry. Oh Lord, forgive me; what have I done? This was all my fault; she looked so angry and upset, her hair was all over the place and her gown yanked down from her shoulders as if there had been a tussle. Then I realised I could do no more. I just had to wait for Johnnie to come and he would reassure me she was going to be fine.

I have no idea how long I sat there, but I was cold and shivering as I kept my ear to the crack in the door. As I sat there, horrible thoughts raced through my mind. I wondered about the children; should I try to contact Mary, the countess, and tell her what happened? But I was sworn to secrecy; besides, I was the reason they had got in to take her. I wondered about all her belongings upstairs, but I did not want to leave my vigil by the door for one minute, in case I missed Johnnie.

Eventually I thought I heard some faint steps and I peeked outside. Some light mist had descended and it was difficult to make out whether it was a man or a woman at the top of the close. As I peered into the gloom, I began to see the figure more clearly. It was definitely a man, for I saw not a skirt or gown, but breeches.

My heart was thumping. It must be Johnnie; he was making his way down the cobbles to me. Soon I would be in his arms and then not long after, we would be man and wife. I got to my feet, stood up straight and pushed open the door.

Chapter 17

Rachel

We rode all night. I was angry and distressed but most of all exhausted, yet I realised there was no point in continuing to struggle. Besides, I couldn't move, so tight were the bonds that tied me to this man. One of my shoulders was bare, one thankfully covered with my shawl. I yelled at him to stop so I could pull it round me, but he ignored me. I decided to conserve my energy and kept my mouth shut. I tried to make out where we were going but there was little moonlight and I could see nothing in the dark, drizzling night. The gallop of the horse soon became a canter, then a trot as the three other horses formed a line in front. I think there was another horse behind too, but I could not move my head.

Through my tears I blinked and tried to see anything that would show me our direction of travel. But I could see nothing in the dark, windy night. I looked down at my hands, trying to remember if I had been wearing my ring when taken, but I could not see even a glimmer of the shiny blue gem. I rubbed my little finger against the fourth finger of my right hand and was overjoyed to find it there. Well, that was a comfort if nothing else, for that was worth a lot, should I need it in the days to come.

I felt the biting wind against my ankles and realised my skirts were pulled up to my knees. I was sitting astride the snorting, foul-smelling beast as if I were a commoner; ladies are surely never meant to ride a horse like this, strapped to a stranger, clothes in disarray.

To take my mind away from the pain across my chest and waist where they had tied me so tight and to help me forget about how frozen to the bone I was, I went over in my head what had happened. Two ruffians in Highland dress had carried me out of my chamber like an animal for slaughter, before strapping me to some other man sitting in a sedan chair. Was this the same man to whose lap I was then bound? I had no idea.

And then, at the West Port, I was transferred by rough hands to this horse in the most unladylike fashion. And now here we were bounding over the countryside in the pitch black as the continuous rain exacerbated the deep chill throughout my body.

I thought back again to the fading embers of the fire in my chambers and, with a gasp, I remembered Annie. What had become of her? Hopefully she was safe; perhaps she had hidden downstairs or had tried to fend off the attackers, though I had seen no one downstairs in the hall. Surely they had not harmed her – please God let her still be alive. A sweeter, more caring person I had never met; she accommodated my every demand in a cheerful and proficient way. She was also lovely to look at, with that delicate nose of hers and stature that was less servant, more lady.

To be honest, she seems to care for me more than some of my children, though Mary, My Angel, was always so special – and kind – to me, and look how well she has ended up. She is also far more attractive than Fannie and the boys, all of whom seem to have inherited James' nose and his scrawny body. I tried to eliminate from my mind the thought that dear Annie had been harmed, for my head was in torment enough.

As the grey dawn broke, I could make out a tall edifice ahead of us, perhaps a tower or a castle with high turrets. The riders all slowed the horses down to a trot and I shook myself to try to waken up from my frigid drowse. The men began to shout at each other in some gruff indecipherable language and I opened my eyes wide. There before us stood a couple of figures bearing flaming torches. The horses' trot dwindled to a halt and the man I was attached to began to untie my bonds. The relief of this was so overwhelming that I was about to thank him, but then checked myself in time. Thank him for what?

One of the other riders carried me off the horse and bore me aloft, thankfully in a rather less undignified manner than that by which I'd been abducted from my chambers in Edinburgh. We followed the servants with the torches to the entrance of the high tower and at the narrow doorway I was put down onto my feet, although my captor held both of my arms tight. I was unsteady on my feet and my thighs ached. I had no strength to do anything, certainly not to attempt to run off, so I just lumbered along beside him.

It felt even colder inside the tower house than outside and I shivered and pulled my shawl round me as I was guided by an old serving woman to a dingy room. I could just make out by the light of her torch that it was furnished with only a wooden bed covered with an uneven mattress and a coarse wool blanket. She pointed it out to me then gestured to a chamber pot beside the bed and beside it a tray with a tankard full of some liquid and a small loaf of bread.

I staggered towards the bed, pulled off a clump of bread and rammed it into my mouth in the most unladylike manner, but I was starving. I took a gulp of the liquid; it was ale, to which I was never too partial. I sat down on the mattress, which was jagged and rough, obviously filled with straw, not the feathers I was used to. But I did not care, I simply wanted to lie down and sleep. The woman hovered by me like an idiot and I took another gulp of the sour ale. It really was not to my taste, but needs must.

"Is there no claret, woman?"

She shook her head and I commanded her to leave. As she turned towards the door, I realised I had no idea where I was.

"What place is this?"

She shrugged and said nothing. Perhaps she was simple; she certainly had a glaikit look about her.

I raised my voice and bellowed.

"How long am I to be here?"

Again, silence.

I shook my head in despair then, overwhelmed by a fatigue that enveloped my frigid body, I lay down on the jagged mattress, pulled the stale-smelling blanket over me and fell at once into a deep sleep.

When I awoke, it was still gloomy but not as dark as earlier. There was a tiny window up high in one of the bare stone walls and I could just make out some silvery clouds. I had no idea what time it was but surely I had slept no longer than a couple of hours; hopefully it was still morning and I could ascertain what I was doing in this midden and when I was getting home.

I flung off the filthy blanket and eased myself off the barbed mattress. My limbs ached. I looked at the cracked chamber pot, sighed and lifted it before removing it to a corner. Once I was done, I strode to the door and tried the handle. It was locked, so I banged on it. No one came so I kept hammering with my fists. Eventually a key turned in the lock and the old serving woman stood there, looking as grey and dim as she had earlier.

"Bring your master here. Now."

She locked the door inside, pushed past me and I watched her go and peer in the pot then collect the tray, which had held the meagre victuals.

"Are you going to bring him or not?"

She shrugged and went out, locking the door behind her.

I banged on the door again with both fists, lifted my head and cried, "Let me out! I demand to be taken home!"

I have no idea how long I waited but another noise roused me from my doze on the vile mattress. I brushed the filth from my bosom and tried to sweep my hair behind my head into the single clasp that had held fast in the winds of last night. I never was expert at doing my hair; where was Annie?

The door opened and a strange gentleman appeared, the idiot servant behind him. I did not recognise him as being one of the ruffians from the night before, but since I could scarcely see in the dark, I could not be sure. He locked the door and walked towards me. I held my head high and stretched out my hand. Be gracious, Rachel, this man is the only means of getting out of this hole. The man ignored my outstretched hand and instead used his right hand to adjust the Highland plaid swung over his shoulder.

"What do you want?"

My mouth gaped open; the insolence of the man. What did I want? Was it not obvious?

"I wish to know why I am here, indeed where I am and when I'm to be going home?"

"Whenever we get word about the crossing, then we'll be on our way again towards the west."

"The west? What crossing? What are you talking about, Sir? I wish to go home."

"It is for your own safety, My Lady."

I screwed up my eyes. "I don't understand, what are you talking about?"

"We must get you to a safe place, but that'll only be when the tides are right."

"What tides?" I was now hollering like a common fishwife.

The two of them were silent, looking at me aghast. My face

must have been bright red and livid with anger. I decided to take a different tack, even attempting a smile.

"Please might you let me know where I am and when I shall be home?"

"You are at my castle in Stirlingshire. We will be leaving here as soon as we've received word and then we head west. But it could take days, perhaps weeks."

I stifled a sob and composed myself by breathing deeply. "Might I have some of my things, please. My gowns, some books?"

The man shook his head. "You can't have your own things, that won't be possible, but depending on how long we have to wait, I could possibly get some things that are necessary for you. What do you need?"

I looked around the drab cold room. "Some wall hangings, a proper mattress, an escritoire, some ink…"

"My Lady, this is an old castle, not a palace. It's only essentials I can get you. You're not to be here long, hopefully. A gown, did you say?"

"More than one gown, at least three and a bodice, a petticoat, a plaid with a pin, some books, hair clasps and some claret; that ale you served tasted like the contents of the chamber pot."

He smirked. "I can promise nothing, but let me see what I can do." He turned to go, the woman by his side.

"Please, please, do not go, Sir. Why am I being kept a prisoner? What have I done to deserve this treatment?" Tears came to my eyes. "When can I go home to my babies? And Annie – my serving woman – what has become of her?"

He turned towards the door and I rushed after him and fell upon my knees, pulling at his legs. "Please, Sir, I beseech you, do not leave me here in this foul place. I am used to fine things."

He wrenched my arms from his legs and flung me away from him then bent his head down to listen to the idiot woman's whispers. Then, standing by the door he announced. "She'll bring in your supper shortly. And there is no claret, only ale." He tilted his head. "Goodbye."

As the door slammed and I heard the key turn in the lock, I heaved myself onto the so-called bed, pulled up the stinking blanket and wept. Once more, I simply wanted to die.

Part Three

Chapter 18

Rachel

The journey by sea was interminable; I have no idea if we spent three days and three nights on that derelict old boat, or one day and one night. I had lost all sense of time in the misery and suffering. And whereas I wanted to die on those cold, wet, undignified journeys on horseback to reach the place they called Loch Hourn, on the boat I wanted to live. Everything was as bad, indeed far worse, than before, but I was determined not to drown. My fear of open water is so great I even chose to cling to the coarse, drunken master as we smacked through the waves while the wind constantly buffeted the patched-up old sloop. The fog that fell some time after we left Loch Hourn was so dense at one stage that I could not make out the figures at the bow, even through the flashes of moonbeam. So, I kept my eyes shut tight for what must have been hours upon hours as we headed west through the night, away from the mainland.

It was now several weeks since my cruel abduction from the lodgings in Edinburgh. We had had to wait an age at the Stirlingshire tower for better weather, which eventually arrived in the month of April. Then I had to endure yet more horseback rides, bound once more as if I were a prisoner, until we reached this sea loch, where I was permitted one day of rest before the sloop sailed. At least by now I had a small trunk of clothes, books and writing materials, but that was my only consolation. I still had no idea where I was being taken and for how long. And most importantly, on whose orders. I had grown weary of asking.

As we rounded the north of a large island the master said was called Skye, the storm battered the already rickety, half-decked sloop and though I'd tried to lie down with my head on the trunk, I spent most of the time holding tight onto the one solid thing on the boat, which was the foul-smelling, inebriated master as he stood at the ship's wheel. The timbers groaned and I could hear the splintering of the rotten bulwarks as I shut my eyes tight and mumbled some prayers to myself. The master was the only man on board who could speak English; the other men only grunted at each other in Gaelic.

After goodness knows how many hours, perhaps even days, there was a faint streak of dawn in the east and the master shouted at me that we were nearing the Sound of Harris. I had not slept at all – how could I? – and my only wish at that moment was not for the health of my five darling children, but that the storm would subside and I would not drown. I kept praying that the rest of the journey – however long that was – would be in calmer waters. Thankfully, with dawn there was a slight lull in the gale and I allowed myself to keep my eyes open for longer.

I also felt the boat was steady enough to sit down, even though there was so much water on the deck. I had long ago lost my inhibitions about what a lady should and should not do and so I sat beside my trunk in great puddles of water, all of my skirts soaked from sea water, rain and urine. I stretched up my neck and was able to see some small islands nearby. The master was kindly enough, even though he stank of sweat and the spirit that he quaffed continuously. He gestured to the islands as we passed and told me the names of each. There was Killegray, there was Pabbay and, to the south, Berneray. Then after some time he told me that to the south-east was a bigger island called North Uist. Eventually, his telescope up to his eye, he pointed ahead.

"Over there, Madam, are the Monach Isles. That's where we are going to land."

"Why? What is there?" I was weak with hunger and lack of sleep so had lost my will to challenge everything in anger, as I usually did.

He shrugged. "That I don't know; I am simply commanded that it's where you're to be put ashore."

He put down his telescope, bellowed orders to his crew, took a swig of whisky then turned the wheel in the direction of the Monachs.

As we approached the Monach Isles, the master told me we were heading for the most easterly inhabited island, which was called Ceann Ear. As daylight fell, I could now make out land and saw that the island was flat, with neither hills nor trees. We sailed in a straight line now and I could make out the shore. The only other thing I could see were seabirds soaring and swooping over the land.

"I cannot see a pier or landing jetty," I said as the sloop hurtled on towards land.

"Pier? Of course there's no pier, Madam. It's a shelving sandy beach; we come to land just before the beach." He raised his telescope again. "Now keep quiet, will you, I have to hear when the keel hits the sand."

I had no idea what he was talking about; I had only seen boats land at harbours with piers and so had no notion of how we were to get off this godforsaken, dilapidated old boat. I continued to sit, holding onto my trunk and stared ahead. As we neared land, I could make out some figures running towards the beach, waving. The men on board our sloop waved back and spoke rapidly in their own guttural language. Now the master shouted at them in Gaelic, so I didn't know what was going on, but he seemed to be steering us directly towards the beach ahead.

I looked up and saw with gratitude that the clouds had parted and the sky was blue. I felt a strange feeling of relief as the boat continued at a slow pace before suddenly juddering to a halt when, presumably, the keel had embedded in the sand. Two of the men jumped out into the water and hung onto the bulwarks, then I saw two men from the island run down the beach and wait at the sea's edge.

The sloop had come to a stop, rocking in the waves as the master continued to bellow instructions in Gaelic. I simply sat, waiting for the vessel to be pulled further up the beach, but soon realised that this was as far as it was going.

"Right, you have to jump out now. The lads there will help you get up onto the dunes."

I looked down and saw only dark water. "But it's too deep, I shall drown."

The master shook his head and pointed at the two men who had already left the sloop. "They've managed fine, so will you." He took a long draught from his flask. "Now get off the boat, we'll see to your trunk."

He pulled me to my feet and pushed me to the side of the boat. I stood, motionless, my fear of drowning returning as I steeled myself to jump overboard.

"I'd hoik your skirts up if were you, unless you want to be completely drenched." He did not even attempt to cover a smirk.

I pulled my gown up to my knees and slithered over the side, gasping as the cold water hit me. It was up to my waist, so my skirts, which now floated around me, were completely wet. I refused to look at the master, who I could imagine laughing as he continued to swig from his flask.

My feet were on firm sand and I flung my skirts aside and forced my weak body through the surf, trying to push my legs faster through the powerful weight of the water. Soon I was on the beach and I collapsed onto the sand in utter exhaustion, my sodden skirts and petticoats a dead weight on top of me. I raised my head to see the men lifting my trunk on their shoulders and laying it down by my side. I had no energy to speak, so I simply shifted my head, leant it on the trunk and closed my eyes.

Chapter 19

William Fleming

I put down my book when I heard the men run past the window. I looked out and saw a sloop approach the beach, with some men on board, waving. I watched as the two island men rushed on towards the shore, one of them wheeling a wooden barrow. I went to stand at my door and saw the most extraordinary sight unfold.

The Monach Islands, where I have lived now for nearly three years, are not exactly full of civilised inhabitants. The entire population of some hundred souls are simple people, cottars who wear modest clothes suited to working on the land or on the sea. Their houses are basic, dirt-floored with no windows and with thatching made from the marram grass collected on the sand dunes.

The only exception of course is the house of Donald Macdonald, tacksman to Sir Alexander Macdonald of Sleat, but he has lived on North Uist since his wife's malady. He now stays on the Monachs for only two to three nights a year, in order to fulfill his job of collecting rent from the islanders, to pass on to Sir Alexander. His house, just like the other wretched ones on the island, is walled with dry-stone packed with earth, but unlike the black houses nearby, it has a couple of windows facing the sea and the floor has flagstones, instead of compressed earth.

And so, when I saw a woman emerge, wet and dishevelled from the dilapidated sloop, and slump down on the beach, as if half-drowned, I could not believe my eyes. For a start, no women ever boarded boats in these superstitious islands; and, though I had of course heard the rumours that there would be a visitor arriving soon, I was not told it would be a woman. Also, I could make out, by a glimpse of the drenched gown and the fact that she wore shoes, that she was a lady.

I watched as the master of the sloop and one of his crew struggled to push a trunk out of the vessel and lowered it over the side to two others in the water. They waded, up to their waists in water, until they reached the beach and deposited the trunk beside the woman, who was now splayed out on the sand, her loose tresses all around. I saw her raise herself onto her elbows, then lay her head and shoulders on the trunk, enclosing its girth with her arms as if protecting it.

I considered going down to the beach to see if I could assist, but knew the islanders would not appreciate my interference, so I stayed there at the door and continued to watch from the one window of my tiny house. Jimmy and Finn at first talked to the crew and gesticulated to the master, who did not appear to intend leaving his vessel. They got down beside the woman and encouraged her to let go of the trunk.

They then helped her get up from the sand and, since she was obviously too weak to walk herself, they lifted her into the barrow, where she slumped down once more, her head dangling over the end, her long dark hair almost touching the sand. Jimmy pushed the barrow through the sand with some difficulty, for she must have been heavy with the weight of water in her clothes. Finn gestured to a boy running over the machair and soon his son John took the other end of the trunk and together they raised it high above their heads.

I then watched this strange procession of a man and a boy bearing a trunk aloft and one lady following, slumped into a crofter's basic wheelbarrow. They continued up from the beach, over the dunes and towards Donald Macdonald's house. Since I lived at the other end of the village I could not see whether she needed help to get up from the barrow, but after some minutes I saw Jimmy, Finn and John walk past my house with an empty barrow.

Five days later, I was about to begin the service in church when I looked over the bowed heads of the congregation to the tiny wooden door, which creaked open. Everyone looked round to see a lady, now dressed in a fine gown, underneath a broad sweep of plaid.

They all gawped as she swept down the aisle between the cramped pews, head raised high, her dark silver-streaked hair cascading loose around her pale white neck. It was impossible to say whether the shocked looks of the congregation were because she was a fine lady or because she wore no hat.

As she passed the few pews of the tiny sanctuary, I noticed she wore a beautiful blue ring that glinted in the late-morning sun filtering through the tiny window above me. She took her seat at the front, in the place reserved for Donald Macdonald and his wife, as if it were her right. Without acknowledging anyone, she sat down, gathered her gown about her and looked up, directly at me. Her gaze was unsettling, those coal-black eyes seared into mine. I picked up my Bible, flicked through the pages and began the service.

At the end, she did not leave first, as Donald and Isabella used to do; instead she waited until each pew had emptied and it was only she who stood inside the church. She approached the door where I stood waiting, then smiled and spoke.

"Reverend, I understood absolutely nothing during that service, not a word." She paused. "I realise you must speak to the people in their own language, of course. But I should like to discuss matters spiritual; perhaps we could pray together in

English. We might also talk about literature? But only when you have time." She continued to hold my gaze, seldom even blinking. "I find there is no one for company apart from my serving girl. Will you call upon me some time later in the week? You know, I believe, where I reside."

"I do, My Lady." I did not even know her name, no one did. "It would be my pleasure."

"Do not expect much." She smiled. "The girl who waits upon me is not exactly versed in domestic matters. Nor can we communicate by anything other than gestures."

And with that, she nodded and swept off, by herself, towards the house at the other end of the village.

Rumours were rife all over the island about who she was and why she was there. Even Jimmy and Finn said they knew nothing, only that a visitor would be arriving from afar. They knew she'd be staying in the Macdonald house, since the tacksman and his wife no longer lived there, and that she was to have Jimmy's daughter Catriona to wait on her.

Apart from that, she was a mystery, though it was obvious from her demeanour and her dress that she was a lady. But who she was no one on the island knew. I hurried next door to the manse, wondering if her lodgings were that much better than this hovel. I knew my house was less miserable than all of the islanders' from those occasions when I was obliged to visit them, but it certainly was nothing like my home back on the mainland.

I sat on the little stool beside the peat fire, prodded the embers and stared into the rekindled flames, feeling somewhat disconcerted. I looked over at my pile of books on the writing table, trying to decide which I might take when I paid a social call.

Chapter 20

William Fleming

On my way back from my visit to old Nessie Maclean in the north of the island, near Gortinish, I strolled over the machair then stopped, sat down on a rock and gazed all around. One of the few things I loved about the Monach Islands was the machair and as I looked down at the clover, harebell, butter-cups and birdsfoot trefoil, I marvelled at the colours – the whites, purples and yellows standing out against the green of the grass.

I had already smelt the wild thyme and trod over silverweed and dandelion. It was a joy, a God-given wonder, that so much beauty could lie beneath our feet. I looked up to the sky and saw fulmars and terns soar and dive along the shore.

On a late spring morning like today, with a bold sun and blue sky and not a cloud to be seen, I felt energised and alive. I was able to forget the putrid smell I encountered when entering the Macleans' hovel as I prayed with Nessie on the filthy mattress her husband called a bed. I was obliged to take a dram, for to refuse would have been impolite, but I did manage to decline the blackened bannock that he'd obviously attempted to make himself while his ancient wife lay dying nearby.

So often during my time on these islands, under the weight of the grey clouds and the battering storms of rain and wind, I wondered why I was here. The congregation did not seem to appreciate my sermons nor my counsel. "It will take a bit of time for them to accept you," the previous minister had told me, and it was clear that he could hardly wait to leave. Well, I was still awaiting acceptance among the people of the Monach Islands, having been here almost three years.

I looked around and squinted into the sun. There was someone walking on the dunes along by Rudha nam Marbh. No one usually walked there; it was not called Dead Man's Point for nothing and these superstitious islanders made detours to avoid the dunes there when harvesting the fulmars' eggs.

I walked towards the beach and was able to see it was a woman; she was wearing a dress. Then I stopped and stood still when I realised it was her, it was the lady from the church. As I approached, I could see she wore a gown of lapis lazuli blue and she swung something in her hand; it was her shoes. I grinned as I saw that this fine lady had had to adopt the island ways.

There was a sudden squawk of seabirds and I saw a fulmar fly out of the dunes near her. She started but did not look afraid, though I hoped she would not get too near one of their nests. They had spat at me when I came across one recently; they can be the most vicious of birds. She moved down onto the beach and I saw her paddle in the water, holding up her skirts a little, so I could see her ankles, white and delicate.

I continued over the machair towards her then stopped. Perhaps she would not want me to approach her in the outdoors like this; it might be unseemly. I would retreat and wait until I paid her a visit; that would be more proper. And so, I stood gazing over at the lady who was oblivious to me standing not far away, as she walked along the sand, her head turned always towards the sea, as if waiting for someone.

Trying to find something to comb through my hair, I realised that in all my time here I had seldom bothered about my appearance. Until today, when I tried to tease my thick locks apart with my fingers and dabbed my cupped hand in a bowl of water to splash on my face. Well, that was how it was living here on these islands. I picked up the books I had selected and went to the door. No one locked their doors here – what was the point? There was nothing to steal and it was the custom that everyone was welcome at any time of the day or night into each other's homes. I remembered soon after I'd arrived being awoken in the middle of the night by a young man prodding me awake. He hadn't knocked, but had just come into my house to ask me to come and pray for his wife who was in labour.

I took my time walking along the machair towards her house, looking out at the swell of the waves as a cold easterly wind blew across the low-lying shore. I passed the Mackinnons' then the Munros' houses, where Anne was sorting out the kelp in her basket and Murdo was milking his sheep into a filthy bucket. I nodded but did not stop to converse. I knew they'd be watching where I was heading, with books under my arm.

I stood at the Macdonald door and looked up. It had recently been rethatched and had more of an air of neatness than a few months before when Donald was last here. I knocked on the door and waited, turning away to gaze rather at the sea than at the low wooden door.

Soon the door was opened and Catriona answered it.

"Come away in," she said, gesturing to a room to her right. Speaking in her own tongue, I asked how the lady of the house was. She shrugged and pointed inside the room.

"Do come in, Reverend," I heard a voice say. And I walked into the front room, which had the window looking down to the sea, so instead of being dark and dingy like all of the other houses, including mine, it was light.

She stood there, wearing the same brown gown she had worn in the church and her hair was up in loose curls around her beautiful neck. Her bosom was covered with a modest edge of lace. This was only the second time I had seen her up close and I realised she must be in her early forties, for she had some fine lines around her full red lips and white and silver streaked through her hair. Yet she seemed to exude the vitality of a much younger woman.

"I do hope today is a convenient time to call?" I said, bowing my head.

"It is. Please sit down on the only other chair in this house." She smiled. "Did the wife of the man who owns this house never entertain here?"

I shook my head. "These islands are not as you might expect." I sat down and put my books on the small table between us. "There used to be more books here, I'm sure of it. But I have brought you a few anyway."

She fingered the spines then grabbed one eagerly and opened it. "Daniel Defoe," she whispered, beaming. "It's a long time since I've read his work." She leant her head to see the titles of the other books. "But perhaps we should begin with this one, Reverend Fleming." She pointed to the Bible at the bottom of the pile.

I hesitated, my discomfort at not knowing her identity increasing. I cleared my throat and was about to speak when the door opened and in came Catriona. She was carrying a knobbly plank of wood onto which was set two goblets and a pewter jug.

"Put them down here," said the lady, gesturing to a space alongside the books. She peered at the makeshift tray. "You can see we don't have any serving trays here. Can you ask her to bring some butter for these bannocks. That might make them less unpalatable."

I did as she asked then watched as she poured some wine into the goblets. She glanced up at me. "I have only two bottles of claret left. I am in dire need of more, but I thought that we must partake during your visit."

"I am flattered. Thank you. But I'm sure I could try to get some more?"

She sat back against the chair and sighed. "That, Reverend Fleming, would be wonderful."

There was silence while Catriona brought in a dish of butter. Once she had gone, I plucked up my courage.

"I feel embarrassed to ask this, but I do not know your name or where you are from. You know by now I am the Reverend Fleming, but please can you call me William? No one else on these islands calls me by it. It would please me greatly."

"Well, then that is what I shall call you." She leant her head to the side. "Did you say islands? I thought there was only one isle here?"

"The Monachs have five islands; we are on the largest."

"I see. Well then, I look forward to hearing more about them."

I smiled. "That, My Lady, will not take long."

She laughed. "Oh, but how rude of me. My name, of course. If you insist on my calling you William, then you must call me Rachel."

She pulled out the Bible from the foot of the pile and handed it to me. Our fingertips met and I swiftly removed my hand to grasp the goblet, which I raised to my lips. She too lifted her glass, smiled at me and took a deep draught.

Chapter 21

Rachel

I had spent only some ten days on the Monachs, which I now know are plural; there is more than one Monach island. And up until this morning I knew even less about them, certainly not from my only companion, the serving girl Catriona, with whom I must gesture with my hands to communicate.

But then William the minister paid a visit this afternoon and I feel that not only do I know a little more about where I am, I might also be able to plan how to escape this godforsaken place, which has no culture, no shops and frankly no food apart from seabirds and bannocks – and certainly no claret. And to think I used to take tea every day from a porcelain cup; and go to assemblies and oyster parties in the city dressed in my best gowns and sparkling jewels.

Also, given the time it took me to get here and those most awful journeys by horse and boat, I must be many miles from home and so I should begin to devise my strategy. I must above all else return to Edinburgh to be with my darling children. They are sure to be missing me; Mary, My Angel, will be so worried. When I think of her I wonder, once more, if she is yet with child.

If so, I hope Fannie is be with her in Inverness-shire to take over the role that, as her mother, I should be fulfilling by her side. Poor Fannie, I doubt she'll ever marry; she has inherited both her father's nose and also his obsession with religion; the girl is always studying her Bible.

And whatever became of Annie? Over the past weeks I have swayed between thinking that she is absolutely fine, then that the ruffians harmed her. I am not only missing her administrations – no one can attend to my hair like she can – but I am also worried about her. What became of her that horrific night in Edinburgh?

I have come to think that I may even forgive my dear husband. I might excuse him for the whore in London, for those political aberrations and even for his demeaning treatment of me as if I were his slave; if only I can somehow get home.

I have spent what must now be over three months travelling, staying in the most wretched lodgings. Admittedly I was overjoyed when the laird at that Stirlingshire castle managed to get a trunk full of things I'd asked for, but that has been the only joy in these past few weeks.

And I still have only two gowns, both of which have seen better days, their colours now faded. It seems unlikely that any woman here on these islands is capable of sewing a gown suitable for a lady such as myself.

After I arrived here, I lay in bed for three full days, exhausted and so low in spirit, this latter not helped by being served vile, fishy-tasting thin pottage by the girl. On the fourth day, she managed to communicate to me that the following day was Sunday and everyone would be at church.

By showing me a Bible written in English from the small pile of books left by the man who owns this house, I understood that the minister might speak English. And so, I rose from my bed, washed myself and took some time trying to get the tangles out of my hair. I dressed as well as I could, considering the poor comforts at my disposal and, after breakfast, I headed for the church.

As I walked along the grassy path, I thought of the breakfasts we used to have at Preston House. There were oatcakes and barley cakes with sweet butter, cold mutton, cold roast beef and proper bread, not these blackened beremeal bannocks that taste only of smoke and earth.

The girl seems incapable, however, of ruining oatmeal porridge and so that is what I have in the morning, even though the consistency is thin, like a gruel served to invalids. At Preston House there was also strong ale and claret for breakfast. I would even put aside my prejudice and drink ale, if the girl proffered it. I sighed as I remembered the groaning table provided for all meals and wondered how I could get some proper provisions. I then took a deep breath of fresh, salty sea air and continued on into the tiny church.

The sight of the young minister was an unexpected joy. He looked to be in his mid-thirties and had something almost naive and innocent about him, with his thick fair hair and freckled complexion. He seemed a pearl among the swine that are the rest of the islanders. As I walked slowly past them all in their overcrowded pews, I noted that they were foul-smelling and wearing drab grey clothes that even the gardeners at Preston House would not be permitted to wear.

When I conversed with him afterwards, I realised how much I had missed speaking English to a civilised person. As I walked back to the house afterwards, I felt somehow joyful, alive. I was, however, under no illusion: I was still a prisoner, though not one confined to a cold, dark room as I had been before.

And so, on a couple of fine days this week I have taken walks along the beach, over the white sand, and have even paddled in the sea. The water is cold yet invigorating. My arrival here last week and the ignominious way I had to wade ashore now seems like a lifetime ago.

Paddling is an activity I would not have permitted for my daughters: to have bare feet in the sea would have been improper. But here I can do as I please. On one of my walks, I was aware there was someone on the dunes watching me, but I chose to ignore them. It was no doubt one of the islanders looking for fulmar nests to steal their eggs. I had the misfortune to taste one of these when Catriona insisted on cooking one for me and I wish never to repeat the experience again. I began to think about the minister's visit later in the week and what on earth she could produce that was acceptable, never mind edible.

When I heard his polite knock at the door, I shifted in the chair a little, so I had my back to the window. I know it seems vain, but I believe my lined face looks slightly less old in a shadow. I also sat fully upright, remembering what Mama had taught me, that posture was paramount for a lady. I am of course fully aware that my looks are fading and yet I must do with them what I can, even in this desolate place. And this gown I am wearing, the copper one, was so ruined in the sea water during that awful boat journey that it now looks simply dull brown.

He took my hand and I bade him sit in the one other chair in this house. And this is the only house on the islands that has been lived in by civilised people; well, they must have taken most of their civilisation with them. There are two chairs, one table, one bed and a basic kitchen for the girl to cook in. There are no books apart from two Bibles, one of which is in English, thankfully. There is a chest in the bedroom, but it is locked and I have tried and tried to open it by screwing in hair pins, but all to no avail.

I poured the claret, taking care not to spill a drop, since I had so little left. I handed him his goblet and after some niceties, he introduced himself, insisting I call him William. I simply said my name was Rachel. He seemed to know nothing about me so why should I tell a stranger about my past? Catriona brought in the beremeal bannocks and I apologised for their charcoal appearance while she went to fetch the butter. I thought of the servants at Preston House and the fine fare I used to serve for callers, the sweetmeats and seed cakes. This girl, though perfectly pleasant, has no idea how to serve guests.

After I had eaten as much as I could of the heavy, burnt bannock, I turned the subject to the books. Though I wanted to talk about the Defoe novel, I felt we ought to discuss matters spiritual and so first we turned to the book of Ruth, one of my favourite Old Testament books; to have a cultured conversation after so long was good.

I then asked him to tell me something about himself as I poured from the jug of claret into my goblet; I had noticed he was sipping his. Perhaps men of the cloth do not drink much – although that old devil, the Reverend Elibank certainly did not hold back when imbibing at Preston House.

"Well," he started, tugging at his hair. He was obviously not comfortable talking about himself. "I was brought up in the Highlands and came here just under three years ago."

"I see. Is this your first parish?"

"Yes, I was otherwise employed before but decided to train as a minister some five years ago." He fingered the Bible on his lap as if seeking encouragement. "It's been, well, a little challenging here, I confess." He looked up at me and smiled.

I finished my claret and set the goblet on the table. "And how often do you speak to your family? Or indeed anyone apart from the inhabitants here?"

"I have letters and supplies sent over once a month from North Uist. That's why I think I can order you some more claret; the boat should be here tomorrow or the day after, depending on the weather and the tides. So, if you wish to write a list of anything else, then I could try to obtain some things and…"

I could not stop myself interrupting. "Oh, a couple of crates of claret, some proper wheaten bread, rosewater, some tea, caraway seeds and hen's eggs, not those rank, fishy seabirds' eggs…" I had no idea who would be paying for these, but that was not my concern for now. I looked around the bare room. "Some more ink and…"

He raised his hand and shook his head. "I apologise, Rachel, I should have said, only very basic commodities. The Uists are not so far from us here but they are still very far from the mainland."

I sighed. Of course, what was I expecting?

"Do you have writing paper to compile a list of essentials? I shall be sending my requests with Mr Macdonald's boat."

I raised an eyebrow.

"Donald Macdonald, he's the owner of this house, he's Sir Alexander's tacksman. He used to live here but it wasn't to his wife's liking very much." He took a gulp of wine. "He now lives on North Uist."

The door flew opened and Catriona rushed in. She did not curtsey or even apologise for interrupting but began at once a garbled conversation with William in her own coarse language. I drummed my fingers against the table until they stopped talking, then she headed for the door. Only there did she remember to curtsey.

William got to his feet. "Rachel, I am so sorry. Catriona has just told me old Nessie Maclean is breathing her last and her husband insists I go to see her one final time. I must go at once."

He took my hand and raised it up and for a moment I thought he was going to kiss it, but he simply bowed his head, dropping my hand with such gentleness, then turned on his heels and fled out the door. I picked up the jug of claret, upended it and shook the final drops into my goblet then tipped my head back and waited for them to trickle down my throat.

Chapter 22

William Fleming

The following week, I was returning from a visit to a family on the south of Ceann Ear and decided to walk around the west side of Loch nam Buadh. It was a fine day and I needed to clear my head after being inside one of the black houses.

They are more like hovels, and this one was packed with a family of seven children, all grubby with soot. I still cannot get used to the fact that the peat fire is in the hearth in the middle of the house and, since there is no chimney, the smoke simply furls around, filling the entire home with fumes and everyone coughs and splutters, spreading germs and ash.

The smoke eventually seeps through the thatch roof, once it has tainted all of the inhabitants. I could not wait to leave, but the mother had just had a stillborn baby and they wanted him baptised. The weight of sadness hung as heavy in the air as the peat smoke.

I was so glad to be back in the fresh air and decided to walk to the western shore of the loch and to the beach at the other side of the island from our village. I walked round the headland and stood on the machair breathing in the fragrant smells of wild thyme and marsh orchids. I bent down and picked one of the purple orchids and pushed it through my buttonhole.

I looked towards the tidal sands between Ceann Ear and the island to the west, Shivinish. I had seldom been over to that island but knew that it was the middle island of the three

Monach Isles that were joined at low tide; to its west was Ceann Iar.

Some of the crofters on our island kept sheep on Shivinish, sailing over there or walking over the sand at low tide during lambing time. I peered ahead and was sure I saw someone over there; I would have thought it was too early for the lambing season, but evidently not.

I continued to walk towards the shore, looking over at the small islet, when I saw a flash of blue. And then I realised it was her. I had not seen her for several days; I had had so many parish obligations. She had sent her girl over to my house with her list of requests for North Uist for the next boat. Sadly, I doubt many of them will arrive, apart from perhaps the claret, but what use would a lady have of that apart from entertaining. And there was surely no one in this desolate place she could invite to visit her.

What was Rachel doing over on Shivinish? For a lady, she obviously had none of the restraints of most of the ladies I knew. I waved and began to walk over the firm sand towards the land. She could not see me, as she was walking up over the dunes towards the west. I hastened my step, breaking into a run and soon was able to shout over the wind.

"Rachel, do you need any help?"

She turned and stopped still as a stone. Then I saw her shoulders relax as she obviously recognised me.

She stood and waited on the dunes. I could see the sheep turn their heads at the sound of humans.

I rushed up to her and caught my breath. We both stood in the sand staring at each other. I noticed that again she carried her shoes in her hand. Her hair was loose about her beautiful white shoulders.

"Are you all right, Rachel? This is a long way from your house."

She did not look altogether pleased to see me. "I am fine, thank you for your concern."

"Did you know these are tidal sands that join this island with ours? Then at the other side, on the west coast, Shivinish is joined by the sands to Ceann Iar, which is bigger than this, but also uninhabited." I smiled and looked around. "It's all rather beautiful though, isn't it?"

Still she did not look happy. "Yes," she mumbled.

"Were you going anywhere in particular? I think there's only an hour or so before high tide. Be careful you don't get caught when the tide comes in." I looked up at the gathering clouds. "And if the rain starts, it'll be miserable here; there are no houses for shelter."

She sighed. "This North Uist you told me about: is it much farther west? You said it wasn't that far from us."

I shook my head. "No, no, the Uists and the mainland are all to the east."

I pointed west. "Over there, after the farthest Monach island, Shillay, is the Atlantic Ocean and then, well, I suppose, the Americas."

"So, the only way to get off these godforsaken islands is in that direction, across the sea?" She pointed east. "Not this?"

I nodded and looked at her as she turned back round. She had tears trickling down her cheeks.

"Rachel, I'm sorry, are you unwell?"

She wiped her tears on the back of her hand, breathed in deeply, then whispered, "I need to get home, William, I need to get off these islands and back to my home in Edinburgh, to my family. I thought if I came over to this island I could ask someone who didn't know me to take me on a boat to North Uist." She looked at me once more, her eyes filled with tears. She stretched out her hand and took mine. "Can you help me? Please?"

I looked down and noticed the beautiful little orchid. I plucked it out of the buttonhole, stretched out my hand and gave it to her. Our fingers touched and I experienced the same frisson I'd felt when our hands touched over the Bible at her house.

"I will do everything I can, but I'm not sure what I can do. The boat has been and gone, it won't be back for a couple of weeks."

She hung her head and touched the flower in a distracted manner.

"But we shall try to make a plan." I looked up as the dark clouds rolled towards Ceann Ear. "But let's go back quickly. There's a storm on its way."

We walked over the machair towards the village and she stopped and gazed down at the carpet of tiny wild flowers. "It's all really rather pretty, isn't it? What are these flowers called?"

I told her the names of all the flowers and herbs I knew and she breathed in deep as her delicate nose hovered over the fragrant ones.

"I'm used to structured gardens. Where I lived there is a formal garden. It's so special, people come from far and wide to visit. There's a maze full of honeysuckle and tall hedges of elder matted with briar and serried ranks of roses. It's strange, all those visitors used to come and see it but, apart from my first visit, I never really saw the attraction. But this" – she stretched out her arms – "this is beautiful, wild."

I looked back at the storm rolling in. The sky in the west was now black. "Rachel, we'll have to hurry to get back in time before the rain."

She nodded and stepped along beside me. I couldn't help but notice her pretty feet. The island women had gnarled toes, flat feet and misshapen bunions; Rachel's were fine and delicate with long toes. The skin looked so smooth.

The first drops began as we reached the village. "I would invite you to my house, William, but I have no claret left."

"Come to mine, I have both claret and brandy. It won't take me long to stoke the fire."

She followed as I led her through the unlocked door and as I looked around, shame struck me. What was she, a fine lady, seeing? My house – a two-room cottage – was little better than a byre for animals, though at least it did not smell quite as bad. It was also larger than the hovels of the islanders. I swept some things off the chair, drew it near the fire and bid her sit down. She did and watched as I tended the peat fire, perched on the stool. I could feel her gaze upon my back and it unsettled me. Soon I got to my feet and picked up two goblets. They were grimy, so I rubbed them with a cloth beside the bowl of water. I grabbed a bottle of claret from my store and placed these on the table. I looked around and saw I had nothing dainty to offer her to eat. But then I recalled the bannocks at her house.

"I'm sorry, Rachel, I have nothing fine to offer you to eat. Nell won't be in till tomorrow; she bakes my bannocks."

She chuckled. "If I don't see another beremeal bannock ever again, I won't be unhappy. Let's just have the wine." She nodded at the bottle and I opened it and poured for us both. While I was doing that, she lifted her skirts a fraction and put on her delicate shoes. I saw not only her long elegant feet but also her fine ankles.

Then, as I took my first sip, I gazed over my goblet at the lovely face that was worn with sadness. I put my drink down and bent over the fire to cover my discomfort. "Sorry, Rachel, it's still cold in here. Let me stoke the fire some more. Then tell me about yourself."

She took a deep draught of wine then tipped her head back, eyes shut as if in prayer. She cradled the goblet as if it were a precious jewel and said, "I am not quite sure where to start."

"Just tell me something about why you are here?"

She shook her head and her hair tumbled loose around her shoulders. "If only I knew that, William, then things might not be as hard."

Chapter 23

William Fleming

By the time I'd drained the last drops from the bottle into her goblet I simply did not know what to say. I was still none the wiser as to why she was here. What she had told me was that she had given birth to seven children, two of whom had sadly died. Her eldest daughter had married an earl a couple of years earlier and her other children were either studying (the boys) or being educated to be a lady (the other daughter).

Her husband was an important law lord and, though she did not say so, I believe he must be devoted to her; she lived in the splendour of his family home where her portrait was hung on the wall alongside those of his wealthy ancestors. Her life seemed little different from any other lady, certainly those I had known when I was growing up, until she described that awful night back in Edinburgh.

"But I still don't understand, Rachel. In fact, there are many things that make no sense. Why would Lord Lovat have you kidnapped so brutally and brought here? You say he is an acquaintance of your husband, but why would he do this? Also, why has your husband not tried, over these many weeks, to find you?"

She sighed then lifted her empty glass and I leapt to my feet. "Let me fetch another bottle." I rummaged around under the small kitchen table and found not only another bottle but a plate with last night's lobster. There was still half left. I sniffed it; it seemed fine.

"Can I offer you some lobster? That's all I seem to have that is acceptable to eat."

"That would be lovely, thank you, William. It's so strange, when I lived in Preston House lobster was a delicacy, served in fricassees and fine French bisques. Here they are so common, they're eaten regularly, even by the common inhabitants."

I brought the lobster to our table with the claret. "Here is a cloth for your hands; I always find lobster a messy business."

"Yes indeed. I used to leave all that to my cook but now I'm doing so much more for myself."

"I invariably eat them outside, but perhaps not today."

We looked out through the open door at the rain thundering down. The sky was still black. I went to light the lamp and she smiled. "I can never quite get used to that smell."

"What, the lamp?"

"Yes, Catriona told me – well, gestured to me when I complained again yesterday – that it was the oil of some bird?"

"It's fulmar oil; I agree the odour is rank."

"It's like the seabirds' eggs she keeps insisting on cooking for me. I cannot get beyond the stink!"

She looked through the open bedroom door to the pile of books by my bed. Thank God I had pulled up the blanket that morning before I went out. The state of the bed was not suitable for a lady to see.

"May I?" I nodded and she walked in, with me following behind.

"I see you have some Shakespeare. I'd love to read that. Might I borrow one of his works?"

"Of course. And I also thought you might like *The Pilgrim's Progress*?"

She nodded. "Though I rather think the Defoe you left at my house last week is more applicable. I feel like Robinson Crusoe washed up on this island."

"There are worse places."

"Oh, I know all about those. The castle I had to stay in for weeks in Stirlingshire was filthy and damp and I seldom saw daylight. I would have died had it not been for my strong constitution."

We returned to the table and began on the lobster. She lifted up a claw, sucked the juices out noisily then put the empty shell back on the plate. "I do like lobster very much; it is about the only decent thing I have had to eat here, apart from crab."

I refilled her goblet then waited, hoping she would answer some of my questions. When I thought back to the conversation, I realised she hadn't told me much.

"William, as to your questions about why I thought it was Lord Lovat who had had me so brutally abducted, I have spent these past few weeks wondering exactly the same. But then I thought back to one day at another castle between Stirlingshire and Loch Hourn and understood. There was a girl there who waited upon me and she spoke some English. When I asked her how this was possible when all around her spoke Gaelic, she told me she'd been raised by nuns who had spoken both Gaelic and English. It was only when I noticed her cross herself every time she entered my room that I realised.

"'Are you Roman Catholic?' I'd asked her.

"'Yes, My Lady.'

"'Is the master a papist too?'

"She shrugged and muttered, 'I suppose so.'

"And then I realised that I was staying or journeying with papists and that Lovat, whose men abducted me in Edinburgh, must be behind this whole thing. I remember recognising the red plaid of those brutal Highlanders. As a devout Highland papist, he saw me as a threat to his plans. His brother was killed at Killiecrankie; his entire family were in favour of the papist Old Pretender being on the throne. Though Lovat has always denied being a Jacobite, for his own political gain, he obviously is and wanted to do away with me."

She wiped her hands on the cloth and flicked away some tiny shreds of lobster meat on her gown.

"But Rachel, why would he want to get rid of you? Why not, say, take this up with your husband? He is a devout Protestant gentleman, from what you say? None of this makes sense."

She sat very still for a moment, staring into the flames. Her cheeks were now a rosy red from the fire.

"William, I do not know why Lovat chose to attack me and not my husband, for surely I am innocent of anything." She looked at me, imploringly. "But all I want to do is to get home, to my babies. Do you understand that?"

"I do. I have no children of my own, of course, but I have siblings and can remember my mother's solicitousness when the younger ones were ill or had even simply fallen over."

"So, you will help me?"

She stretched out her arm and her fingertips brushed the back of my hand. I felt the hairs on my arm bristle.

"I will do everything I can, Rachel. I hate to see you, a kind lady of such intellect, always so distraught." I looked out of the door at the pouring rain. The water had begun, as it always does, to drip through the poor thatching, in the corner above the kitchen.

"The boat should be here in the next couple of weeks, so you could try to get a letter sent with it to Donald Macdonald to ask that you be released and sent back to your family. He will surely understand and…"

"No, don't you see? He is obviously in with them. It is his house I am staying in; he must be part of it all."

"I don't see how." He frowned. "Indeed, he is a very pious man and a disciplinarian."

"There must be someone else we can trust."

"Well, we could entrust the boat's master to take the letter to someone else I know on North Uist. He is a minister there, an elderly man, Murdo MacInnes. I feel sure he would not question anything. But who on the mainland will you send your letter to?"

"I have been thinking of that, William. I have had plenty time to think, in the monotony of my existence here. My first plan was to try to escape by myself, but then, thank God, you found me on that other island, otherwise I might have been marooned there at high tide. My second idea is to try to get a letter to Mary, who is now Countess of Kintore. There would be little point involving my sister for no one would believe her, whereas My Angel now has influence. Though I wonder why she has not sent out search parties for me already. But then I thought, perhaps she is expecting a baby or has indeed given birth and is lying in. Her husband's family were staunchly anti-Jacobite and so she could surely elicit his help."

"Rachel, do you not want to trouble your husband? Is he not the ideal man to try to bring you home?"

She downed the liquid in her goblet. I refilled it, marvelling at her capacity for wine. My mother had but two glasses then turned bright red and took herself off to bed.

"No, he is so often away on business, as I said – in Edinburgh and London. I wonder if he has had a period of mourning for me; I am sure he thinks I am dead. Mary will have more time to concern herself and, besides, she would not have given up hope."

"Very well, let me find some writing paper and my quill. Shall we write it now?"

She beamed. "Yes. And then I wonder if I might take to bed thereafter. I am weary; but this has been the most propitious of encounters, William. I am so grateful to you."

She stretched out her arm again and, with her long slender fingers, caressed the back of my hand right to the tips of my short stubbly fingers. I did not – could not – move until she had stopped.

"Now, shall we begin to write that letter, William? Where is your ink?"

Chapter 24

Rachel

I did not tell William any falsehoods; I was perhaps only a little sparing with the truth. Why should I trouble this charming, naive man with the vicissitudes surrounding the politics and morality of my Lord Grange? Why should he know about the trauma I endured as a child or that the momentary pleasure during those weeks before our marriage dissipated soon after the wedding vows had been uttered and I realised my husband did not truly love me; he simply lusted after my body for a while. And of course I was suitable to provide his heirs. No, he need not know more about my life; all I wanted to do was escape from this place. And he, the Reverend Fleming, was my only way out.

I sat on my bed trying to untangle my hair. It really had suffered over the past few weeks, not only with the weather and the tortuous journeys, but also because my dear Annie was not with me to patiently tease out each tress and then set it up with clasps to look nothing less than remarkable, even given the grey streaks now.

How I missed the girl – especially when I compared her to Catriona and her incompetence. I had no idea whether Annie could cook, but Catriona certainly could not; this and the constant need to mime in order to communicate was so very wearing.

This morning, for example, I asked her if we might eat something different. I had had enough of her weak broth flavoured with little but greasy mutton or, worse, seabird. When she tried to cook some limpets, even those she managed to ruin, having cooked them for about an hour; they were so tough I could hardly even chew them.

So, I suggested she try a crab soup; we had had this on occasion in Preston House and it had always gone down well. But there was a certain spice that was required for the receipt – mace, I seem to recall – and since there were no spices in this prehistoric kitchen, I thought I might go out to the machair and collect some wild herbs to add instead. But first, in the unlikely event that within the locked trunk in my room were some spices – perhaps some brandy too – I attempted once more to fiddle with the lock. I pushed and wriggled in some of my hair pins but the lock held firm. I was so frustrated, I kicked it hard, which did nothing but hurt my foot.

I set off towards the machair and there bent down to collect some wild herbs – thyme I recognised and there was another herb that William had shown me the other day. It was called yarrow and he said the locals made tea with it, to cure melancholia. I know what would cure that for me and it was boat-shaped.

In old island folklore, he told me, yarrow was said to conjure up visions of future sweethearts; some put it under a pillow to dream about their future partner. What utter nonsense, but these are simple peasants who will believe anything. All I wanted was to add it to some crab soup to give it some flavour. I put some in my pocket beside the thyme, then picked a couple of those tiny orchids and some beautiful blue harebells, while thinking back to the perfect garden we had at Preston House where I had first met James.

There in the herb garden the gardener grew thyme, of course, but also savory and marjoram, French sorrel and camomile. I cannot recall what the cook used each for, but I knew that thyme and perhaps yarrow would add a new taste to the soup. And who knows, perhaps the herbs would also prove of medicinal benefit. I believe the islanders boil up certain herbs for maladies such as coughs and constipation. They even use certain seaweeds for rheumatics and indigestion.

I stood up straight and looked out to sea, where the terns and fulmars were soaring upwards then plummeting down into the waves. I screwed up my eyes and stared towards the horizon. There was something out there, far away. Was it a boat? I now knew the direction I looked towards was east and that was where North Uist was; could that be the boat bringing my supplies? If so, William said I was to hand my letter to the master and state that it had to go as soon as possible to the Reverend Murdo MacInnes.

I ran down over the floral green carpet to the dunes then down onto the beach. I stood there gazing at the horizon; it was definitely a boat approaching. I turned and strode up to William's house and knocked on the door. There was no reply, so I continued on to my house, fetched the letter and returned to the beach where I waited, barefoot like the natives.

The boat juddered to a halt in the shallow waters and I remembered those few weeks ago, having to jump overboard to eventually set foot on dry land. I watched as two men threw down their oars and leapt over the side where they stood, waist-high in the water. By now I'd been joined by a dozen or so islanders, all running over the dunes towards the beach. There was still no sign of William, which was odd; everyone on the island would be aware the boat was here. I would simply have to hope the master of the birlinn spoke English.

The islanders ignored me as they rushed past and waded into the water. The remaining two men on board the boat began to hand boxes and bags overboard to the men, who then carried them high above their heads to the islanders, who had formed a line from the boat to the beach. As they deposited the things on the sand, I wondered where my own were. I looked inside a couple of bags but could see only oatmeal and barley. Why on earth would they ask for more of the only grain they could grow here? Why not wheat flour?

Once the cargo was removed, the two crewmen stayed by the boat, holding on to the sides, and the other two men came ashore. One removed a scroll of paper from his pocket and began to look at the goods, then to his paper. Presuming he must be the master, I approached, nodded and smiled. The man's long dark hair was tied back behind his neck and his swarthy looks reminded me of a picture I had once seen of the Barbary corsairs from many decades before. He ignored me so I coughed to attract his attention.

"If you please, Sir, I have something for you."

"Oh, and what would that be?" His voice was gruff.

Thank God, he spoke English. I handed him the letter.

"Can you see this name and address?" I pointed to the minister's name and address, which I had written large, in case he was a poor reader. "I need this letter delivered to this person, the Reverend MacInnes – and no one else – as soon as possible. It contains a letter for my daughter, the Countess of Kintore."

He shrugged. "And why would I do that, My Lady?"

"Well, Sir, I thought you might like to do a lady a favour."

He leered at me, staring very obviously at my bosom. "I repeat, why would I do that?"

"Why, because..." I was trying to control my anger. I breathed deep while deciding how to answer. I had never heard such insolence from a person of inferior rank.

He looked me up and down once more, his gaze stopping on my hand. "Nice ring you've got there. Lapis lazuli, is it?"

I lifted my hand up and looked at my ring. "Yes. Now will you deliver this?"

"Possibly, if I can."

"Please, Sir, will you promise?"

He grinned. "I will promise to try my best." He turned and began wading into the water.

"Please, I would be so grateful."

Without turning his head round, he raised the hand holding the letter in the air and tucked it into his shirt. Then I suddenly remembered my claret.

"Captain, one more thing," I shouted after him, "is there not a box for me?"

He stood in the water, looking at me, then turned to peer inside the boat. He spoke to one of the men, who ducked down then lifted something up. Oh, thank God, there was my wine.

I beamed as he gestured to two of his crew, who waded through the shallows to reach the beach. The islanders had all scurried away through the dunes with their cargo and so, I stood alone on the sand, waiting. William was still nowhere to be seen. How I would get the box up to my house I had no idea. I would have to go and fetch Catriona's dim cousin John to assist.

The box was laid at my feet and it was only when I bent over it that I noticed the line of red seeping out all over the sand, down to the sea. I lifted the lid and, to my horror, saw smashed bottles and puddles of red. I thrust in my hand to determine how many bottles were broken and pulled out one good bottle. I fished around again, my hand red from the claret but now also bleeding from the shards of glass. There was only one unbroken bottle.

I raised my hands in the air and yelled to the master, "What happened to my wine?"

"The sea was rough, My Lady," a voice came over the waves.

"Wait!" I bellowed, standing barefoot in the sand, staring down at the red-stained wooden box, bleeding into the sand.

"Come back. What am I meant to do with this?"

He shrugged and turned to shout at his men, who picked up their oars. With that the boat slipped off the sand bank and off into the darkening sea.

I sat down on the sand, clutching the one bottle of wine as salty tears streamed down my cheeks.

Part Four

Chapter 25

Rachel

I lay flat on my back on the edge of the dunes watching a butterfly flying towards the machair. It was pale blue, with a dark line around the edges of the wings and a frilly white fringe. It was fluttering above a patch of wild flowers and then it alighted on some birdsfoot trefoil.

William told me this was the male butterfly and the female was a dull brown colour. I thought it was strange when he told me that, but he then explained that with most birds it is the male who is the more colourful of the species, the females often being merely dull and brown.

So why, I wondered, are humans so different? Of course, men can wear shiny buckles and ruffs around their shirts, but on the whole their colours are far more muted than ours. Although, as I looked down at my brown dress, I realised I was becoming an island lady, all bright colours faded from my attire. I smiled as I stroked my arms, once white as alabaster, seldom outdoors and, if so, always covered.

Here on the Monach Islands my arms and face were exposed to all weathers and for the past couple of weeks, to extraordinary sunshine and heat. My arms and face were a golden brown, a colour that only a few months ago I would have been ashamed of; now, I find it not unappealing. And William agrees; he told me only yesterday how becoming the bronze hue was, with my black hair and dark brown eyes. He flushed and turned away when he told me; he can be so shy at times.

I smiled as I thought of him, while lying on the warm sand, watching the butterflies. This was so relaxing after the night before: I had had a terrible night's sleep, the nightmares from the past recurring. I went back to when I was twelve, to that dark night standing with my sister, who was grasping my hand so tight it was bruised for days after. We were watching as the men hoisted my father's body down and dropped it onto a barrow. We then had to trudge after the cart all the way to the West Port, where my uncle lifted something off a spike; my sister told me later it was our father's hand.

By this stage, I was peeking through eyes screwed up tight; I had seen enough, I could take no more. Why my mother had wanted us to witness it is still a mystery. She could simply have sent the men to do it, but no, she insisted that night, and for several anniversary years thereafter, that she wanted us all to be there.

Her reason perhaps was to show what evil was, to convince us never to commit crimes ourselves, never to let such shame stain our family; she had never forgiven him. Well, whatever her reason, it had had the opposite effect on me for now not only was I tormented by the memory, but I also felt my father had been wronged. He was not mad, as others implied; he was trying to correct a wrong. He was misunderstood.

And so was I, I mused, while watching another butterfly, this time a large white one, fluttering towards the red clover beyond. From the moment of his hanging, I had always felt I was defined by my father and his so-called crime; and then, much to my mother's joy, I had become simply someone's wife. Well, I still am James' wife, if only he could attend to his husbandly duties and rescue me.

I yawned and realised I was thirsty. The serving girl had taken to hiding my claret. Two crates arrived with the last boat but I am given only one jug each morning. When I ask her, she feigns ignorance, but I know she must be hiding it. I am becoming increasingly frustrated with everyone and everything on this godforsaken island. And yet, looking around at the blue sky and colourful machair, I thought how pretty it looks in weather like this.

I stretched my arms above my head to protect my eyes from the sun and stared at my golden-brown hands. One finger was marked with a white band where my lapis lazuli ring had been. After much anguished thought, I'd ended up giving it to that scoundrel, the master of the boat, the week before, to make him promise to deliver my letter to the North Uist minister. Three months after he said he'd try to deliver my first letter, I knew he hadn't.

William suggested that, with such a rogue, the only way was to bribe him with some sort of payment. Since I had nothing of value apart from the ring, I had no choice. He had agreed at once and so now I await news from My Angel, Mary.

꙳ ꙳

The sun was still high in the sky and the turquoise water shimmered in the heat. I had no idea what time it was but Catriona said sunset was late in the summer months; for all I knew it could be five o'clock or eight o'clock. A welcome breeze was blowing in from the machair behind me as I looked back towards the village. There was no one around and nothing to be seen, just some smoke coming through the roofs from the peat fires. Perhaps it was supper time and they were all inside their houses, eating their bannocks and fish.

I ought to return to see what horrors the lass had cooked for me. The cormorant soup last week had just about finished me off; she had added some seaweed, as if to enhance the flavour. Since I have been growing strangely fond of Catriona, even though she hides my claret, I felt obliged to eat it all. I still want to gag at the very memory of it – greasy, like poor mutton broth, salty as the sea all around and with chewy lumps of flesh, as if from some ancient cockerel, but tasting of fish.

I was about to get to my feet when I saw a figure at the opposite side of the beach. I peered across and saw it was a man and he appeared to be removing his clothes. What glorious freedom there is in being a man; I too would love to remove my clothes, the heat today had been unbearable. I leant forward and saw, to my delight, that it was William. He wore only his breeches and I saw him turn his head towards the village as if checking no one was watching, then sprint towards the sea and fling himself into the waves. Oh, how I should love to do that, to feel the cool water against my hot skin, to taste the salt on my lips.

I looked around to check no one was there then got to my feet and began to walk towards the water, my bare feet padding on the soft, warm sand. At the water's edge, I hesitated then held my head high and entered the water; if a man could do this, so could I. My fear of water could surely be overcome; it was illogical. As long as my feet were on the sand, I would be fine.

The feeling of the water – still chilly even after two weeks of intense heat – was bliss. I shut my eyes and raised my head to the blue sky. As I pushed myself through the waves, I recalled the last time I had been forcing my skirts against the weight of the water: the day I had arrived here some four months earlier.

As I thrust my legs through the surf, I saw William had stopped swimming and turned around. He saw me and began to swim in my direction. I smiled as he approached, his hair wet and tousled, his strong shoulders emerging from the water as his body surged through the water. And I realised I had not seen a man's bare shoulders for many years; James and I had slept apart for so long.

Soon he was in front of me and he smiled. We did not speak; he simply took my hand and drew me towards him. His eyes held mine as he leaned in close. He kissed me and I tasted the salty tang. We stood in the shallows for some time, our bodies clasped together. Then he looked up at the village and sighed. "I'd better go home. Someone might see us. They'll be coming outside soon to tether the animals." He swallowed and shook his head. "Forgive me, Rachel."

"William, there is nothing to forgive and I for one do not care what those peasants think. Let's go over there," I said, pointing to the dunes. "Come with me. Quick!"

And so we ran to the marram grass and lay down on the hot sand. As I tried to unlace my gown, he attempted to help me and I could not help but giggle, since it was not easy dealing with the heavy, sodden frock that clung to my body. Though anxious at first, he too began to smile and together we began to peel it off. Then I lay back down upon the sand, the shingle crushing into my legs and the sharp grass scratching my back, but what of it? I was free, at last, without a care in the world; no longer a condemned person, I was a woman once more.

Chapter 26

Mary, Countess of Kintore

When Mama told me how wonderful it would be to be a countess, I believed every word. And at first, it was all rather splendid. To be mistress of Kintore Castle and to have a household of so many servants, and to have anything I desired, was all so new. I forgot about the things I missed about my life before I married the Earl: Edinburgh, Preston House, my family, my friends. But then the novelty wore off. Here, living in the middle of nowhere on the west coast of Scotland, with only a long sea loch and the squawk of seabirds outside, I had no one to speak to. Of course, his mother was always around, but since John was forty, Lady Arabella must be at least sixty and looks so ancient, she can hardly last through dinner without falling asleep. Plus, there is his sister and her strange twins, but they are all such dull company; it is as if they have never known how to smile, never mind laugh.

And then there is the main problem. Mama had of course warned me how it would be in the bedroom and so I was well prepared. But she had said that during each confinement and while the baby needed its mother's milk (she insisted I feed the babies myself) I would be spared his attentions in bed.

But this is where I am most bereft. I have all the gowns I require, I have lands and rooms aplenty, too many servants to give daily tasks to, but I have no baby. For two long years I have waited and still, every month, along comes my reminder that I am barren. His sister tries to confide in me, telling me not to worry and that everything will be fine; but how can it be? Is it because I am too young? Or perhaps he is too old; he is, after all, only two years younger than Mama. Whatever the reason, I am beside myself with grief every four weeks, regular as clockwork. It makes me miss Mama even more.

She was the only one I could speak to honestly about how I felt, and she listened as I told her my worries. But now she's gone, there is no one in whom I can truly confide. My sister Fannie is coming to stay soon and, since she is now seventeen, I could possibly speak to her about it. Perhaps she and I can do something special together, something to take my mind off it all – though trying to tear her away from her Bible studies might be difficult. My chaplain is already aware he will have to conduct more frequent services during her stay. She is used to morning and evening worship at home, which only Papa encourages. The rest of us think once a day is enough.

The chaplain, Alexander, has been a comfort to me in times of worry, though obviously, since he is a man, I cannot tell him why I am in despair every month. I wonder if the Earl is perhaps a little jealous of Alexander, with whom I would far rather spend time. Anyway, he will be busy for the next few weeks with Fannie's spiritual needs.

I will at least be able to speak to Fannie about Mama. I often think back to that day some nine months ago when we held her funeral. I told Aunt Jean I could not believe Mama was dead, but she scoffed at the suggestion. But I simply do not understand what could have happened to her. If she had been ill, Papa would surely have told us.

I wondered if to spare me and my siblings the shame, she had perhaps been sent away somewhere to restore herself to full health. She had admittedly had some outbursts of rage that, I now realise, were not conducive to being a lady. Perhaps she had agreed to go somewhere for the sake of her mental health, for physically she has always been as strong as an ox.

But I simply cannot imagine she would disappear like that, without even saying goodbye. The boys are of course fine about it, they just get on with their lives, but I – and I'm sure Fannie too in her own queer way – grieve her sudden departure. Papa does not seem to be concerned or ever look crestfallen on the rare occasion when I have spoken to him of Mama. Indeed, he simply changes the subject.

I must go now and instruct the servants on preparing Fannie's room, for it is only two days until she arrives. She will be exhausted after the long journey so might need at least a day in bed to recover. I just realised I had forgotten to tell Chef about her strangeness around certain meats and how she will not eat anything that wobbles.

⚭

"Lady Kintore, there is a letter for you." It was the third week of Fannie's visit and we were sitting in the drawing room looking out at the howling gale.

Fannie had just about calmed down after being served Chef's excellent rosewater-flavoured carragheen jelly at luncheon and though she kept giving me looks, I ignored her and simply spoke – or rather, shouted – to deaf Lady Arabella instead. It really is about time she got over this ridiculous childhood nonsense about wobbly food.

She sat scowling by the window as the rain lashed against the panes. The servant entered and bowed low.

I took the letter from the platter, looked at the handwriting and gasped. "It's Mama's writing. Fannie, come here. Quick! She's alive. Praise the Lord!"

I slipped the paper knife along the top and pulled out the parchment.

I ran to the lamp where the light was better and held it underneath. Together we read it out loud.

Mary, my dearest Angel,

I have written three times before, but I now know they have never been delivered. This letter I feel sure will find its way to you. I have said the same things in each letter and it wearies me to keep repeating my plight, so all you need to know is that I was abducted in the most brutal manner from my chambers in Edinburgh one horrid cold night in January, kept in some miserable and filthy castle in Stirlingshire for several weeks, then taken — and all this on horseback, no comfortable carriage — eventually to the sea where we sailed past Skye and North Uist. I am sure we set sail from somewhere in Inverness-shire and so I hope I am not far from you; I have no idea exactly how far away your castle is.

For the past five months — or perhaps six by the time you receive this — I have been held captive here on the Monach Islands, which comprise five tidal islands. I am not ill-treated, but I am lonely and miserable most of the time, although amid all the ignorant, uncultured natives, there is one kind human, a gentleman who happens to be the minister. This, I am sure, would please Fannie.

"Mama remembers me too!" Fannie beamed.

"Of course she does, silly. She is writing to me because I am older than you, that's all."

Fannie was always craving Mama's attention and affection.

Please do not tell your father about this letter, nor indeed any of your brothers. And perhaps your husband the Earl should not know either, for fear he might inadvertently pass on the information. But if you could find a way somehow to come to fetch me, I should be so grateful. I do hope you are by now with child and are busy preparing a beautiful nursery, so I have no idea how you could do this, but if you could somehow plan a rescue, even if you cannot come yourself? I am miserable without my dear family. Alone and dejected. Please come and save me?

  Your ever loving mother

Fannie and I sat staring at the letter for quite a while until I suddenly leapt up and rang the bell. "We must call for a map, we'll find out where these Monach Islands are. Then let us go and rescue Mama!"

Chapter 27

William Fleming

Sometimes I wish that we kirk ministers could go to confession like our papist counterparts and confess our sins, for truly I have sinned. Father, forgive me. She has beguiled me since she arrived on the island some seven months ago. She has such an allure, a charm that has been drawing me in slowly over these past months. I tried so hard to forget about her and to concentrate instead on my parishioners, but their drudgery often got me down and it was so enlightening to speak to an intelligent, cultured person. I confess, however, it was not simply the intellectual appeal; though she must be nearly ten years older than me, she is still a beautiful woman and I am so enthralled by her, I have seldom felt such lust. I prayed and prayed for a way out, but this time, none came.

And so we are now lovers and though I continue to lead worship in the kirk and deal with my parishioners' needs and try to avoid her eye in kirk every Sunday, I spend as much time as I can with her. We never meet now in our homes for our servants would be too suspicious. So, we contrive to meet somewhere out of sight of the natives.

Last week we met up near Gortinish, the week before up at Dead Man's Point. But yesterday, having checked the tides, we met on Shivinish, the tidal island directly to the west. I had taken some boiled crab claws and of course a bottle of claret. We met over at the south harbour then headed up over the bay towards the beach, where we lay together on the sand then ate with such an appetite and she asked me, as she always does, to tell her more about the wonderful butterflies and flowers and herbs of the machair. I picked her some of the wild flowers and she took them in her hand, declaring that they would brighten her drawing room and then she would dry them between paper to keep forever.

I had translated a Gaelic poem about the machair on the island of Benbecula that I had come across and recited that to her as she lay back on the sand, her beautiful eyes shut in concentration as she listened. As I got to the last line, she raised her head and looked all around.

"I have never seen such loveliness; this place is truly magical. I thought I was an educated woman, but I had never even heard of the machair. In the city we are ignorant of so much of the wild beauty of the islands."

I nodded and was about to pour her another cup of wine when I heard a noise. I looked down towards the harbour and noticed a small boat out at sea, heading in.

I told her to keep down as I watched two men get out and haul their boat up onto the shingle beach. They then headed north by foot towards the easterly headland of Ceann Iar and I remembered that of course it was time to shear the sheep here before the winter and bring the fleeces back to Ceann Ear. A fulmar flew out with a great flapping of wings from the dunes nearby and she sprang up from the sand.

"Keep down, Rachel," I hissed. "They might see us." My heart missed a beat as one of the men – I now realised it was Angus Macleod – turned in our direction, but I did not move and thanked the good Lord he had bad sight; that was why he always had to have young Malcolm with him on the boat.

"What shall we do? Stay here?"

I shook my head. "No, they'll be some time, gathering the sheep into the fank then shearing them. Then they'll wait for the tides to change so they can sail the boat back with all the fleeces to Ceann Ear."

I peered west where they were already beginning to gather in the flock.

"You go first. Keep on the sand but head directly back over to Ceann Ear. I'll follow in a while and head up to Gortinish on the sand first. They won't see you. If they see me, I'll say I was visiting the Macleans up north and decided to take a walk over to Shivinish."

She nodded and stood up.

"Please try not to be seen, Rachel."

She leant over and kissed me then sped away, towards the harbour and then back to our island.

I watched her arrive over on Ceann Ear and thankfully she did not turn round to wave. I waited until I felt it was safe and then stood up and walked over the clover, wild thyme and orchids towards the north. I held my head low as I walked, trying to think about the beauty of the machair; but all I could think of was that this must not happen again. This has to stop. I cannot risk what took place here not that long ago occurring again.

Chapter 28

Rachel

I had been looking at that chest — what the locals call a kist — for long enough. There was obviously something in it and I was determined to find out what. Why would Isabella Macdonald have left it here, locked, when she left the island? Since there was so little else to occupy me when I was not with William, it was beginning to torment me.

I have no idea how Donald Macdonald's wife could have survived a year on the Monachs with no others of her intellectual equal, apart from her husband, and presumably he was away often on the mainland. I had asked William what she did in this stark house and he said he did not really know as he had little to do with her, communicating with her and her husband only after church.

At first, he had said he could not even recall her name, which seemed strange since they would have been in the front row of the kirk every week and he would have surely talked to them. But he said they were not on informal terms as they had never asked the minister in for a meal or even a drink, which seems to me strange, when I think of all the times we had to endure the pompous Reverend Elibank at Preston House after church on Sundays.

She apparently had her own maid from the mainland with her, so at least she could communicate with the servant, unlike Catriona and me, constantly gesturing as if we are deaf mutes, even though I am trying to learn some Gaelic words. At least she now has the measure of my hair and how it needs a good fifty brushes every morning to bring out the lustre.

Today had not been a good day: it was a whole week till my next shipment of claret was due to arrive and I had to make do with that vile liquid Catriona calls ale. I do not know whether it is that, served by the girl as my morning draught, or the nightmares of Father that make me gasp for air and feel quite queasy sometimes. When I discovered what the so-called ale is made from – gorse – I realised it must be that. It tastes like everything else does: of fish and rotten eggs.

Catriona has been rather strange with me over the past few days and I wondered if those two natives over on Shivinish had seen either myself or William that day a couple of weeks ago; I have not seen him since, so have no idea what happened when I left him. William had been very nervous about being seen, but I am sure we were not. Well, let them gossip if they want; I don't care. The liaison takes my mind off the fact that I am basically a prisoner, albeit not within the four walls of a prison. And as for William's reputation – his is surely so untarnished they will believe me to be the mature seducer and exonerate the blemish-free young reverend.

My girl had left for the morning to go and see some ancient relative on the south of the island. So, I wandered outside and round the back of the house, where she usually sits plucking her smelly seabirds and I prefer to keep far away from the stench and the flying feathers. It was early autumn, there was a chill in the air and as I breathed in deep I could smell the rain approaching.

I saw an axe sitting beside a wooden plank and went over to pick it up. It wasn't big and thankfully was not too heavy. I tested the blade against the tip of a finger; it was sharp enough. I took it inside and put it on the kitchen table.

I poured a cup of the vile ale to quench my thirst then went to look once more at the lock on the kist, trying to work out how to smash it open subtly. I would prefer Catriona not to know I had broken into it. She had gestured to me a couple of times that it was firmly locked and she had no idea where the key was. The last time she was out, I scoured every drawer and cupboard in case it was hidden. I can't explain why I had become obsessed by it; perhaps without my claret for a while, I was convinced that it was full of wine.

I went to collect the axe, peered at the lock and, before I lost the courage, took a swing at it. The axe slipped down to the floor and slashed into the rug. Thank God my bare foot was a good six inches away. I shook the lock and saw it was still intact. I tried again and again, now swearing like a fishwife as I was becoming increasingly frustrated.

James used to scold me for using such language; well, there was no one here to hear me so I could curse away. At last, the lock sprung open and I flung the axe to the floor. I yanked open the lid and sat down beside the chest.

I fumbled under a black cloth lying over the top and cast it aside. Underneath were piles of books and journals, which I pulled out and placed on the floor. Surely there must be some claret at the bottom? It didn't take me long to empty everything and sadly I saw there was no wine.

Only one heavy book, some journals, almanacs and smaller books. I lifted out the large tome and opened it; to my delight, I saw it was a 1623 edition of Shakespeare. I flicked through some pages and counted: it contained thirty-six of Shakespeare's plays. Well, this would keep me going through the long winter ahead. I felt joy at the prospect at reading it and yet also despair at the thought of having to stay on in this place for an entire winter.

I reached down to the base and brought out a small dark brown bottle and a beautiful cream-coloured silk bag with a drawstring. I uncorked the bottle, sniffed then smiled with relief as I downed the contents – a rather fine medicinal brandy. I pulled the bag open and brought out a tiny white cotton gown, a little woollen hat and two white linen caps – baby clothes. Did Mrs Macdonald have a baby while she was here? Though I am sure someone told me – it must have been William – that they had no children.

I took a couple of the journals over to the chair and opened them. Two pages were stuck together and, when I prised them open, I saw they were full of dried flowers that, even though crisp and brown, I recognised from the machair. There was some daisies, dandelions, harebell and blue speedwell. Some months ago, I would have had no idea what they were but William was a good teacher.

I began to read the journal and as I read, my eyes opened wide. After one page I ran to the kitchen to pour a large goblet of the hideous ale to steady my nerves. I returned to the chair, downed the cup and continued to read. I could start to feel the rages I thought I had tamed some time ago return. My insides churned up in anger and despair as I turned one brittle page after another.

Part Five

Chapter 29

Annie

I stood up and peered round the door at the approaching figure. He was walking with a brisk step towards me. I pushed the doorknob and tiptoed onto the step. As he approached, I thought I detected a slight limp; actually, no, he was staggering, as if he was drunk. I suddenly shivered all over; what if this man was not in fact my Johnnie? I slunk back a little into the shadows and waited.

He emerged from the gloom and at once I realised, from his frame, that it was not him. I gasped and tried to step back inside but an arm grabbed me and pulled me out into the close. I still could not see his face, half-hidden by a swathe of plaid, the same red plaid I had seen on the Highlanders who had taken My Lady. I smelled brandy and sweat but tried not to gag as he dragged me down the close where it was narrow and dank.

"Sir, who are you? What d'you want of me?"

He pushed me up against the cold stone wall of a tenement and slipped the plaid from his head. I thought I recognised him but was not sure how. It was still too dark to see his features clearly, but he spoke like a gentleman.

"There is no reason for you to know my name, but given your status as a serving wench, you may address me as Sir."

I shrank back, trying to avoid his malodorous, alcoholic breath; he must have been in the tavern all day and all night.

As he attempted a smile, I raised my head. I would not be intimidated by a man, even though he was obviously a nobleman. I thought of My Lady and knew she would not stand any bullying, even from one of higher social standing.

"Sir, I was given to believe that Johnnie would be here. The men earlier said he would be here presently. Where is he?"

The fat man belched and I had to turn away as a smell of rotten eggs and fish enveloped me.

"Annie, Annie. Why would you think young Johnnie would come back for you?"

"Well, because he promised me he would. We are to be married and…"

He shook his head and chuckled. "Johnnie did not promise anything. If he had done so, he would have kept his word, I can vouch for that. He told me you had kindly agreed to assist with Lady Grange's removal for her own safety and for the protection of her family, this family of whom I am so fond."

I was beginning to worry. Who was this ogre and what was he doing here? He obviously knew Johnnie and My Lady's family. I tried to wriggle away from his grip on my hands against the wall, but he held fast. I let out a scream and he clamped one hand over my mouth.

"Annie, Annie," he said, smirking. "It's no use. There is no one here to see or hear you, so do not even attempt to flee. He leant his head back a little and looked me up and down, as if appraising my size. "Yes, Johnnie was right, you are about her height. He has done well."

"Sir, please let me go. I don't understand where my Johnnie is, but I don't care now. I simply want to get back inside and to my bed."

"I'm afraid that won't be possible, Annie. You have lived a good life, you've been a faithful servant to that harpy all these years and now she is gone. But instead of allowing you to go with her, I decided that you would serve her one last time."

"I ... I don't know what you mean, I..."

He released his grasp with one hand, quickly crossed himself as he muttered Forgive something under his breath, then suddenly pounced upon me, his hands round my neck. I tried to twist away, but he was too strong. I kicked him in the groin and he jolted back, but his hands remained firm. I felt my body go weak and limp and soon I had no energy to fight back. I shut my eyes and waited for the end. My final thought was, how could I possibly serve My Lady when I was dead.

Chapter 30

James

I had not seen Lovat since the funeral, which was several months before, although we had communicated by letter. I was now on my way to meet him at Clerihugh's, our usual watering hole, to discuss the situation on the island. I knew I could trust him, but there were just a few issues that bothered me.

When I asked him what had happened to the serving girl, Annie, he wrote that she had been paid off handsomely and was now living up north, near his castle, with one of his Highlanders; I had no idea she had helped Lovat's men gain access to Rachel's chambers. I had spent all those years watching her bow and scrape to my demanding wife, thinking she was as loyal as a lapdog. It never ceases to amaze me what people will do for money – and love. Or, in my case, lust; it was sadly this lust that caused me to spend twenty-five years of my life with a harridan.

Lovat had been under suspicion again by the authorities so had written to tell me he was keeping a low profile in Edinburgh. When he needed time in a civilised place away from his primitive castle, he went to his town house in Inverness. But his first wife's family were always hanging about there, waiting to harangue him at any opportunity. Well, he hadn't done himself any favours by his behaviour towards Amelia. At least Margaret was a far better choice for his second wife and, as he always said, she was biddable.

And I know, my darling, that you are still awaiting the news that we too are free to wed and you will become my wife, the second Lady Grange. But even though we had the burial at Greyfriars Kirk, I still need to have word from Simon about how Rachel is faring on the remote island and if anyone is aware that she is still alive. We have waited this long, my love, I know we can hold on a short while more.

I was first to arrive at Clerihugh's and had already drunk half my ale when I heard his raucous voice. I looked up to see him limping over to my table.

"What's wrong with your leg, Lovat?" I asked as he heaved himself into the chair opposite.

"It's not my leg, it's my foot, my big toe. Agony to walk." He turned round and bellowed at Young Hugh to fill his glass as he raised his bandaged foot upon a stool that a lad rushed to bring him. He is so slovenly but has such authority.

"Gout. Too much excess, says my physician. Don't overdo the sweetbreads, kidneys and oysters, he commands. And ale!" He shook his head. "Really, Grange, is life then worth living?" He grinned and leant towards me. "But you know what they say about a man with gout?"

"Not that fable about sexual prowess?"

"Yes. And it's true, it's no myth. You see, when you have plenty of bed rest – which I have to do to show my doctor I am heeding his advice – there is an incubating effect on the reproductive organs." He beamed then drank from his glass of ale.

"And your physician agrees with this hypothesis?" I smiled.

"There is no need to ask him. You just ask Jeannie Wilkie down in Advocate's Close."

"I will do next time I find myself in need."

Young Hugh came over to take our order and I listened as Lovat ordered a ragout of kidneys and some eel pie.

The servant turned to me. "And Your Lordship?"

"I shall take the same and perhaps some hare broth first. I have a mighty hunger on me."

I took a long drink of ale.

"So, have you been up north to your castle since we last met?"

"I had such an urge to go back to France recently, thinking of my old love, Marie, d'you remember her?"

I nodded, remembering the Gallic beauty who had borne him a child and who for some reason seemed to love him as much as he did her, even though she was but a servant.

"Indeed, I had intimated to my colleagues at The Sheep Heid I would go on their behalf, try once more to speak to someone at the royal court. But my advocate in Inverness said my exile was still in place."

"Really? I thought the banishment from France was only for ten years after the 1715 Rebellion?"

"Not according to him. I daren't risk it, Grange. Besides, with this damned foot of mine causing me such grief, I can't travel far. Even getting here today from Duddingston was a trial." He picked up his drink and narrowed his eyes. "They say you've been to only a couple of meetings there, Grange. You are still for the Cause, aren't you?"

I leant across the table and whispered. "Yes, but as I have told you so often, Lovat, I can't risk going in the daylight. I prefer not to go in summer, for fear of being seen."

He shrugged. "Well, as long as you're still with us."

"Of course." I leant back against my chair as Young Hugh brought the food to our table. "But there are other matters I must speak to you about."

He speared a kidney from the ragout with his dirk and rammed it into his mouth before masticating noisily. I wanted to hand him his napkin and tell him, as I used to tell the children, to keep his mouth shut, but I controlled the urge and asked, "Rachel. Tell me her news. How does she fare on the Monachs?"

He chewed with gusto then swallowed. "As I wrote to you in my letter, she has her own house on the Monachs, a stone-built cottage with glazed windows, simple yet sufficient accommodation and has even some books from the tacksman's wife. I was told what these were, if you are at all interested: a Shakespeare, Pope's essays and Bunyan, to name but three."

"You never mentioned there was another lady on the island. I thought they were all Gaelic-speaking peasants? Don't let her get in with anyone, she's scheming, devious."

"The tacksman, one Donald Macdonald, left the Monachs well over a year ago, something to do with his wife's malady, but he goes over from North Uist every few months to keep an eye on things. My kinsman on Skye keeps me in touch."

"Is she in good health?"

"Thriving, I hear. She can't speak to anyone there apart from the minister, who I imagine treats her as a fallen woman. No one else understands anything other than Gaelic. So, there's no means of becoming friendly with another soul."

"And there's no way she could leave the islands?"

"A few of the natives have birlinns for the fishing and also to check on the sheep on the nearby tidal islands. But even as persuasive and manipulative as we know she is, she cannot speak to them, nor they to her."

"And so, she has no communication with anyone off the island?"

"The man who does the regular run over to North Uist has strict instructions that he must not accept anything from her. He's a bit of a rogue, but unless she's got money to bribe him, he will obey my man."

"She would have no money with her, the servant girl always held that in her purse. And Annie, the girl is fine?"

Lovat lifted his bowl of broth up with two hands and tipped the contents down his throat. The dark liquid dribbled down his chin. I had to look away.

"As far as I know, yes. Oh, another thing I recall my man telling me: she has crates of claret delivered regularly, but I presumed you would be happy to pay me for that?"

"Of course, I spend much less on her nowadays than I had to before. I suppose she can't give up that dependence she has on wine. She used to insist it was the only way to forget her father's atrocity."

Lovat harrumphed then wiped a hunk of bread around the dish of ragout. "Mind you, I did wonder if we might have to move her elsewhere."

"Why? You just said there was no way she could get off the island?"

"Have you forgotten what you said about her wily ways? If she learned Gaelic, she could easily plan an escape. She could get in with someone and perhaps try to get one of their birlinns."

"We can't allow her to break free. Think what damage she would do to my career."

"And also to my reputation, Grange. If she knows about your Jacobite leanings, she most certainly knows about mine and I refuse to end up in prison; certainly not for a mad crone such as your wife. She is a loose cannon."

"Lovat, one thing Rachel is not is a crone. Though age and claret have withered her somewhat, she is still a striking lady."

He shrugged.

"What can you do to prevent her escaping?"

"There is one other place I can have her sent. Have you heard of St Kilda? A barren rock even farther away from the mainland. They have a boat going there only once a year so there's no danger of her escaping, even if she gets in with the islanders."

"Well, that sounds ideal, Lovat. Should this happen soon?"

"No, no, until I hear something untoward, there is no need. But that is our back-up plan. It will perhaps be not quite as, how shall I say, civilised, as the Monach Islands; the St Kildans are semi-naked barbarians who live in hovels and eat nothing but seabirds." He paused to spear another kidney. "But we have that option."

He wiped his greasy lips with a napkin then stood up, screwing up his face in pain as he rested his not inconsiderable weight upon his right foot.

"I must go, but I'm in town for at least a fortnight. Can I hope to see you at Duddingston in the coming few days?"

"I shall be there one evening soon, Lovat. Thank you."

I watched him hobble towards the door as I downed my drink and beckoned over to Young Hugh to pay. I tidied the mess my companion had left on the table then stood up to leave, heading back down the High Street to Niddry's Wynd. Fannie had just returned from Inverness-shire and my sister told me I ought to go and see her to hear all Mary's news, though to be honest, more than ten minutes with my serious, pious daughter is almost too much to bear. We shall no doubt first pray together, she and I – though I can only hope she desists starting our invocations praying for her mother's soul as she invariably does.

Chapter 31

Mary, Countess of Kintore

Alexander my chaplain laid out the map before me.

"Are you sure you still want to make the voyage, My Lady?" He looked directly at me, the gaze from his clear blue eyes piercing, as usual.

"Yes, I do. I had hoped my sister would come with me, but she is of a sensitive temperament and wanted to go back to the security of Edinburgh before she starves to death." I smiled. "My chef's food is not to her taste. The last straw was a dish of sago at luncheon then tapioca at supper. She is such a baby when it comes to proper food. And these puddings were flavoured so beautifully, one with rosewater, another with ginger."

He smiled patiently. "Everything is set in place for the journey, My Lady. I am keen for us to take another servant along, but you think just your maid will suffice?"

"Alexander, with you as my guide in matters both spiritual and now also navigationary, I shall be perfectly fine. My husband has come round to the fact that I am accompanying my chaplain to his presbytery meeting, as ladies sometimes do. The fact that, when on North Uist, we might take a journey across the sea to some outlying island is of no consequence; and certainly not anything the Earl need know about."

I smiled then looked down once more at the map.

"So, we sail to North Uist and, while you attend to your presbytery duties over at Lochmaddy, I shall reside there with

Lady Macleod at Claddach for three nights to allow me time to recover from the journey." I pointed to the east then west coasts of North Uist. "Then we shall take the boat over to the Monachs. That cannot be too arduous a journey, surely?"

"It will be the middle of October when we arrive, My Lady, and the Hebridean weather is seldom predictable. But provided you need stay only a couple of days on the Monachs, that is plenty of time for us to be back here before winter sets in."

I nodded. Apart from Fannie, Alexander is the only other person who knows my reason for going. My husband believes I am going to visit Lady Macleod in Claddach for social reasons. "I presume you have not told your brother we are coming over?"

"No, I've said nothing; indeed, it's some time since I've heard from him. I don't know if he can attend the presbytery meeting; it might be difficult for him to get away from such a remote parish."

"I am unusually nervous about seeing Mama again. Her letter was so strange. I have thought and thought about who could have abducted her and why. Obviously, Papa had nothing to do with it, but I used to hate one of my father's acquaintances, Simon, Lord Lovat, and I have been wondering about his role in the abduction."

"Lord Lovat? Isn't he that papist who many are convinced is a Jacobite?" Alexander frowned.

I nodded. "I can't think why, but I have always mistrusted him. Even at Mama's so-called funeral in Edinburgh he was there, sidling around silently like a snake, so smug and self-important. Now, I know Mama was often not an easy person to be around; indeed, latterly she and Papa had terrible fights, but she is still my loving mother and I am so worried about how she might be. She said she felt alone and dejected; I do hope her strength of character remains intact and she has not given over to excessive drinking. My brothers used to say she was more fond of her claret than of her sons." I bit my lip; I ought not to have mentioned this to my chaplain, but it was true. Besides, he will soon meet her and testify to her character for himself.

I went towards the window and looked out at the grey loch towards the west. There was a light mist, as usual, but I could just make out the headland that marked the way to the islands. What was Mama doing out there? How awful to be so alone; but she is strong, she will be fine.

Alexander came to the window seat to join me. "Many ladies these days drink often and for many reasons other than thirst. You, My Lady, are an exception. Your rectitude and fairness are exemplary."

"Fair? What do you mean by that?" I frowned. Admittedly I am always kind to my servants.

Alexander flushed a little, combed his fingers through his thick ginger hair and turned back from the window and the drizzle. He glanced round at me, his clear blue eyes gazing straight at me as if into my very soul.

"Fair of face and of mind." He leant towards me as if to study my face closer then jolted back and stood up. "Now, My Lady, shall we go to the chapel for our morning prayers?"

Chapter 32

Catriona

I thought she was dead. She lay slumped on the chair by the window, the axe by her bare feet. There was a trickle of dark brown on one foot, which at first I thought was blood, then I realised it came from a small bottle by her side. I tiptoed towards her, my heart racing. I could smell the fumes as I bent over her face to check her breathing. So, she was just intoxicated again, though how she could be on the gorse ale, I don't know. There must have been alcohol in the bottle on the floor.

I picked it up and sniffed. I had no idea what it was, since no spirit was permitted in my own home. But this was obviously strong liquor, to help satisfy her needs. I sighed and looked around. What a boorach – there were books and journals strewn all around. The kist was smashed open and it looked like she'd taken everything out of it. I had had no idea what was in there, it wasn't my place to ask, but I was told it had belonged to Mrs Macdonald and that her husband would be collecting it one day for her. That was quite a while ago.

When she and her husband had left, quite suddenly one day two summers ago, the rumours abounded. No one had actually seen her leave the house and get on the boat, just him. And so, people began to wonder if she had in fact left; but since there was really nowhere to hide on these islands, was she perhaps dead? That was what I kept thinking anyway. She was very snooty about us island folk and refused to have anyone else to help her, only her maid Elsie. We all used to wonder what she would be cooking for her mistress and master; certainly not fulmar eggs and bannocks.

There was talk from others that, in fact, the couple had boarded the boat together, along with the maid, and were now living happily over the sea on North Uist as was anticipated all along, and she had a bairn and was far more content than she'd been on the Monachs. She hated it here, so her departure was hardly a surprise, but for it all to happen to suddenly…

My Lady stirred and I leant over to see if she wanted any help getting into bed. I felt sorry for her; after all, she wasn't a bad mistress, often a little demanding, but what a life for her. She'd gestured to me one day that she had five children; how could she bear to be parted from them. And what was she doing here, a cultured, educated lady all alone among us, simple Hebridean folk?

"Do you want to get into bed, My Lady?" I said in my own language but gesturing with my hands as we always did when communicating. She opened her eyes wide and shook her head. She looked terrible, but possibly no more haggard than she has for the past few weeks – so pale, as if she was going down with some ailment. She said something to me, sweeping her hand towards the guddle all over the floor. She lowered her eyes and I wondered if she was apologising.

I began slowly tidying everything up, placing the books in one pile and the journals and diaries in another. I kept looking up at her, but she just lay there, silent, watching. There was a pretty silk bag, and I noticed it was filled with baby things. I thought back to the chatter about Mrs Macdonald, that she could not have babies. So, why would she have kept baby clothes hidden in her kist?

I began to pack everything back into the kist and then she stamped her foot. She bolted upright and grabbed one of the journals from me. Its pages were bulging, as if they had things stuck between the papers. She stood up and went to put it under her pillow, then lay down on her bed, crossing her arms over her chest. I was going to ask if she wanted anything, but her eyes were shut. However, she was not sleeping; when I shut the lid of the kist, I could hear a noise. I looked over to the bed and saw that her shoulders were shaking in silent sobs.

Chapter 33

Mary, Countess of Kintore

After two days, I felt I'd rested sufficiently after the arduous journey by sea to North Uist. We had disembarked at Lochmaddy, where Alexander stayed on for his meeting, while I continued west with my maid Meg to Claddach and to the home of Lady Macleod. She was such a kind hostess, concerned that I shouldn't overtire myself and indeed keen for me to stay in bed, but I insisted that I was perfectly well and eager to have some fresh air. She is at least fifty and has forgotten, I think, how it is to be some three decades younger.

We took a tour around the delightful gardens and ended up standing on the shore, looking out to sea towards the west. The day was clear and crisp and the visibility good. As we stood at the seashore, I asked what we could see on the horizon.

"Those are the Monach Islands, Mary, where you are keen to go in a few days' time. Though I do think you might reconsider. They are uncultured peasants there; you will have no company worthy of a lady such as yourself."

"Lady Macleod, I am keen to visit to accompany my chaplain, who wants to see how the kirk fares. He has heard rumours that the kirk is in decline and he is charged with looking at the fabric of the building, then he will report back to the next presbytery meeting."

"I see. Well, as long as it is a day visit. There will be nowhere to stay. The only decent house belongs to Donald Macdonald, who is now a neighbour of us here at Claddach. In fact, let us invite him over for supper tonight if he is free and he can tell you more about the islands. I shall invite some others living nearby too."

"That would be wonderful, thank you so much." I took a deep breath of the salty sea air and followed Her Ladyship back to the house, where she immediately wrote a letter to this gentleman, inviting him to Claddach that night.

⌒⌒⌒

"Countess, I heard you are eager to visit the Monachs. Might I enquire why?"

Donald Macdonald had been placed at my left side and we were conversing over the crab soup. He was about forty years old, with thinning grey hair and a plump face that matched his rotund body. He'd already finished his plate of soup before I had even taken my second spoonful.

"Yes, I am hoping to go, two days hence, with my chaplain. He has presbytery matters to deal with there."

He frowned. "What matters would these be? I am tacksman for the Monachs and so am fully aware of everything that may need addressing on the island."

His tone was rather haughty, but I smiled and explained about the essential repairs to the church roof.

He shook his head. "Oh, is that all? Well, pray do not trouble yourself by going there, My Lady. I can assure you that last time I was there it was holding up fine."

"And when were you last there, Mr Macdonald?"

"I am due to go soon; I have been away dealing with other matters and am long overdue a visit. I have simply not had time. There are many matters here to occupy me."

"I hear the winter weather can sometimes affect stone walls and roofs; perhaps the presbytery are worried that another harsh winter might be detrimental to the building. And since I hear there is only one church for the island, that would leave many parishioners without a place of worship."

"It won't come to that, My Lady. And I repeat that I would not recommend the voyage. It is no place for a lady."

"Oh, and why is that?"

The soup plates were being cleared and I sat back as the wine was topped up in his glass; I had not touched mine.

"The peasants are both ignorant and unwelcoming. They speak no English, have no education and eat little but seabirds. Also, there is nowhere for you to shelter, apart from my house. And that is occupied at present." He glanced round and my face must have betrayed my displeasure at his manner. "I am sorry to say, My Lady."

"Did you not use to live there?"

"Yes, but now I prefer to visit only occasionally. It is unnecessary for me to live on the island all the time."

"Might I enquire if your wife – I presume you are married? – lived on the islands with you? How did she find it there?"

He dabbed his lips with his napkin. "My wife, sadly, is dead. Her time on the Monachs was not happy. Not happy at all."

"Oh, I am so sorry, I had no idea you were a widower."

He took his glass and drank deep. "How is your husband the Earl? I have never met him, but I hear good things said of him."

Why was he changing the subject so suddenly? Was he still too grief-stricken to talk about his wife?

"My husband is fine, thank you." I looked over the table at Lady Macleod, who was talking animatedly to another neighbour, the Laird of Kirkbost, who looked so old and frail he might die at any moment. She had not mentioned Mr Macdonald's wife, so perhaps I should not enquire further. The candles flickered on the table as the doors opened and the servants brought in the next dishes. There was a wonderful rich smell of venison and chestnuts and port wine wafting past. Another dish, of Scotch collops, garnished with force-meat balls and pickled cucumber, was placed before me.

"The Reverend Fleming is extremely keen that I accompany him to the Monachs when he returns from Lochmaddy and the presbytery meeting. I therefore feel it my duty to go. It will no doubt only be a day trip and, provided the weather holds, the day after tomorrow is the planned day for our expedition."

Mr Macdonald had been raising his glass to his lips when he suddenly froze. "Fleming, did you say?"

"Yes, that is the name of my chaplain, the Reverend Fleming."

"Fleming. I see." He downed his glass of wine and beckoned a servant over to fill it.

"How long has he been in your household?"

"Oh, I can't say, probably just a little over a year, perhaps more."

"When did you say he is arriving here at Claddach?" His tone was brusque.

"I did not say. Tomorrow, late in the evening I believe. Why is it of concern to you?"

"I will require a word with him as soon as he has arrived."

I did not like the attitude of this man at all, presuming he could address me, a countess, in this way.

"I cannot say if this will be possible; my chaplain answers to me," I said, smiling sweetly then turning to Lady Macleod's spinster daughter Frances to speak to her. I ignored my other companion for the duration of the supper and made a mental note to forget to tell Alexander about his request; what had our journey over the sea to do with him?

Chapter 34

James

Fannie might not be as pretty or as talented as Mary, but by God, right now she is a useful daughter to have. What she told me this morning shocked me to the core. First, she insisted we say prayers together and, as usual, she intoned on behalf of her mother's soul while I drummed my fingers together, wishing she would hurry up.

I was spending time with her only because Jean insisted that I make more of an effort. According to my sister, she was unlikely to make a good marriage unless her confidence grew, since neither her looks nor her charm – or lack of it – would suffice.

At last Fannie began to tell me all about the recent trip to her sister. She described in detail what it was like to stay for three weeks at Mary's grand castle, what they had done each day and what food they had eaten, as if that was of any interest to me whatsoever. Fortunately, I had a bottle of brandy to my side; she of course drank nothing.

She then proceeded to tell me all about the outrageous allowance the Earl gives his wife for clothes and for running her houseful; and she not even twenty. She told me of walks along the shore of the sea loch and of time spent in the family chapel under the tutelage of the young chaplain with whom, if I read her words correctly, Fannie seemed a little in love. I made a note to ask Jean to follow this up with Mary. Fannie would make the most perfect minister's wife.

At last, just as I poured my third glass of brandy, she got to the most interesting piece of news. I could tell she was desperate to tell me.

"One day, Papa, a letter arrived for Mary. She was in such a state of excitement, for she recognised the handwriting at once," she exclaimed triumphantly.

She looked at me, as if waiting to see my reaction. I shrugged, wishing she would hurry up with this tale. I had business to attend to.

"It was Mama's writing!"

I confess I have absolutely no idea how my expression must have appeared, but I do know I said nothing. For quite some time, I was so stunned, my mouth hung open, limp with the shock.

And so she continued. "The letter was from some remote Hebridean islands called the Monach Islands. The Reverend Fleming told us that this was a small archipelago to the west of a big range of islands called the Uists, North and South. And they were far away to the west, miles by sea and land from Mary's castle on the coast."

"Go on," I urged, at last finding my voice.

She straightened her shoulders, as if about to make a great pronouncement. She looked very pleased with herself. Encourage her in her every endeavour, Jean had said.

"Please continue, my dear." I attempted a smile.

"The letter was indeed from Mama and in it she told us of her brutal kidnapping from her Edinburgh lodgings and now her exile – well, no actually, a better word is imprisonment – on these remote islands. And so, having at last found a means of communication, she wants Mary to come and rescue her. And as soon as possible!"

She gazed at me, waiting. I chose my words carefully. "Fannie, dearest, I do not see how this is credible."

I thought about what my sister would advise me to do and so took her hand in mine, something I do not think I had ever done.

"Your mother is dead. We know that, the minister conducted the funeral. Do you remember?"

"Stop speaking to me as if I were a baby, Papa. Of course I remember, it was not even a year ago. I was there, we all were, at Aunt Jean's; it was awful. She is not dead, the letter proved that she is alive. Isn't it the most wonderful news you've ever heard!"

"No, Fannie, it is not, for surely this is written by some imposter, a fraudster who wants something from us, or more likely from your wealthy sister."

"No, Father, I do not see how that is possible, it is Mama's writing." She began to snivel.

"Fannie, my dear, there are many bad people in the world. Some people will do anything for money and…"

"But there was no mention of money in the letter. None at all. Mama simply asked to be saved from her ordeal!" She was wailing now.

"And do you think that, if someone were to send in a rescue mission, they would find your mother? No, they would not, for she is dead. What they would find would be some man determined to get his hands on Mary's husband's money somehow. Mark my words."

I withdrew my hand so that she could use her handkerchief to wipe her face. She really was not a bonnie girl and her runny nose and constant snivelling were not adding to her appeal. I looked away and hoped my words sufficed.

"But I don't understand, Papa. Why would someone do that?"

"Because, my dear girl, there are many bad people in the world." I stroked her hair, thinking that there was someone I must see as soon as possible. "Now, why d'you not go upstairs and lie down on your bed for a couple of hours? You must still be tired after the long journey. I shall ask Mistress Wilson to bring you up a restorative tea. How does that sound?"

She nodded and slouched out of the drawing room, sniffing into her handkerchief.

As soon as I saw her reach the stairs, I leapt to my feet and strode into the study, where I pulled out the drawer for some paper.

I dipped my pen into the ink and began to write.

> *Dear Lord Lovat,*
>   *I hope this finds you well.*
>   *I am sorry to inform you that a calamity has occurred: news has travelled to me from the remote Monach Islands. A letter purporting to be from my wife has been sent to...*

I stopped and shook my head. No, this would not do. I could not risk putting anything to paper, it was too dangerous. I took the paper and ripped it up into tiny pieces then threw them onto the fire, prodding them with the poker until they burst into flames. I would have to go and find him myself. It was time to put the St Kilda plan into action.

I sped upstairs to my chamber, locked the door behind me and opened the trunk. I took out the coats and breeches, leant into the bottom and pulled out my hat with the white cockade. I tucked it under my coat and unlocked my door, then ran downstairs, where I rang the bell. The housekeeper came hirpling out of the kitchen.

"Mistress Wilson, a calming tea for Fannie in her chamber, if you will. She is resting after the journey."

I turned to the lad, who had darted up from the cellar stairs. "And Bobbie, fetch my carriage. I must go at once to Duddingston."

Part Six

Chapter 35

Mary, Countess of Kintore

A ferocious storm blew in the following day. The wind battered against the windows, rattling the panes and sending an icy draught everywhere. The rain was relentless, lashing against the windows, making it well-nigh impossible to see out. Only the stable boys ventured out, to check on the horses. Lady Macleod and I sat by the fire, trying to keep warm. It was chilly in her house and I always felt the cold. I shivered and pulled my shawl more tightly around me.

"Lady Macleod, from your experience of living here, how long might this awful weather last?"

She shook her head. "When it comes in like this, with hardly a warning, it can last some time. Three winters ago, it rained for almost a month. We were nearly flooded, too, even though the house is high up above the shore."

I sighed. "It's October now, so if it's not cleared in a couple of weeks, it will be impossible to take the trip, I fear."

"I said the very same thing to Frances at breakfast. What does your nice young chaplain say?"

"Just that we must wait. But we both now appreciate that if it is still as bad in a week or so then we must return home, for we still have to take the boat to get back over to the mainland."

"You know you are most welcome for however long you need to stay, but your husband the Earl will be keen to have you home."

I nodded.

"Shall we take some tea, Mary?"

"Thank you, that would be good. Something to pass the time."

She rang the bell and the maid arrived.

"Bring us some tea, please. And," she turned to me, "will you take some of Cook's seed cake?"

"Yes please. Oh," I called after the servant, "ask the Reverend Fleming to come and see me."

She bobbed and scuttled off.

"My Lady, I've spoken to several locals about this weather and they now all agree it is set to last for a few more days. But if at least the rain clears in a day or so, shall I try to go myself to the Monachs? Presuming the wind has died down a little?" My chaplain stood beside me, whispering as he gestured out to the west.

"That is what I have been thinking about, Alexander. Earlier I thought that would make sense but now, I think not, for what if the storm returned with a vengeance and you became marooned over there? Then I should have to return home alone. I do not think my maid and I should travel without you; my husband would be most distressed."

"So, what's to be done, My Lady?"

He stared at me, his piercing blue eyes unsettling me.

I leant in towards the window where the rain continued to pelt down and the wind howled and swirled.

"I shall write a letter to Mama," I whispered, "and, if we find that, after a few days, we are unable to make the journey, then I shall have it sent to Donald Macdonald's house near here. As tacksman, he must surely have to go over to the Monachs soon and he can risk being stranded over there, whereas we cannot. He said the other night he had not been for several months."

I came and sat down again beside Lady Macleod. "I presume Mr Macdonald would take a letter over to the Monachs for me?"

"Of course, my dear. And that is by far the most sensible option."

The maid entered with a tray of tea and cake. "And now, let us all have some refreshment and warm ourselves up by the fire." She stabbed the logs with a poker and I watched as the flames flickered and danced.

Chapter 36

Donald Macdonald

So, she wishes me to be her messenger. The high and mighty countess has commanded that I take her letter to the Monachs. Well, we shall see about that.

I received Lady Macleod's note asking me to pay a visit. Although the old dear can be rather tedious, always talking about the same subjects – the weather, the fluctuation in the price of tea and sheep – she never asks me about Isabella. To be honest, no one does these days; they know I will just clam up and change the subject at once.

Ah, Bella, how foolish you were, how weak and pitiful, a disgrace to your sex. What on earth could he have had that I, your husband of ten years, did not? Well, you are not here to answer that question; and your demise was no one's fault but your own.

I have often pondered the reasons why you did it, Isabella. I know of course how you did it: you made a strong tea of rhubarb leaves and drank it down. When I interrogated your maid Elsie about it later, she said you had asked her to pick some rhubarb, that you had a fancy for it, sour though it was. You were taking notions for strange foods and now of course I know why.

Instead of cooking the stalks, you boiled the leaves to make a toxic drink. And then you insisted your maid bake scones for some family of ingrates with a dozen children, and take them to their home on the west of the island, near Loch nam Buadh. And so, while Elsie was away there and I was over on Ceann Iar trying to get the rent from Daft Hamish, you did it.

I have often wondered how it felt, to know your life was about to end, as you writhed in agony alone, dejected. It's strange that he never even bothered about you after I found out the truth. What a coward he must be. When I asked Elsie why you did it, as she sobbed pathetically over your vomit-covered, soiled body, she said she had no idea. And I believe her; she had no inkling. How devious you both must have been, to have kept it from even your maid. Now she serves in my house here on North Uist and we never mention Bella at all.

What I ponder also these days is, did you actually intend to kill yourself by imbibing the rhubarb-leaf potion? Or was it just to bring on a miscarriage? Even as I say that word, I feel nauseous; and this is why I can never forgive you. We had waited for a child for so many years and then you met him and suddenly became with child; and this after we had not shared a bed for anything other than sleep for many months.

It makes me so angry, but I must lighten my mood by turning to other things. The countess' chaplain is the Reverend Alexander Fleming. Surely, the chance that he is related to William Fleming is slight, but I have discovered that he is indeed so. Why is the church being so tardy replacing William on the Monachs; I presumed he had long gone. Good God, I told them over a year ago I wanted him gone – he is of no use to me now, refusing to talk, to tell me who it was – but the man is still there.

I thought he could be sent somewhere even bleaker, St Kilda perhaps might suit him well. I believe the Reverend Murdo MacInnes, in his role as head of the local presbytery over in Lochmaddy, deliberately defies my instruction for he knows where I stand on Presbyterianism. Yes, of course, I went to church every Sunday when we lived on the Monachs, but Fleming could see into my heart. Dear God, he even witnessed me kneeling to pray at wee Morag MacNeish's funeral. How stupid I was, such a papist gesture, but it was just the day after I'd found Bella and was in such a state of grief or, more likely, anger, that I paid no heed. I should have stayed away but the father was one of the best men on the islands, so I went to be there for him; but I was so distracted I found myself kneeling when we were invited to pray.

~~~

I set off for Lady Macleod's house, well wrapped up in my plaid, and strode over the moor. The weather was foul, the rain pouring down in torrents and the wind howling and swirling all around. I shook the water off my plaid and stamped the mud off my feet before entering her hall, where I waited for my audience. Soon, an earnest young man with piercing blue eyes arrived and introduced himself.

"Mr Macdonald, I am the Reverend Alexander Fleming." He inclined his head a little, but kept his steely gaze upon me.

"I am pleased to meet you, Reverend Fleming. Are you related to the Reverend William Fleming by any chance?"

He paused, smiled, then nodded.

"William is my elder brother. Of course, you must have met him while you lived on the Monachs."

"Indeed I did." I tried not to sneer. "Every Sunday; and at other times beside."

"And that is why I am so keen to go there – first of all, to check on the kirk roof, but also to see him. It has been more than two years since we last met."

"I see. And has he plans to leave the Monachs soon, do you know?"

"Not that I know of." He looked out towards the west through the rain-lashed window. The storm showed no sign of abating.

"But, Mr Macdonald, you perhaps are wondering why the countess invited you to call today?"

I nodded.

"She is, sadly, indisposed this morning, but requested that I ask you a favour on her behalf."

"A favour?" I raised an eyebrow. Why would that haughty scrap of a girl believe I should want to help her?

"Lady Kintore wishes you to take a letter for someone who lives on the Monach Islands. Sadly, she is now unable to go and this storm, even after a whole week, is not subsiding. I find that not only Her Ladyship but not even I can sail, for it is too dangerous for now and we must return home as soon as possible."

Oh, I see what she wants me to do – to be emissary for her and deliver a letter to the woman I now realise must be her disgraced mother, living in my house. Good Lord, why had I not made the connection earlier? Well, bad breeds bad and this young upstart countess can think again if she presumes I will be her lap dog.

"Of course, Reverend Fleming. I should be delighted to help. I cannot say when I shall be able to sail, but as soon as the wind dies down, I will be on my way."

He took something from his pocket.

"Here it is, Mr Macdonald. Her Ladyship will be most grateful, I'm sure."

I accepted the letter, nodded then headed for the door. "I am sure she will be. Goodbye, Reverend Fleming."

"Good day, Sir."

I strode outside, the letter tucked into my belt. I decided to take the shortcut home, along the shore, and when I got to the dunes, I cowered down in the marram grass to shelter from the blast of wind off the sea. The rain had stopped pelting down and there was only a light drizzle.

I retrieved the letter from under my plaid, broke open the

seal and opened out the parchment. As I read the childlike handwriting, the raindrops fell onto the page, making the ink run. I screwed it up tight and walked towards the headland where I flung it into the grey, tormented sea. As I walked home, I was light of step as I thought how pleased my Lord Lovat would be with this turn of events.

Chapter 37

James

I do not understand how a storm can last so long. There has been a gale and torrential rain in the Hebrides for over two weeks now. Unprecedented, Lovat says. Unfortunate, I say.

I met His Lordship at Clerihugh's, where he gave me news of the inclement weather holding up proceedings. It was a month since we had met and formulated the plan to take Rachel off the Monachs and to St Kilda.

"Grange, not only can no boats get over to the Monachs right now, but we also have no chance of getting her to St Kilda before next spring."

"What do you mean, man?"

He winced as he hoisted his bandaged, gout-ridden foot up onto a stool.

"What I mean is that there are no boats able to sail out to St Kilda over the winter. It's just too dangerous. Never been done."

"So, what do these St Kildans do for supplies over the long dark winters?"

"They eat seabirds and their eggs. And porridge, sometimes cooked with a puffin in it."

I screwed up my face in disgust.

"They store their oats in their hovels over the winter; often it is so wet they're mouldy, but they eat them anyway. I tell you, Grange, it's the end of the earth. The peasants are even more wretched than those on the Monachs."

"So, if she can't go there, where can she go?"

Lovat sighed deeply. "Grange, there is nowhere else. Winter is nigh and I can't risk any of my men and their boats to transport your shrew of a wife. She is safe where she is. She can just stay put all winter."

"But what if Mary gets help over to her first?"

"Are you listening to me, man?" He thumped his tankard on the table and drew nearer. "No one can get over. It's hard at this time of year to sail to the Monachs without risking life and limb. Only people who know the waters well would even attempt it."

"So, she'll be safe there till the spring, do you reckon?"

"Yes. There's nowhere for her to go. And, who knows, she might succumb to a malady over the long cold winter and then our worries will be over." Lovat smirked. "Then you can marry your wench in London."

"She is not a wench, Lovat, I have told you before; she is a fine lady." I picked up my ale. "And as to maladies, Rachel is as strong as an ox; she is unlikely to succumb to anything, apart from alcohol poisoning."

He shrugged. "And what of your daughter, the countess? You told me her sister is easily persuaded, but what of Her Ladyship?"

I bent down and held my head in my hands. "I don't know, Lovat. She's a different person, strong, solid. She can't be fobbed off like Fannie. What's to be done?"

He got to his feet, grimacing with the pain as he put his not insubstantial weight on his foot.

"Grange, I have done more than any friend could have, under the circumstances. It's up to you to deal with your children yourself. I have enough worries with my own brood."

And away he stomped, leaving me to contemplate what on earth I would say to Mary.

Chapter 38

Rachel

The winter dragged on and on. The storm had lasted nearly a month, by which time most supplies had run out. My claret had finished long ago, but strangely this had not affected me as much as it would have in the past; I seemed to have lost my great urge for it. God knows why. Perhaps the corks in my last box were tainted.

When there was a sighting of the first boat on the horizon, some time in late November or perhaps early December, everyone in the village rushed to the beach. It was a clear, crisp, cloudless morning and the birlinn could be seen from far away. I stood barefoot with the islanders on the sand and watched as they pointed out to sea. The nearer the boat got, the more they began to grumble and mutter in their own tongue. Soon some of them turned and fled over the dunes, away from the shore. I gestured to Catriona to try to find out what was going on. And then I understood: on board was another man, not just the master and his two crewmen. And it was he they either seemed to fear or loathe, for even those who stayed were whispering under their breath, their faces tense. Even I, hearing the muted Gaelic, understood. How they must all detest the tacksman.

This was Donald Macdonald, in whose house I lived. Well, this should be an interesting encounter, I thought, as I stood firm in the wet sand. I looked around and saw there was now only myself, Catriona and another three islanders waiting, expectant.

The boat navigated the dangerous reefs near the shore and shuddered to a halt on the shelved beach and the two lads leapt overboard with their ropes.

Soon a stranger jumped overboard and waded through the surf to join us. He was stockily built and had a balding head. His fat cheeks were blotchy and his nose red and bulbous. I raised my chin and tried, unsuccessfully, to tease out my locks with my fingers as he approached. He stopped before the five of us and we waited. I had hoped he might address me in English, but he spoke Gaelic in a harsh guttural tone to the natives, who turned and fled, including Catriona. I stood still and gazed at this man, my captor on the Monachs.

"I had hoped to find a lady living in my house, but I see she has become a native." He gestured to my attire. I looked down; I was so used to wearing the native dress now, I had forgotten I had it on. My dress was brown and tatty, just like the local women, but I did refuse to wear the island headscarf to cover my crowning glory, my beautiful hair, so I had draped the scarf – fetchingly I thought – around my shoulders. The dress might be ugly and unattractive, but it was much more comfortable, and with far fewer buttons and fastenings than my two gowns, which were so shabby and also far too tight for me these days. My figure was becoming less elegant, stout but not in a comely way; it certainly couldn't be anything to do with Catriona's cooking. Bless her.

I raised my head to stare straight at his pinched features. He really was an ugly man. "Sir, I am unused, even on these barbaric islands, to being addressed in such a disrespectful manner. If you care to neglect my needs in matters of dress, then how else am I supposed to appear? Naked?"

He smirked. "My apologies. I was simply taken aback at your attire."

"Yes, well, as I said, unless I am furnished with a new wardrobe soon, I shall be wearing even more tattered clothes.

And by the way, I believe you are aware that it is right and proper to address a lady as My Lady?"

I leant my head down towards him.

"Have you brought me my claret? And some proper eggs, not these vile seabirds' eggs my girl feeds me constantly."

He scowled. "My Lady" (he pronounced the words as if spitting them out) "I am not here to be your messenger, but in my role as tacksman. And since you are living in my house, I shall not be staying overnight but shall be returning to North Uist late this afternoon. I must therefore be on my way." He gestured to the boat. "The master there has some supplies, I have no idea if any are for you." He started to walk past me towards the village and I ran to keep up.

"Mr Macdonald, have you no letters for me?" Why was there nothing from My Angel after all this time?

"I told you, ask the master. Though why would anyone write to you?"

I stormed after him. "How long must I be kept here?"

"That I do not know, it's not my decision. And now, excuse me, I do not have long and I have rents to collect."

And he strode on towards the dunes, where he turned and shouted, "Do you know where the minister is? The Reverend Fleming?"

I shrugged. "Where he always is, I presume. In his church, praying for redemption."

Chapter 39

William

I heard the kerfuffle down on the beach. I'd spotted the boat on the horizon and knew that not only would all of my parishioners be down there, waiting, but she would be too. I disappeared into the church and continued to pray.

Ever since that unforgettable visit by Rachel, I had kept as low a profile as is possible on these small islands; apart from visiting ailing parishioners, I have simply been in the church every day, trying to repair some of the damage after the storm; the thatch on the roof was not as badly affected as many other homes, but I still needed to try to patch it up.

I had hardly seen her at all. She continued to come to church and, at the start, glowered at me from the front row in a defiant manner. But after a few weeks, I realised that she was not sitting in the front row – I had not noticed her because she now wore island dress and blended in with the other native women. After the service I went past the pews to the entrance as usual, looking from left to right, before my eyes fell upon hers; she wore the brown uniform of the island women, but without donning one of their patterned headscarves.

As I stood waiting for the congregation to emerge, I studied the wooden door, which was almost hanging off its hinges after those weeks of battering in the terrible storm. We badly needed money for repairs and that was something I would have to speak to the presbytery about – if only I could get a message to them; or, as a last resort, I would have to mention it to Donald. That prospect did not fill me with joy.

Rachel had arrived at my home some three months ago looking, I must say, quite shocking. Her skin was always weather-beaten these days, but her eyes, usually clear and large, were bloodshot and like slits in her pale face. For the first time, she looked her age – which I now know is 42. She had always taken time to groom her hair, which was so beautiful, but that day it was dishevelled and tangled; it gave her a wild look.

She had on her blue gown, which admittedly was past its best, but I also noticed a split in the material around the bodice and that the hem was torn. But then I recalled with embarrassment that I might have been the cause of those rips.

I was alone in my house, busy hunched over my desk writing Sunday's sermon, and she had simply wandered in unannounced and sat herself down by the fire.

She had a bulging notebook on her lap. I leapt to my feet.

"Rachel, how are you? I have not seen you for some days."

She neither smiled nor indeed changed her grave expression at all.

"I have been in bed. I have had some sort of strange malady; it came upon me after I discovered the contents of Isabella Macdonald's trunk."

I swallowed.

"Are you perhaps aware of what was in the trunk, William?"

I shook my head. "Can I get you some refreshment, Rachel? I believe there is some wine left, or I could see if…"

"Claret will suffice," she commanded, and I ran towards the kitchen.

I returned with a bottle of claret and two glasses and poured her drink in silence. I confess, my hand was not steady as I poured. I knew what was coming.

She didn't thank me for the refreshment, just took one sip then replaced the glass on the table.

"William, I fear you have been lying to me."

"What do you mean, Rachel?"

"Do you remember I asked you about Donald Macdonald's wife? And you said you knew nothing about her, not her name, nothing; indeed, you said that you were barely acquainted."

I nodded and took a gulp from my glass.

"It appears this was not true; indeed, it seems that you lied to me constantly." She opened the journal on her lap. Dear God, I now saw what was bulging. Bella had obviously kept all of the wild flowers from the machair, dried them and put them in a book.

"It would appear that you and Isabella – Bella as I believe you called her fondly – were not only acquainted, you were intimate. And you picked flowers for her from the machair – the daisies, dandelions, harebells, heather, orchids – all of the pretty flora you also picked for me. It would appear…"

She turned the pages of the journal

"…that you and she met on the remote beaches of this island and also over on Shivinish and once on Ceann Iar. And you were not simply entering into discourse on the price of tea. There in the dunes, where we too met, you lay with her. And not just once or twice, but often. So often that she…"

"Rachel, I am so…"

She thrust the palm of her hand in my face, leant closer and hissed. "I have not finished speaking." She sipped her claret and began again, her voice now shrill.

"You fornicated in the sand so often, it appears that she became with child and since her husband could not give her a child during those ten years of unhappy marriage, she was delighted. But then, disaster ensued. She writes, by the way, that no one else on the islands knew, not even her maid. How did you keep these nefarious goings-on a secret for so long, William?"

There was a sudden noise and we both looked round. The door had swung open in the wind. I held my head in my hands as she continued.

"Then, when she told you her joyful news, you panicked. The cuckolded husband would come to know – for she was already growing fat – that she had been with another man, for it was some time since they had lain together. And so, instead of being gracious and godly, you threatened her – is that the correct word? – with eternal damnation, saying she must not tell him who the father was. Some swarthy islander, he must be allowed to think. What a coward you are, William Fleming."

"Rachel, this is not true, please let me explain."

"No, not yet. For I am sure you are aware what happens in personal journals. A lady pours her heart out in her diary; she does not invent fiction."

She turned another page and I downed my glass. Again, I knew what was coming.

"So, she agreed, under duress, not to reveal the identity of her lover, but then things took a turn for the worse, didn't they, William? Her husband found out about the baby and he of course wanted to kill the man concerned, but she persuaded him that they might have that long-awaited child after all, move back to North Uist together with the child and forget about her lover. But then you rejected her, told her you had never loved her, that the baby would be born an abomination, and she was then so heartbroken, she decided to get rid of the child."

I bit my lip. "Rachel, this was not my doing, she had…"

Again, she raised an imperious hand. Having looked tired and ill on arrival, she was now emboldened, full of vigour.

"And so, the last entry in this journal is her sending off her girl to get some rhubarb."

She lifted the journal and read from the page: "'I told Elsie I had a notion for some nice rhubarb; it was the season. But little does she know what my intentions are with it. I shall rid myself of the child and forget the entire miserable encounter and return to North Uist anyway.'"

She closed the diary and continued.

"I cannot of course speak to my girl Catriona, since we don't share a language, but we now communicate by gestures and understand often what we need to say. So, when I put this to her, she told me that, given the strength of the potion, it must have killed her. Dead. What an agonising death she must have suffered. And then her husband left the Monachs alone, still not knowing the identity of his wife's lover, the cause of her demise."

She leant back against the chair. "What a tragedy, what a waste of a life – no, of two lives. And what say you to that, as a man of God?"

Even though I tried to contain my emotions, I found I could not and began to weep, while mumbling feeble excuses, but I knew Rachel was right. She was the only person now to know I had been responsible for Bella's death. Donald had questioned me over and over when Elsie had suggested to him that "the minister might be able to help identify the man".

I decided the best route was to tell him I did know but could not betray a member of my congregation by sharing information given to me in confidence. I have always suspected Donald has papist leanings, so I threw in a reference to Roman Catholic priests having their lips sealed after confession. The man hates me for so many reasons and wants rid of me, but the one thing he demands of me, I cannot possibly give. Oh, the deceit I have become embroiled in.

I managed to control my pathetic tears and looked up at Rachel as she closed the journal, arose from her chair and headed for the open door.

"I might see you at church, William Fleming, and I want you to know this: I will not betray you by speaking of our trysts to your feeble-minded parishioners, but from today you will not see me alone. Ever."

She stepped onto the threshold and raised her voice. "In return, this is what will happen: if you do not enable my rescue, through my daughter the Countess of Kintore, as soon as possible, then believe me, the rumours will start to fly across these wretched, godforsaken islands."

As she stormed out, I nodded my head, for I knew she meant it.

Chapter 40

Donald Macdonald

I just had time before the boat was returning to North Uist to call into the church. I had to see the minister and try again to prise out of him what he knew. Though what on earth is the man still doing here? He is a constant reminder of my wife's unnecessary death as he alone knows the identity of the man who seduced Bella.

I had had an exhausting day going from house to house, listening to the same story of how the storm had blown away so much topsoil, there would be nowhere to grow oats and barley for their porridge and bannocks next spring. The turf had been torn up and there was now even more sand covering the islands. They were all in despair and the storm was the excuse most of them had for not paying me the rent due. Some of the simpletons were obviously hiding, refusing to answer their doors, but most just said they were struggling and they would pay next time. Next time; how often have I heard that story!

I walked towards the church and noticed the wooden door hanging off its hinges; this storm had done so much damage. I pushed the door open and walked inside. It smelt musty as usual. He was there. He turned on hearing my footsteps and I saw him freeze for a moment, then regain his composure and walk towards me.

"Good afternoon, Donald. I heard you were on the Monachs today. Have you done most of your business?"

"No, I have not, I didn't have time to get over to Ceann Iar but Daft Hamish never pays on time anyway."

He nodded then waited.

"William, why are you still here? I thought I had given instructions for you to leave the Monachs?"

He bristled. "Donald, I think you know by now the way the church here works. It is not up to landowners nor their lackeys to decide who is the minister; it is a presbytery matter."

Lackey, how dare he!

"William, I have come to ask you one more time. Who was the man who caused my darling Isabella's untimely death?"

He looked down at his feet and a thick silence filled the dank building.

"Donald, you know I cannot betray my congregation," he muttered. "There are some things that pass between a parishioner and their minister that must remain private." His eyes opened wide as if he had just had a thought. "To change the subject slightly, Donald. You will be aware that Lady Grange resides in your house here?"

I nodded. "Obviously I am."

"Well, she is desperate to get off the island. Is there any way she could be sent elsewhere? Even over to North Uist? That is still a long boat journey from mainland Scotland, but here she is miserable."

I scratched my head. "Why would I care if she's miserable? And why would you want to help her, William? You must know she is a vixen, a shrew, the most disloyal of wives and also that she comes from a family of lunatics? Why, I saw her this morning down on the beach looking even more native than the natives."

"I do not know about her family history. But surely you could see it in the goodness of your heart, Donald, to free her from this barren place? Can you search your Christian soul? She is used to Edinburgh society, balls and oyster parties. Here there is nothing but seabirds to eat and no company at all, certainly not in her own language; and there is no one of her class. At least on North Uist there are some noble families she could stay with perhaps?"

I raised my eyes heavenward as I thought of a plan.

"William, you seem very keen to help this lady. Even though she deserves nothing at all, after her disgraceful behaviour to her husband in the past."

He opened his mouth to speak but I held up a finger.

"But I see a possible solution." I looked towards the door where the daylight was fading into dusk. "This is not something I have time to go into further today as I must get the boat back over to North Uist before nightfall. But here's my thinking: you will tell me the name of my wife's lover, and I shall endeavour to have Lady Grange removed from the Monachs."

His eyes narrowed.

"What do you say to that then?"

He gulped like a sinking fish. "I ... well, let us discuss this the next time, Donald. But I can see the idea has merit."

"Good, then let us during my next visit – as early in the spring as possible, weather-wise – converse as two gentlemen over a glass of brandy at your house. You have brandy, I presume?"

He nodded.

"Good." I turned and headed for the open door. "But I do expect you to have packed your belongings and be prepared to move to a new parish soon after. You have been here long enough. And now I must be on my way. Until the next time, William. Farewell."

There was no reply from inside the sanctuary as I headed out into the gloaming.

Chapter 41

James

I pulled my plaid tight round my shoulders as I sat in my carriage on the way to Duddingston. It was December, so I should not have been surprised at the freezing cold, but I must be getting old; the chill spread into my very bones.

I shivered too when thinking of the letter I had received earlier from Mary. This was her second correspondence after I had written to her about what Fannie had told me. And I tried to fob her off with the story I had told poor Fannie, that the letter from their mother was in fact from fraudsters, keen to get their hands on Mary's wealth. As I had feared, Mary was having none of it and in her letter she was all for me raising an army to go and fetch Rachel.

When I repeated the trope about swindlers after her money, I heard nothing for a few weeks. Until this second letter this morning. It caused me not a little concern.

> *Papa, I do wish you would treat me as a fellow adult and not a child. Please do not forget I am now a countess and not only able to make important decisions myself, but also to understand the difference between truth and lies.*
>
> *Fannie you might be able to placate with tales and fabrications, but not I. As your eldest daughter, I demand to know the truth. Surely you must be able to find out whether indeed Mama was abducted in a shocking manner from her*

Edinburgh lodgings and taken, after the most undignified
and horrific journey, to the remote Hebridean islands. And
it occurred to me, what has become of Annie, her girl? She
cannot simply have disappeared; there was no mention of her
from Mama in her letter. And what of Mama's jewels? I have
neither seen nor heard of their whereabouts. Surely, if she
had indeed died, I would have been given her jewels, to divide
between Fannie and myself? Not that I need any; my husband
the Earl provides me with enough from his family vault.

Papa, I do feel you are not being altogether realistic. It was
Mama's handwriting and I am convinced that she is on these
Monach Islands. I know she is still alive and I fully intend to
go and find her. Unfortunately, this will not be possible until
the spring, but when the better weather begins, I shall return
to North Uist and to the Monach Islands with or without
your help.

Your loving daughter,
  Mary

Dear God, when did my eldest daughter become so
stubborn and resolute? Obviously, she takes after her mother
in more ways than one. How on earth does her husband put
up with her? Well, he is a weak, feeble-minded man who is
past his prime and so presumably just puts up with his young
wife's foibles.

I peered out from the curtain as the horses slowed down
over the cobbles. The lights of The Sheep Heid were visible
at the end of the village. I brought out my hat with the white
cockade, placed it on my head and descended from the carriage,
while wondering why my life has become so complicated.

"Lovat, there are more problems in my family."

My old friend shook his head and sighed.

"But before we speak of Rachel, first of all I must know exactly what happened to the girl, Annie, on that night back in January? It has been bothering me."

We were sitting at Lovat's favourite snug window seat. He had his back to the window and I sat facing his mighty frame, just able to make out figures passing by outside, in the dark drizzle of Duddingston village. Lovat was already the worse for wear and I was trying to keep up with him by ordering an ale and a chaser of brandy at the same time. He had just told me he and other Jacobites had been discussing the next uprising against the king and that my involvement would not affect my high office. Since this was clearly ridiculous, I decided to change the subject.

He leant back against the lattice pane and sighed.

"Grange, I thought I told you, you needn't worry about her."

"But I want to know what happened to her. Could she suddenly arrive back at Preston House and tell someone what happened on that night?"

He chuckled. "That would be difficult. In fact, impossible."

"Lovat, did you have her killed?"

"Grange, my old friend, what an accusation. Number one: no, I did not have her killed. And number two: do you remember watching the pall bearers at your sister's house on the funeral day struggling to lift the coffin upon their shoulders? Do you think it could possibly have been an empty casket?"

I stared at him, dumbfounded as the realisation dawned. I leant towards him and whispered. "Please do not say she was in my wife's coffin?"

He shrugged. "How else were we to make the funeral as real as possible, James? I have heard of unoccupied coffins that are too obviously empty as the men swing them onto their shoulders as if they'd nothing but a feather inside them. I have also heard of stones being piled inside, but no matter how many you put in, they rattle."

He raised his hands in the air. "Grange, there was no other way. Besides, she was the ideal body – same height as your wife, though weight-wise, a little slimmer." He patted his paunch. "Well, our servants always are."

"So, you had her killed and instead of disposing of the body, you laid her in the fine coffin you insisted I buy for the burial at Greyfriars Kirk?"

"Are you getting deaf, Grange? I said I did not have her killed."

"I don't understand."

He picked up his goblet and drank deep, shaking his head as if irked by my ignorance. At last I grasped his meaning.

"You did not have her killed; you killed her yourself, Lovat? Dear God, what have you become?"

"What have YOU become, Grange. It is YOUR reputation we are saving."

I slumped back against the chair as I took it all in. So, Annie was dead. The girl who had served my wife for so many years, and so loyally, was killed in order for the lie we had fabricated to ring true.

I frowned. "You didn't make her suffer, I hope, Lovat?"

"Not at all. It didn't take long." He looked over my head and beckoned to the server. "Johnnie, bring us some oysters, would you?"

I shook my head, picked up my glass and downed it in one. What webs of deceit we were spinning.

Part Seven

Chapter 42

Rachel

I stood on the beach, the cold water lapping at my bare feet, looking over the sea at the skerries and the glint of moonlight on the rocks. Even in the dark, this place had the capacity to look strikingly beautiful. I was taking my usual evening stroll over the sand, looking out to sea, hopeful, wishing. It was some three months since a boat had managed over to the Monachs and there had been talk that they would be able to land again soon. I didn't hear this myself, of course; it was only Catriona who told me in our now well-established code of communication.

I had not ventured out in daylight since I'd had the meeting at the manse that day with the minister. I had no wish for the company of others; only Catriona was my loyal and faithful aide. Dear God, I had even become used to her vile seabird broths and stews, but I did draw the line at fulmar eggs; those I could not stomach.

I had read most of the Shakespeare from Bella's trunk and was now becoming agitated as I had nothing left to read. There was no possibility of me borrowing books from the minister, for I refused to see him again. He was dead to me. I had stopped going to church; let the natives talk, if they wanted. Instead, on Sunday mornings, I read my Bible and contemplated what a miserable life I now had.

The moon was bright tonight and the stars were luminous. I gazed up at them in wonder, breathing in deeply as the sea air chilled my nostrils. I pulled my scarf more tightly around my hair – the peasants' headscarf I'd vowed I would never wear. Well, what do I care now? I looked down at my brown dress; even in the dark, it looked drab and dull, but brown or grey is how I felt, constantly. I was colourless now.

I presumed the islanders would all think me mad, the erstwhile grand lady who no longer goes to church. The lady who dresses in shabby attire and goes barefoot as if she's never known fine gowns of Persian silk or dainty embroidered slippers. The lady who eats cormorant soup and bannocks, as if she had never tasted lobster bisque or rosewater tablets.

Sometimes, when I am on one of my night-time walks along the sand, I pick up long feathers from seabirds and push them into my headscarf, trying to remember the feel of a fine ribbon or even a sparkling jewel adorning my beautiful hair at the many assemblies we went to in those early years.

I even came to wonder if I was losing my mind. Admittedly, when I had my claret, I did not care as much, but even when my taste for wine had returned, and while I still had supplies, I savoured it, rather than glugging it down like a parched animal. But as for madness? My father was mad, many had insisted. Why else would he have killed a man in cold blood? Well, I believe it was for justice and for fairness.

I still had the nightmares and when I woke up in the morning sweating and trembling, remembering that night when I'd peered through my cold little fingers at the grotesque bloodied hand on the stake, my girl Catriona, just like Annie, knew what to do. She brought me my drink and then the memories were soon soothed away.

I wandered back up the beach, scuffing my feet against the drifts of sand and shingle, then stopped at the dunes to look out to sea once more. When would a boat come? How I longed to be rescued. I still believed My Angel would somehow manage to get help, but when and how?

A light was on in the minister's house and part of me wanted to go straight there and rage against the injustices the world had served me, both before he had come into my life and also after. But instead, I headed for my home where my bed and the dying peat fire awaited.

Chapter 43

Catriona

I was hanging out the washing, looking far out to sea, when I screwed my eyes up tight as I thought I saw something on the horizon. Was it possible? Yes, it was a boat. I let out a sigh of relief. It had been some four months since the visit from any boat – even Mr Macdonald's – and everyone's supplies were low. And so, as I gazed out to sea, I hoped and prayed that this was the supply vessel and not the tacksman's boat.

I ran to the shore where a few of the other islanders were waiting. We all said just what I was thinking, please God let it be Gruff Gordon the boatman with the provisions. Our islands had gone through such bad times.

First of all, there was the storm, battering the land and blowing away all of the topsoil. Everyone is now so worried about the grain this year. And then there was the minister, or lack of. He took the service as usual three Sundays ago and no one has seen him since. Angus Macleod had realised three days later that his boat was gone. Why the Reverend would want to set out in another man's boat in conditions that were not at all ideal, with early spring squalls, was a mystery. Angus had raged and raged; where would he get another boat from? How was he to get the fleeces back from Shivinish and Ceann Iar?

He and his brothers had barged into the minister's house, expecting to find some sort of explanation. But there was nothing, not a note, nothing. The minister's help, Nell, had no idea why he would leave. So, the minister had abandoned his church, his parishioners – and his duties. No one talked of anything else. When I'd told my mistress, her features took on an expression even more sad than usual and she took to her bed. She has been there ever since.

We all peered out at the boat, now making its way around the skerries towards our beach. By now there were a couple of dozen folk with me, all pointing and chattering. Please let it be Gruff Gordon, so we have our supplies. But then big Jim MacNeish said it was not the master and two crewmen in the usual birlinn, but a bigger sloop and there were three other people aboard. Panic swept across the sand.

"It's the tacksman with helpers to get all our rents. We've no chance to escape this time."

One man fled away over the dunes.

"Maybe it's a new minister?"

"Or our old one being hauled back?"

We all continued to stare at the boat as it slowly approached, heading south round the reef then straightening up west towards the shore.

Morna beside me pointed out to sea. "That looks like a woman. Look at the hair."

And sure enough, we could now see that it was a woman with a hat on top of a head of blonde hair.

"There's another woman beside her, look."

There was a smaller woman, with a scarf over her head; and a tall slender man stood beside them both.

"Thank God, it's not Mr Macdonald."

"But who is it then?"

"They'd better have our supplies, that's all I care about."

We were lulled into silence as the sloop sailed slowly towards the beach then shuddered to a halt on the shelf. No one moved, for it was now obvious that the taller woman with the hat was a lady and it looked as if the other, shorter, woman was her servant. The tall man wore a dark gown over his breeches and a black hat over his red hair. Who on earth were they?

Wee Jean jumped up and down. "It's the new minister and he has a wife and servant with him. Oh, praise the Lord!"

We all agreed that was possible, so the men rushed forward to help the women over the side of the sloop, trying not to get the hem of the lady's gown too wet.

She stood on the sand in dainty red slippers and gazed up at us all as if she had never seen anything quite like it. She stared at us as if we were foreigners, which I suppose we were, to the likes of her.

She then turned to the man, who took her hand and led her towards us. Her step was slow, faltering, as if she had never walked on sand in her life. The girl stepped slowly, timidly, behind. We all gaped in wonder at the beautiful gown the lady had on, adorned with pearls and jewels. This was a very fine lady indeed – quite young, only in her early twenties I would think – but obviously someone of importance. When they reached us womenfolk, the man spoke in a Gaelic that was not of these islands, and yet it sounded somehow familiar.

"Do any of you know where Lady Grange resides?"

I gasped. It was someone to rescue my mistress!

And soon it dawned on me why he sounded familiar. This man was obviously a relative of the minister; I could now see the resemblance, the nose and eyes were the same. The Reverend William must have gone away to organise her rescue. Praise the Lord indeed!

Chapter 44

Mary, Countess of Kintore

I had great difficulty stepping up the beach as the sand kept sinking under my feet. My red slippers would be ruined, but I most certainly was not going to go barefoot like the natives who had lined up to greet us.

At first sight of them, I was nervous, thinking they were perhaps savages, like those tales I'd heard of explorers encountering barbarous, man-eating natives in lands far away. But this was Scotland and I put all such notions to the back of my mind and thought of my poor mother.

I raised my chin and stared back at them all; most were gawping at me as if I were Queen Caroline herself. Alexander began to speak to them in Gaelic and I turned to stare at him. This foreign tongue was so alien to me. Then one of the native women raised her hands in glee and started babbling back at him. "Your Ladyship," he said, turning to me, "this girl says she is Lady Grange's servant and we may proceed forthwith to see your mother."

I could hardly believe it. After so many months, I was finally going to be able to see Mama. I wondered how she looked. Surely her fine clothes must have made her stand out from these natives in their drab brown attire. I wondered if this girl did her hair as well as Annie had always done. And, yet again, I wondered what had become of Annie.

The girl – whose name was Catriona, Alexander said – led

us up over the dunes towards the little village and what could be described as its houses. These had walls built of dry-stone, packed with what looked like great clods of earth. The roofs were thatched with some kind of reed or grass.

I could see no chimney and when I asked Alexander about this he told me the smoke from their fires simply made its way through the roof, the soot blackening everything inside the houses, in which apparently the animals live as well as the natives. Dear God, I do hope Mama is not being kept in one of these ramshackle hovels. There was now great chattering and prattling from behind and I turned round to see the remaining islanders speak to each other excitedly as they hauled boxes and crates from the boat up the beach.

When we came to a larger house, still with the dry-stone walls and thatched roof, but with a proper doorway and windows and a chimney, Catriona ran inside and we could hear her shouting. And as Alexander and I stood on the threshold, with Meg just behind, we heard a cry of joy. I could recognise Mama's voice anywhere. It was her!

The girl rushed back to the door and beckoned for me to follow. I did and soon came to an open bedroom door. As I entered, I saw someone, a poor-looking soul, in bed and looked around to see where Mama was; she was obviously nursing an invalid. The island woman in the bed was elderly, her hair flecked with grey; I could see the same drab colours of the natives' clothing around her shoulders and neck.

But I soon realised there was no one else there and so my gaze returned to the figure in bed, who was sobbing and holding out her hands to me as if in supplication. Dear God, it was Mama; what had they done to her? Her hair, which used to be glossy and lustrous, was tangled and in ugly clumps; her skin was pale and her eyes bloodshot.

"My Angel," she cried. "My Angel, at last you have come to fetch me. Come closer, Mary, come over here."

I crept over to the bed and took her hands. I noticed her nails were filthy and as she opened her mouth to smile, I saw that some of her teeth were now black.

She pulled me into an embrace and I could not help but notice that the odour from her body was not pleasant; I must get Meg to fetch my phial of scent and something to clean her teeth. She was now sobbing and her tears drenched my shoulders. I pulled back a little, to check once more it was indeed Mama. And at last I found the power of speech.

"Mama, it's many months since I have seen you; are you quite well?"

This was clearly a ridiculous thing to say, but I was too stunned to think of anything other than platitudes.

She sighed and gestured to her girl to bring in a chair for me. I turned round and noticed that Alexander had politely stayed next door, for which I was grateful. Once I was seated, the girl shut over the door and we were alone.

Mama began to pull the bedclothes down, so I saw now not only the collar and scarf, but the whole of her drab attire; it looked as if she was wearing the same brown dress all of those native women had on. What had become of her? Where were her beautiful silk gowns? She then flung the rest of the covers off and pushed herself to the side of the bed. She swung her feet on to the stone floor and stood up. And then I realised.

I could do nothing else but gape at her vast belly protruding out from the dull serge cloth of the shapeless dress; she was heavy with child. She grabbed my hand and placed it on the mighty bulge.

I stared at my white, well-manicured hand and then at hers, grubby and with black dirt under each fingernail. I then looked up at her beaming face with those blackened teeth and I wanted to retch, but I knew I must be strong. I was still without words, so it was up to my mother to speak.

"I have been unwell, Mary, for many months. But now you

are here, I have hope." She lifted my hand away, took the bell by her bed and rang it. "Catriona, bring us some wine; we must celebrate the arrival of My Angel!"

Chapter 45

Rachel

Oh, consummate joy; she has come! At last, after so many months in this wretched place, My Angel has come to rescue me. I could hear the commotion down on the shore, but had neither the energy nor the will to go to the door and see what was happening. I was just wondering how long it might be until Catriona would arrive home, hopefully with my claret, when the door sprang open and there she was, babbling in Gaelic. And then a minute later, Mary stepped into my bedroom.

She looked exquisite, so elegant and fine, wearing a gown that would not have looked out of place at the royal court. Her hair was coiffed in that way she'd always favoured, piled up loosely on her head under her bonnet, and there were jewels in her hair. But the expression on her face was a picture. Her look of utter horror at the sight of my room, shabby and smelly, was admittedly shaming, but I had lost all capacity for abashment. And what must she have thought on seeing me, for elegance and stylishness I'd lost long ago, ever since I had arrived on the Monachs.

The expression now on her sweet little face was one only a mother could see through. She was trying bravely to cover the disgust at what was all around and, especially, before her. But then, when I got out of bed and she saw my belly, her mouth hung open in disbelief. I thought she might faint, had she not been seated.

I took her smooth, dainty hand and placed it on my stomach, hoping the baby would start its rolling and turning, but it was still. It has moved little in the past couple of days now, but that is because my time is nigh. She was utterly silent, just staring at my face then at my belly, and even when Catriona knocked at the door and arrived with refreshments, she said nothing.

The girl had opened a bottle of claret that had just arrived on the boat; Jimmy had kindly delivered my crate. She put out some of her bannocks as usual and again I looked at Mary's face. Her expression was not this time of revulsion, but of incomprehension. What were these coarse grey bannocks that looked so different from the dainty wheaten ones we used to have at Preston House?

At last she spoke. "Mama, what has happened to you?" She gestured at my whole body, starting with my face, then of course at my belly.

I had to smile. All these months of waiting to be rescued and I had not even thought about the reaction to my reduced state; well, reduced status, but not diminished in body size.

"Mary, I have suffered so much, it is beyond your comprehension. But let me simply say that I have never been so happy in my entire life as I am now, seeing you, my darling girl." I stroked her soft cheek. "Now, when can we leave this damned, godforsaken place?"

She shook her head, probably shocked at my language. Then she took a sip from the goblet. "I see you still have your claret supplies, Mama, so things cannot have been that bad."

"Not that bad? Have you any idea what I have had to suffer while you all carried on with your lives of privilege and luxury?" I realised I was not speaking but growling and obviously frightening her, so I leaned back and took a large draught of wine.

She stood up and went to the door. "Can you cover yourself up please, Mama. Or get back into bed. I want you to meet my chaplain; he will decide when we can leave here. But not immediately, I know that. He too has business to attend to."

"Business? What business? I want to get off these islands at once!"

She stood at the door, pointing to the bed. "I shall bring him in now, Mama. Please get into bed. And compose yourself."

I did as I was told and pulled my hair back off my face, to try to tame the tangles. I drew the bedclothes up to my neck and waited. Soon she entered with a tall gentleman who, Dear God, looked so like William, it took my breath away.

He bowed and approached the bed. "Lady Grange, the countess says you are keen to leave as soon as possible. I must see my brother first then hopefully we can leave in a couple of days. I hope this will be suitable."

"Your brother?"

"Yes, the Reverend William Fleming."

I slumped back against the pillow. "He is gone; he disappeared without a trace some three weeks ago." Catriona had just intimated, before she showed Mary in, that the minister must have gone to find someone to rescue me; but now it would seem not, as he had clearly not been in contact with Mary, or his brother.

"So, you have not seen him recently?" I asked.

"Not for a few years; and no letters for well over a year. Our mother has been heartbroken." He shook his head. "I don't understand. Why would he leave without any word?"

I sighed as I realised, finally, what a flimsy, weak man he was.

"I am so sorry to hear this news, My Lady." He looked genuinely shocked. "I will go to the church now and pray. Then we can decide what to do. I do not want our return trip to be delayed too much, but the countess will obviously need to rest for a couple of days at least after the long, arduous journey."

"After the long, arduous journey? In the comfort and ease of a boat where she has servants with her to bow and scrape and look after her every need?" I was aware I was raising my voice, but I did not care.

"Was she the one who was bundled ignominiously onto a horse which carried her all night long in the middle of winter? Then held captive in a castle dungeon for weeks, before being flung into a leaky boat that sailed through rain-lashed waters for days then washed up here on these godforsaken islands? I think not." I paused to take a breath. "Her Precious Ladyship can, I feel sure, put up with a little discomfort, unlike the many, many months of sheer agony her mother has had to suffer." I was shouting now, but I could not stop myself.

They both stared at me in horror and I was about to continue my tirade, but a searing cramp made me gasp in agony. The pains had begun, all of a sudden, and with a vengeance.

Chapter 46

Catriona

The young lady flew through the door to fetch me and her maid. The expression on her face was enough to tell me what was happening. But I had been planning for some weeks now what to do, so I ran through to my mistress and gestured where I was going then returned to the maid who stood stock-still by the fire.

I motioned to her to boil some water, clanging the big saucepan down in front of her and hoping she at least knew how to tend a peat fire.

I ran through the village to Old Bessie's house and rushed in. "The baby's on its way, Bess. Can you come over straight away? Remember she said the last two babies were really quick."

"Aye, but that was some years ago; she's old now, could take much longer," she mumbled, dragging herself up from the fire.

"Please hurry, Bess."

The old woman picked up a cloth bag lying on the bed then turned to me.

"And what about the payment you mentioned?"

"Yes, it's all in hand."

"And double for keeping it to myself?"

"Yes, yes," I said, though I had no idea how my mistress was in fact going to pay her the usual rate, never mind double. I watched as she wrapped herself in her shawl and then hobbled out the door behind me. I glanced towards the sea, which was now rough; the wind had got up and the waves were thrashing against the skerries. The boat on the shore had been hauled up high on the beach; the new arrivals would not be going anywhere soon. I noticed a figure disappear into the church and realised this must be the minister's brother, off to pray; well, what else could a man do at times like this? This was a time for women only, although I wondered how useful the countess might be in assisting at childbirth.

I took Old Bessie into the house and straight into my mistress' bedroom. She was writhing in agony, her head arched back and her eyes shut tight. The daughter just sat there, immobile, her face screwed up in horror at her mother's pain.

She said something to me, but I had no idea what it was, so I ignored her and she continued to sit watching as Old Bessie got to work, bossing me about in short snarls. Soon, the maid rushed in with boiling water and a cloth and spoke to her mistress, who waited till My Lady was through the next contraction before speaking. I got the gist of it.

"Mama, Meg has attended three of her siblings' births. Would she be of use to this old woman?"

"Yes!" my mistress shouted as the next pain arrived and she howled like a wounded animal.

Dear Lord, Jeannie had told me how sore it was, but I had no idea the pains were quite as bad.

The young lady snapped her fingers at me, but I avoided her. Could she not see everyone was busy? She then stood up and went over to her mother – at last – and took her hand. Her maid handed her a wet cloth and she used it to mop her mother's sweaty brow.

After only perhaps an hour or so, Bess was shouting that the baby was coming soon and to fetch a clean cloth. I ran to fetch the only clean sheet in the house and put it on the bed beside Bess, who was now telling my mistress to push. I have no idea if she understood the Gaelic, but she had done this many times before so surely she knew what to do.

Soon she gave a great wail and her face turned even more ruddy as she squeezed her eyes shut and pushed and pushed.

Bess kept nodding her head and speaking in her soft way and soon a noise was heard. I was up at the top of the bed by my mistress and her daughter when I saw Bess lift up the baby, hale and hearty-looking, as it cried out loudly.

"It's a girl, a healthy girl has been born. Praise the Lord," said Bess, wiping blood and muck all over her dress while the countess looked on in horror. Then Bess gave the baby to her mother, who took her in her arms and kissed the bloody head. The young lady winced and looked as if she was about to be sick.

"Look, Mary, here is your little sister."

The countess got up slowly and approached the bed. She patted her mother's arm and stared at the slime-covered baby. Her maid brought over a basin of warm water and proceeded to bathe the little one, who continued to cry and cry. There was nothing wrong with her lungs.

My mistress leant back and smiled. "Her name will be Rachel. I wanted to call Fannie that, but my husband did not allow it. And so, this little angel will be Rachel."

She turned to her daughter. "Mary, perhaps your chaplain can baptise her?"

My mistress beamed even more as the baby was handed to her, all clean now, and she put her at once to her breast. Her daughter bent over and stroked the tiny baby's cheek. I saw a smile break out on her pale face and I swear she had a tear in her eye.

Chapter 47

Mary, Countess of Kintore

I had no idea childbirth was quite as bad. I'd obviously heard people say it was awful, the pains so intense you wanted to die; and sadly so many mothers do die. But to watch my own mother go through the agonies of having to push out a baby was hideous; and then to witness the immediacy of the transformation from agony to bliss was astonishing.

At first, I simply could not believe my mother lived in such wretched circumstances. She told me she hadn't left the house for some three months so no one else on the island, apart from her girl Catriona, knew about the baby. As she suckled the tiny little one, she talked and talked. Her kidnapping had been unspeakably brutal and the journey here so unbelievably vile, I simply could not take it in. And the question of who was behind it all bothered me.

"Mama, may I ask you something?" I was whispering. Little Rachel had gone back to sleep, laid down alongside the bed in a makeshift cot fashioned by the girl from a drawer. I had Meg search my things to find the softest plaid to wrap the child in. "Do you know who might have organised your abduction? And why?"

"I'm sure Lovat was behind it all, but he's a canny man with so many contacts in high places. It would be impossible to prove."

"Lord Lovat? But why would he do that? He was at your funeral too, Mama" I shivered at the memory of that day,

looking at the coffin, refusing to believe she was in it. What
or who was in it? And now here I was, sitting in front of my
mother, who had just given birth. Who was the father? That
was obviously the next question I wanted to ask but could not.

"Lovat has always had your father's ear. I think I know why,
and he used to see me as a threat. You might not have heard,
but he treated his first wife abominably; it would be indelicate
of me to tell you what happened, but let me just say that he
was not a gentleman. Indeed, he is crude and arrogant. And
he did not like the way that I, a mere woman, stood up to my
husband."

"Mama, some of your behaviour was not always ladylike."

"And what does that mean, Mary? Does that mean that I
cannot contradict my husband in any way at all, merely because
I am a woman? It is unjust, so much of it is; I have had plenty
of time here to contemplate such things. I was simply not
willing to follow in the footsteps of all those downtrodden
and mistreated wives and he did not like it – your father, that
is. And so, I believe he must have told his friend everything."

I leant over the cot and stroked the smooth cheek of the
sleeping baby; she was so adorable when she slept. When
she was awake, I admit I was rather nervous; I had seldom
handled babies before; I saw Aunt Margaret's and Aunt Jean's
for minutes only before the maids took them away to their
nurseries.

"Mama, how does it feel when you suckle?"

"Wonderful." She beamed. "Well, to be honest, a little
strange at first, but then you remember that you are the source
of life for a tiny helpless creature, which fills a mother with
such joy." She glanced at me then down at the cot. "You and
your husband have not managed to…"

I shook my head. "No, and I don't wish to discuss it, Mama."

To change the subject, I looked around at the tiny bedroom.
"The chaplain came round to the back door earlier when you

were napping, to say that the wind was getting worse and we wouldn't be able to leave until it had died down, but it will give you time to recover your strength."

She nodded and smiled. "Will you sleep here? There is no other bed, but we could share and…"

"No, no, Mama, I would not even consider it. You need your rest and you will be feeding her throughout the night. Do not concern yourself, Mama. Alexander said that my maid is making his brother's house habitable and I shall stay there with Meg."

"And your chaplain?"

"He will sleep in the church; it is just next door. He says he wishes to be in God's house to contemplate the mystery of his brother's disappearance."

I raised an eyebrow.

"But Catriona will be here with you if you need anything in the night, Mama."

"No, she goes home at night, Mary, I do not wish to…"

"It is all arranged; well, Alexander has of course been speaking to her for me as I have no idea what she's saying."

"I suppose she can sleep by the hearth. She is used to that in her own home."

"I have given her suitable remuneration."

"Thank you, My Angel."

"And I also paid the old woman who delivered the baby. I paid her handsomely for her trouble – and for her silence, too. You seem to have managed to conceal it all from the other islanders."

"They were never that interested in me after the initial curiosity, but that was when I attempted to maintain the aura of a lady."

I sat down again and looked at my mother in the bed. Her hair was such a mess, but she did look less haggard now. "Mama, will you let Meg do your hair? She's rather expert at mine, I am sure she can do yours nicely."

She shrugged. "Mary, I have forgotten how it is to have well-groomed hair. As you can see, I have taken to wearing native dress and even bare feet. It is actually quite liberating."

She smiled.

Really, this would not do. "We can have gowns made when you are back at Kintore. And Mama, I was going to ask if there is a woman on these islands who can feed the baby? I know you told me you want to do it yourself, but just to help you return to your former strength and…"

"And to appear more ladylike, while some filthy peasant suckles my child? No, I shall be feeding her myself. And that is that. Besides, I think there are only a couple of nursing mothers on the islands and neither lives that near." I turned to the door. "Isn't that right, Catriona?"

I looked around to see her girl carrying in a tray of broth and a spoon. I had already refused food as the stench coming from the kitchen and the sight of the girl plucking seabirds at the back door made me retch.

"She has no idea what I am saying but we communicate. Somehow. Thank you, Catriona." Mama shuffled up the bed and took the food from the girl.

I looked outside through the tiny window into the moonlit night. The wind was howling and I could just make out the waves buffeting the rocks by the shore. "I think I ought to go now to my lodgings, Mama. But I will be here tomorrow morning."

I stood up and kissed her forehead and she grasped my hand. "Thank you, My Angel, thank you."

She lifted up the spoon and stirred her broth. I held my breath as I took my leave, for the overpowering smell of rotting fish coming from her bowl made me feel sick. What a wretched place this was.

Chapter 48

Catriona

Three days later, the wind had just begun to die down. They were talking about leaving soon, which seemed rather too early, as it wasn't long after she had given birth. Most island women are back working a day later, but I just thought for a lady it would be different – but then, what do I know? At least with a calm sea and dry weather, the child would be comfortable. This morning felt like spring, at last. There was less of a chill in the air and the lapwings had returned to the machair.

The young countess was sleeping at the minster's house and his brother ended up sleeping at the kirk, which must be terrible as there's no fire in there and the floor is so cold and damp. But there is no choice. The countess and her maid came over on the second day with supplies.

There were some bannocks, but not thick and grey like ours; these were thinner and golden. The girl said they were made from oats, not barley. Communicating with her was like trying to speak to my mistress; we eventually got the gist of what we meant to say to each other. They also had some butter and a mutton ham, which Meg sliced up thinly and gave to my mistress. She loved it and kept asking for more.

The maid was actually quite helpful with the cooking; I thought she would only be good for brushing hair and getting her mistress dressed, but I think she was maybe from a croft as she knew about milking and how to make a peat fire.

The difference in my mistress was unbelievable. Not only was the agony of childbirth over – I think she had been dreading it, given her age – but also there was the joy of seeing her daughter and knowing she was about to leave the Monachs. I was bracing myself for that time, as I'd come to be fond of her, even though initially she had not been easy. But that was hardly surprising, given what she had come from.

So, on the evening of the third day, the countess handed the baby over to her mother, reluctantly I thought. At first, she had been awkward holding the wee one and didn't know how to rock her to sleep. But now she was always wanting to cuddle her when my mistress was not feeding her. She kissed her mother and came through to the kitchen to collect Meg, who had everything ready for her. She smiled as she moved towards the door; it was obvious she was happy the wind had died down and the next day they would be leaving.

I had given my mistress her evening claret as usual and had seen that she didn't need anything else, so I lay down to sleep on the hearth, where there was still a little heat from the peat. I don't know how long I'd been asleep when I heard a noise. I turned my head so I could hear better. It wasn't the noise of the baby crying. It was more like footsteps coming towards the house.

And then, all of a sudden, the door flew open. It was a clear, starry night, so I could just make out two figures standing there. One had a lighted torch and I was just able to see that they were Highland men, dressed in plaid. I leapt to my feet and was about to speak when they rushed over and put a hand over my mouth. One man tied my hands behind my back then the other released his hand for a moment to tie a gag around my mouth.

I started to kick out and opened my mouth to scream but then I saw the dagger at my chin. They took the chair from under the table and tied me to that, around my ankles and my arms. Dear Lord, what was happening? They flung me and the chair into a corner where I could neither move nor speak.

But I could see. And soon I saw them emerge from the bedroom with my mistress over one shoulder and a gag around her mouth. She swivelled her head around, but I don't know if she spotted me there in the dark. Her eyes were imploring; how could they drag her away from her nursing bed? Was the baby all right? Please God, let little Rachel be unharmed and still sleeping, unaware of what has just happened.

I tilted my head to listen and could make out the faint swish of oars. Presumably the boat had just arrived, in the middle of the night, with the sole purpose of taking my mistress. Where were they going?

This could not possibly be the minister's rescue mission I had convinced myself about. I managed to shift the chair and my legs about so I could see out the open door and to the clear, starry night and I thought of her, bound and gagged, with those two ruffians. I began to cry, at first gentle tears, then massive sobs as I worried about the baby.

Chapter 49

Mary, Countess of Kintore

There was a loud banging on the door and I sat up in bed and looked around. It was still dark outside and I had no idea what time it was. I pulled on a plaid, ran to the window and looked out to where I could just see dawn breaking over a calm sea.

"My Lady, you must come. Quick!" Meg stood there at the door in her nightgown, her feet bare; there was panic in her eyes.

I ran through to the other room and there was Catriona with a bundle in her arms. It was the baby.

"What's happened?"

With gestures and gesticulations, I soon realised Mama was gone; they had come to take her in the night. Oh, dear God, has she not suffered enough?

"Go and fetch my chaplain," I shouted at Meg, who sprinted for the door. I sat down and the girl handed me the baby. She was starting to girn and I put my little finger in her mouth; she sucked it with such a strength, I knew she was hungry. How on earth could we feed her? Oh, why can't the girl speak English?

After about five minutes, Alexander arrived, his hair tousled and his eyes half-shut with fatigue. I relayed what we had gleaned from Catriona. "Ask her if she saw who took Mama?"

Little Rachel began to cry with a vengeance. "Then ask her to go at once and get a wet nurse."

The girl told him all she had seen then bolted out the door.

"It was dark," said Alexander, rubbing his eyes. "But she

said she could see it was two Highland men wrapped in bright plaid and they must have taken your mother from her bed, gagged her then thrown her over their shoulder and the next thing she heard was a boat being hauled down the beach and the oars setting to work."

"Why did she not do more to stop them?" I was now walking back and forth, rocking the baby to try to soothe her.

"She couldn't. They had a dagger and they tied her up by her arms and ankles to a chair and flung her, all bound up, in a corner. After quite some time trying, she managed to wriggle her way out of the hand ties then untie herself." He shook his head and frowned. "I am so sorry, My Lady."

"You don't think this is somehow related to your brother's disappearance – and his attempt to rescue Mama?"

He sighed. "I have given up on William; I've no idea where he is. And so, no, this was not his doing; besides, why would he hire ruffians? We must sadly forget about him; I cannot imagine what Mother will think."

The baby was looking sleepy again; she gave me one last bleary look, blinking her beautiful black lashes, then closed her eyes. I had managed to get her back to sleep; under normal circumstances I would be proud of myself, but there was nothing normal about this situation.

After what seemed like hours, but was probably only half an hour, Catriona arrived at the door, pulling into the house a grubby-looking girl with bright red hair who looked to be no more than a child herself.

They gabbled a little and Alexander said something, then Meg gave her a chair facing the wall, so Alexander could not see her expose her bulbous breast and guide Rachel's rosebud lips to the nipple. There was a gratifying sound of sucking and we all sighed with relief.

"Please thank the girl and tell her she will be paid. Does she live nearby?"

"Not in the village, but just a bit west, towards Loch nam Buadh. She'll have to go straight back to feed her own."

"How old is she?"

Catriona asked the girl and then Alexander nodded. "Fifteen."

So young – but this was a new world I was living in and it all seemed like a terrible nightmare. But at least I knew I could leave this wretched place, and I could decide when; whereas Mama was being taken to God knows where, and not of her own volition.

Meg made tea, which she then brought to me at the table. There was only one other chair, so Alexander had to stand above me as if he was a sentinel on watch. I took a sip and looked out the window where a weak sun was rising over the sea to the east.

Was that where they had taken Mama, back to the mainland? How was I to find her now? I turned round as the girl lifted Rachel onto one shoulder and patted her back. I smiled and gazed happily at her sleepy little face, blissful now she was sated with milk.

But soon I snapped out of my reverie when I suddenly remembered my responsibilities. Dear God, what was I to do with the baby?

Part Eight

Chapter 50

Mary, Countess of Kintore

The sweet sound of Catriona singing the lullaby drifted through from the bedroom to where I sat gazing out at the sea, now calm and turquoise under the clear blue sky.

> *I left my baby lying here,*
> *Lying here, lying here,*
> *I left my baby lying here,*
> *To go and gather blaeberries.*
>
> *Hovan, hovan gorry og o,*
> *Gorry og o, gorry og o,*
> *Hovan, hovan gorry og o,*
> *I never found my baby, O!*
>
> *I heard the curlew crying far,*
> *Crying far, crying far,*
> *I heard the curlew crying far,*
> *But never heard my baby, O!*
>
> *Hovan, hovan gorry og o,*
> *Gorry og o, gorry og o,*
> *Hovan, hovan gorry og o,*
> *I never found my baby, O!*

It was late spring, some two months after Mama's abduction – we were still here as Alexander tried to find out about his brother, with the bad weather delaying us further. I was now familiar with all of the Gaelic songs the girl sings for the baby, but this tune affected me especially, with its haunting melody.

When Alexander translated it into English for me, I was shocked. But then he explained that the islanders believed a baby left unattended could be stolen away by the "wee people", sometimes replacing them with a foundling. Pagan nonsense, he had grumbled. I just wished it was not such a lilting tune; sometimes I couldn't get it out of my head.

Meg and I had moved into Mama's house as it was less cramped than the minister's home and less wretched than the islanders' homes. I went one day, with Catriona carrying the baby, to the young wet nurse's cottage and saw for myself one of the hovels the islanders live in. Jean could not come to us that day as her own child was ill.

She and a woman I presumed to be her mother were giving him a tea made by boiling up some herbs gathered from what they call the machair. This, Catriona told me, was to try to reduce his fever. The girl was distraught, but she sat down to feed little Rachel while her mother laid the sickly baby down to sleep, his little chest puffing up and down with an alarming wheeze.

The house was filthy, the floor covered in animal detritus and crumbs. It was dark and smoky from the fire in the middle of the room. Surely the soot and fumes in the air were not good for the boy, but we could do nothing to intervene. Just as we were leaving, a young man arrived and ran straight over to check the sleeping baby. He glowered at us and I realised he resented both our presence and the fact that his wife was nourishing our healthy little girl as well as his sickly little boy. I told Meg to give him a coin, which he snatched without any thanks.

We took our leave, Catriona carrying little Rachel close to her chest, wrapped in a shawl. As we walked home over the machair, she pointed out the beautiful flowers – yellow, white and blue – and I felt once more a strange joy. There was something so tranquil about this place. Despite what had happened since our arrival, I experienced an inner peace I had never found when I was in Edinburgh; and certainly never living in my husband's castle at Kintore.

As we approached the village, I looked up to see Alexander running towards us, with some men trying to catch him up. He was waving at us and as we got nearer, I saw he was flustered and red-faced.

"My lady, there is news." He stopped to catch his breath. "The wreck of a boat has been washed ashore on the next island. I must go at once to Shivinish. The men think it might be William's boat."

We watched the party of a half-dozen men striding across the dunes towards the other side of the island and the tidal sands.

~~~

Rachel was lying on my lap kicking her tiny feet as I stared at her adorable little face, stroking the soft plump cheeks, marvelling at her beauty. There was a sudden thud at the door and Alexander wiped his boots on the mat and entered. He removed his hat, inclined his head and pressed his hand against the wall as if to prevent himself from falling. His face was grey, his eyes bloodshot. Dear God, was he crying?

"Sit down, Alexander. What's happened?"

His head drooped as he slumped onto the chair. I lifted Rachel upon my shoulder and inhaled the intoxicating smell of that warm, downy head.

"There was a wreck of a boat, it was Angus Macleod's."

I nodded and waited.

"One of the younger lads – Angus' nephew Domhnall – had wandered further along the shore. You've not been over to

Shivinish, My Lady, it's the next tidal island to this one, quite small. At the northern tip there's a spit of land that almost reaches Ceann Iar; there's only sand banks and dunes between them."

He stood up and went into the kitchen, where I could hear him speak to Catriona. She hurried in with a mug of ale. "Excuse me, My Lady, my throat is parched," he said, gulping down the beer.

"Young Domhnall shouted to us all to join him and when we got to where he was standing in the shallows near the reefs, that's when we saw him. Well, what was left of him. It was a horrific sight."

He paused to take a deep breath and looked directly at me.

"William's body had been washed ashore, it looked hideous, hardly my brother any more; the corpse was grotesque. The men said he can't have got far; it had been a windy night when he'd left so perhaps he had only gone a short distance before getting into problems. They think that he may have capsized – and the currents had been too strong." He took a deep draught of ale and continued.

"The men picked him up and wrapped him in one of their shirts. They're laying him out now in the church. I could hardly walk with them. My heart was breaking." He screwed up his eyes as tears flowed.

I went over and knelt beside him, patting his hand. The baby snuffled noisily.

"I am so terribly sorry, Alexander. What awful news. Please let me know what I can do to help."

He wiped his face with his sleeve and took a deep breath.

"Once we have buried him, My Lady, I must get word to my mother." He began to shake with silent sobs. "It will break her heart. He was her favourite."

Chapter 51

Mary, Countess of Kintore

I am not sure how much more tragedy I can stand. First of all, I had found Mama again after all those months. Then, discovering she was with child was a deep shock, for so many reasons; but the arrival of my sweet little Rachel came to be such a blessing. Then there was the discovery of Alexander's brother's body and the toll that's taken on my chaplain. And now this morning I had news from the wet nurse Jean. I sit at the window watching the waves crash up onto the sand while the storm rages and I try to gather my thoughts.

I must first consider the plight of Jean, who turned up as usual at dawn, but I did not see her till the mid-morning feed. Her cheeks were flushed and her eyes cast down as I entered the kitchen, where she sat nursing Rachel. She looked wretched, broken. She was humming that haunting melody: *I left my baby lying there*.

I shouted for Catriona to come. I wanted to ask her how she was, had something happened? Catriona listened to the girl speak in a faltering voice then burst into tears before stopping to compose herself. In between sobs, she continued in a low monotone. She finished with a pleading look at me. Well, whatever it was she required, surely I could help, if she needed money.

Catriona signalled that she was going out to get Alexander for she and I still had difficulties in communicating. As I watched the girl tenderly stroke little Rachel's plump arms, a thought occurred to me. But I put it to the back of my head and waited for my chaplain.

"My Lady," he said after discussion with Catriona, "Jean wanted you to know that her own little boy, Ruairidh, died last night and though she and her husband are distraught, they know he is now in heaven and at peace. They will bring him to me this afternoon to be buried."

What a tragedy. No wonder she is so upset. That child hadn't looked well at all. So, she will be nursing only Rachel till we manage to organise our journey home.

"And the next part is, well, rather odd, My Lady." He stroked the straggly beard he had grown since we had arrived on the Monachs.

"Pray continue."

"Jean says that since your mother delivered a – I shall translate what she said, My Lady, though you must forgive the insolence – an illegitimate child, you will perhaps want her to go to a good home, to rid yourself of the shame."

I gasped and glowered at the girl, who had turned to face the wall when Alexander entered. All I could hear was the happy suckling of my darling little Rachel.

"Let me finish please, My Lady."

I shut my mouth, sat up straight and composed myself.

"Jean says she and her husband have been discussing it since dawn and she says she would like to bring up little Rachel as her own, now that her own baby is gone. I know this is a shock to you, but the sentiment is kind and…"

"And what, Alexander? You expect me to hand over my own baby – well, my little sister – to this poor destitute child to bring her up in a hovel, dress her like a peasant and then let her die young of some awful disease brought on by the miserable conditions in which they all live?"

I shook my head. "I cannot believe you even bothered to tell me this. Why would you not simply dismiss her nonsense?"

The girl, hearing my voice raised, turned round and stared at me then continued to sing that song.

> *Hovan, hovan, gorry og o,*
> *I never found my baby, O!*

Dear God, the melody was beginning to drive me mad. "Stop the singing! At once!"

I strode over to the girl and grabbed Rachel from her. "You will not be taking my baby. I…"

And then I saw her face, the sadness welling in her watery, grey eyes. Oh, what a wretched life she had. Am I the one to deny her pleasure? I stretched out my arm and took her hand in mine. "Alexander, please tell her to return at her usual time for the next feed. We will discuss everything then with her and her husband."

The girl got to her feet, slowly, as if she were weighted down.

"Tell her I will cover the baby's funeral costs."

And I watched her trudge out, misery hanging heavy on her slight frame, as I hugged Rachel tightly to my chest.

～ ⌢

Alexander sat opposite me and we both sipped the brandy Catriona had brought us.

"Before we discuss the baby, My Lady, I must tell you what we found on William's body as they prepared him for the funeral tomorrow."

"Ah yes, the funeral. And then once the ceremony is over, might we begin to prepare more for our journey home?"

"Yes, though there are matters we must see to here first."

After everything that has happened, I simply wished to be home. And hopefully my maid will find a suitable wet nurse back at Kintore. I am keen to return and surprise my husband the Earl with the joyful gift of a baby. I nodded at Alexander to continue. He looked exhausted, his eyes bleary and red.

"As we prepared William's body for burial, one man discovered a letter inside a pocket of his breeches. It was sodden, so wet it was all stuck together, but I dried it out by the peat fire and just last night, I was able to read it." He prodded the embers in the fire and huddled closer to the flames; it was a bitterly cold night, even though it was late spring.

"The letter was addressed to a Captain Mackintosh who was setting sail soon from Glasgow to the West Indies. William introduced himself as minister of the Monach Islands and wrote that he had been given the captain's name by Gruff Gordon, the boatman who ferries letters and goods between here and North Uist."

"That ruffian who supplies our brandy?"

"Indeed, My Lady. So, after a polite introduction, William wrote that he had been invited to be minister in St Kitts in the West Indies as soon as he could obtain a berth. His benefactor, Colonel William MacDowall, is an established sugar plantation owner there and though based in London now, travels to the island often. I presume it is his desire to have a chaplain for his own household there."

"Why would your brother go there? Is he acquainted with this colonel?"

Alexander nodded. "He's my mother's brother, our uncle. I had no idea William was still in communication with him; certainly, our mother hasn't seen him since he left Glasgow some twenty years ago. He is, well, rather a different personality from our devout mother."

"I see. And how could all of these preparations have been kept a secret from everyone here on the island? And presumably from the presbytery too?"

"That, My Lady, is what I cannot fathom. He must have

been planning it for some time. Perhaps your mother knew about it, but we will probably never know. I have kept the contents of the letter secret from everyone here. The men speak no English and besides, the parchment was sodden when they caught sight of it. But I recall Catriona telling me that when the islanders saw our boat arrive, they'd all hoped it was William returning; they'd presumed he had gone to find help for your mother. The girl said he was fond of her."

"If he was fond of her, why on earth did he allow her to be kept a prisoner here for so long? And why was he not on hand to protect her from what we must presume was a violation?"

I coughed and chose my words carefully. "How else is little Rachel explained?"

My chaplain looked away and drummed his fingers on the glass in his hand. Another thought occurred to me, but just like that one I'd had earlier when I watched Jean nurse little Rachel, I pushed it aside.

"So, what does everyone think happened to William?"

"The winds changed. They'd been westerlies for days, so presumably his plan was to sail east, over to North Uist then journey to Glasgow for the passage to the West Indies. Instead it looks like as he headed north towards Stockay, the winds suddenly changed and he was forced back towards Ceann Ear and probably towards Rudha nam Marbh, Dead Man's Point. There's been more than one shipwreck on those reefs. And from there, the boat – and his body presumably – floated around the islands to wash up on Shivinish."

"It seems as if, instead of doing a heroic act and saving my mother, he stole a poor islander's boat then escaped by himself, abandoning her. Why would he do that? A man of God?"

"I have spent the entire night praying that God would give me an answer, but I am still perplexed. Only one thing occurred to me and…." He stopped and shook his head.

"And what?"

"Nothing, My lady." He turned to look outside where the rain was pelting down. "There was one other thing I hesitated to tell you. In the sanctuary is a wooden stand for a Bible. Since none of the islanders can read, only the minister uses it. I lifted the book up yesterday and saw something underneath the bible. On closer look, I saw it was letters scratched into the wood. The words were: *Forgive me, Father, for I have sinned.*

I stared at him. What did this mean? I opened my mouth to speak but once again he silenced me with a raised hand. "And now I beg your forgiveness, My Lady. I must go to prepare for baby Ruairidh's burial. I shall return afterwards with his parents to discuss the mother's proposal."

And before I could insist he stay and elaborate on his thoughts, he had exited abruptly, leaving me to consider the plans for our immediate departure from these wretched islands.

Chapter 52

Rachel

Even when I consider the hardship I have suffered over the past year and a half, it is nothing compared to the misery I must endure now. It is so much worse in every respect. I am exceedingly weary in this godforsaken place, with no one for company but a glaikit serving wench; her bannocks make the memory of Catriona's seem as if they were baked by a chef trained at the French court. The only sounds here, apart from the roaring of the wind and the crashing of the waves onto this barren rock, are the shrill squawks of guillemots and solan geese.

I sit in this dark, windowless hovel that is now my new "home" and try to remember my fine life of old. I am once more dressed like a native in a coarse brown flannel smock, with only a shabby plaid to keep me warm against the icy blasts swirling around this lump of rock all day long. I gaze at my bed of straw and at the peat fire in the middle of this two-roomed "cottage", though the nomenclature is a little exaggerated since the next room must surely house animals in the winter, for even now in early summer, it stinks.

Nearby is what they call a "cleit", a small dry-stone domed structure where they store the vile sea-birds I have to eat daily. At least on the Monachs I had some fish, crabs and lobster to vary the dire diet of oily fowl. Yesterday, my serving girl Seonaid brought in two seabird eggs and broke one in half then proffered it to me raw. Obviously, I refused, but she simply shrugged, tipped her head back and drank it down while I watched in horror. Not only is she a barbarian, but she has no idea how to serve a lady. The only one variation to the tedious diet she provides me with has been mutton and it is the toughest meat I've ever tasted. The beasts here must live for so long, they end up inedible and stringy.

But first of all, I turn reluctantly to my abduction from the Monachs. I had just given birth to my darling little baby Rachel a few days earlier when I was hauled ignominiously from my bed, filthy hands clamped over my mouth so that I couldn't alert Catriona. I was dragged, kicking all the way, down to the beach at midnight, under a full moon. There, a fetid muffler was tied around my mouth, so I was unable to speak and I was bundled onto a sloop, which set sail immediately. Even with the moonlight it was too dark to see my assailants properly and I knew that, unless I flung myself overboard to my death, I had no other option than to simply sit, so this I did, shaking with silent sobs. Eventually they removed the cloth from my mouth and I watched as we sailed away from my tiny babe towards what I think was the west, for we passed between the top of our island and Stockay. Dear God, were we going to the Plantations? I remember William once telling me the West Indies lay somewhere far away to the west of Scotland.

I was proffered a flask by one of the two sailors and I took it gladly. It was a bitter-tasting ale, but I gulped it down. Soon my breasts became full and as the milk leaked out, another wave of sadness overwhelmed me as I thought of my darling baby's sweet little lips. Where were these two ruffians taking me? I couldn't see what colours their plaid was, so had no idea whether this was another of Lovat's evil schemes.

As we sailed out into the open seas, the small vessel pitched and tossed. And whereas on the interminable journey to the Monachs I had felt such seasickness, now I was inured, or perhaps simply so profoundly sad, having been wrenched away from my newborn baby and my eldest daughter, that I was numb.

Blood was seeping out from the rags between my legs onto my smock but I had no energy to rage against the injustices meted out against me; so I sat stupefied, detached and silent for many hours. Did the journey last eight hours? Ten? Certainly no less, for a hazy dawn broke in the east and daylight at last meant I could see better.

Eventually one of the ruffians yelled something indecipherable and pointed ahead. There on the horizon was land. Jagged peaks rose from the water and soon I could hear the piercing screeches of seabirds as they swooped and dived around us. I continued to stare ahead, wincing at the pain in my breasts as milk leaked onto my smock.

Soon I noticed a row of houses up from a beach and I let out a sigh of anguish as I realised they were taking me to yet another island. And I knew for sure this was not the Plantations; it was far too cold.

Then I saw a near-naked native run down the beach and plunge into the sea. He was soon joined by several others who all swam towards our sloop and dragged it ashore. Deadened as I was now to emotion and numbed to pain, I simply let myself be guided overboard and dragged through the waves until I reached the beach, where I collapsed onto the dried seaweed and shingle in sobs of misery.

I lay on my blood-soaked smock awhile then, at the sound of whispering, opened my eyes. What I saw first were feet, one pair shoed in some kind of sandals fashioned from seabirds' feathers. The others were bare feet strangely arched with gnarled, claw-like toes. I looked up past the drab brown clothes at filthy faces and wild hair. These were obviously the island men coming to greet me. I got to my feet and looked beyond the natives towards the small hamlet, where they led me, and to the stinking hovel in which I now reside.

The people here are ungodly. There is no minister and I have no means of asking whether there ever has been one. Unlike the Monachs, where I could converse with William and communicate in some way with Catriona, this is impossible here; no one speaks English.

They stare at me as if they have never seen a lady and I try not to breathe in as I pass them, for they do indeed smell of rotting fowl and fulmar oil. This oil I now know is not only used as fuel, but also as a primitive medicine.

In my cottage, I sit at my door on a low stool and my back hurts, but they have no chairs. I dread to think how my posture is suffering. Through my low door, I see the other hovels, all of which have doors facing in the same direction as mine, north-east, presumably to protect against the prevailing wind.

Every morning I watch the men head off towards the cliffs with their ropes slung on their backs and return some time later with their prey, mainly solan geese, but, just like on the Monachs, also fulmars and guillemots. I now also know why the men have feet shaped in that odd, claw-like way; their toes must have adapted over the years, probably centuries, to clambering up and down the cliffs, grasping on with their arched feet, as they hunt for the seabirds.

The cottages are all rudely built of stone and the thatched roofs are secured by rope made of twisted heath and weighed down by small boulders to prevent the thatch being blown away. The wind here is even more powerful than on the Monachs and also relentless.

The landscape is pretty; there are plentiful flowers in the grass, but it is not as beautiful as on the Monachs; the more I think back, the more I realise I was content there. Here I am in a constant state of melancholia. And I have no claret to raise my spirits. The natives brew ale and, after much nagging,

Seonaid brought me some the other day. It was vile but I drank it down. When I tried to ask her how they made it, she ran off and brought me back some nettles, which she thrust before me. No wonder it has a dire effect on my digestion.

Most days, I walk along the village street – if it could be called a street – and then up to the cliff face to try to see if I can find out more about my location. Even on a clear day, there is no land to be seen, apart from a couple of rock stacks nearby. And so, I still have no idea where I am, nor even the name of this place.

This morning I walked to the end of the village, heading towards the burn. As I passed the last house, I heard a song and stood still to listen. A girl was singing the most beautiful melody, which was both pleasing and yet haunting. She sang in Gaelic so I have no idea what the words meant but there seemed to be a chorus.

> *Hovan, hovan gorry og o,*
> *Gorry og o, gorry og o…*

She stopped singing and I realised the noise I heard now was sobbing. I peered inside the hovel and saw a figure rocking back and forth by the peat fire. It was too smoky to see well, so I went inside and coughed to alert her to my presence.

A young girl, her dark hair matted across her cheeks, looked at me and I saw her large brown eyes were filled with tears. In her arms was a baby and even from where I stood, I could hear the loud wheeze from the tiny child's chest.

The girl did not smile, but I went towards her and looked closely at the baby, who was perhaps only a few days old. His face was livid red and I put my hand on the wet brow. Dear God, he obviously had a raging fever, why was she standing right beside the fire? I tried to explain to her it might be best to unwrap the baby from the thick woollen shawl and cool him down, but she just stared at me.

I motioned to her with my fingers that I had given birth to eight children and she allowed me to take the baby from her. I unwrapped the filthy shawl and stared at his stomach. Where the cord had been cut was the most awful, red, pus-filled sore. I bent down to look closer and smelt the stench of fulmar oil. Had the midwife used that putrid oil to clean the cord?

I gestured that I was leaving but would be back and as I headed out towards the cliff, I could hear that stirring melody follow me. Once on the hillside, I looked around for the herbs I wanted. Soon I found them, gathered a bundle of St John's wort and some butterwort and headed back as quickly as possible to her house, where an older woman now stood, adding more peat to the fire.

I looked around and found a bowl, where I piled the yellow flowers and green leaves of the St John's wort then grabbed a small cup and began to pound down on the contents. I was trying to mash everything up to create a poultice, as William had told me this was done by the Monach islanders to cure an infection. I had no idea if it would help the baby, but the child might otherwise die.

Billows of smoke filled the room and I was soon aware that the song had increased in volume as more women entered the hovel. Soon the pulverised mixture released enough moisture and so I squeezed the flowers and herbs between my hands and took it to the baby, where I placed it over his stomach. I motioned to the girl to keep her hand clamped there while I looked around for a cloth to fix it in place.

Then I pointed to the older woman to give me some boiled water in a beaker. In my other pocket I had the purple butterwort flowers and I dropped a couple into the water and mashed it all down. I then gestured to her that this needed to be strained and given to the baby once it was cool. William had explained another day on the machair that butterwort was made into a tea and given to help relieve chesty coughs.

The women, now all joining in the lullaby, were crowding around the girl and her baby and so I left, the haunting melody still ringing in my ears. As I walked back down to my own hovel, I felt once more a crushing sense of sadness, both for the baby in that poor young mother's arms and for my own baby, whose mother ached to hold her in hers.

Chapter 53

Mary, Countess of Kintore

I was rocking little Rachel in my arms at the window while Meg packed our bags. She had just fallen asleep when I peered out of the window through the mist. Was that a boat down on the beach? Soon I could see a figure heading this way. As he approached, I realised it was the factor, Donald Macdonald. Well, this ought to be an interesting encounter.

"Meg, there's a visitor. Do not rush to let him in."

I sped next door to put the baby down to sleep, tucking the blanket around her warm little body, shut the door behind me and went to take my seat by the window.

He entered, his jaunty swagger undiminished, and inclined his head, before taking the other chair in the room. He looked around.

"It is so strange for me to enter my own house and yet always as a guest."

Why did he need to speak so loudly? His deep voice echoed throughout the room.

"I believe you are adequately recompensed for your trouble. So, what brings you over to the Monach Islands this time, Mr Macdonald?"

He leant against the chair back, stretching his feet forward. Even in his posture, he was an insolent man. I did not trust him – I knew my letter to my mother had never arrived, but I was not sure who was at fault. Donald Macdonald himself, or some third party he'd entrusted it to? "Well, My Lady, it seems as if your chaplain has become my minister."

I bristled. "The Reverend Alexander Fleming is his own man, he is no one's possession."

"Oh, I had thought differently when we spoke at our first meeting several months ago at Lady Macleod's house."

I was about to argue back when I could hear a noise from the bedroom. It was the gentle whimpers of the baby. I thought it best to leave her for now.

"As you no doubt know, Alexander has decided to take over his brother's parish. Once he has escorted me home, he will return to take up his position. I am very sad to see him leave us but totally understand his reasons."

"To atone for his brother's sins?"

Really, this man was too much. "What sins?" I snapped. "His brother is dead."

"Well, stealing a boat for one, abandoning his flock for another. And as I am sure you must have heard, there have been rumours that not only was he heading for the West Indies, but he was perhaps escaping the terrible consequences of one of his dalliances. Stranger things have happened on remote islands. A child, it seems, was…"

The baby's cries were now too obvious. "I am not interested in rumours and gossip, Mr Macdonald."

I got to my feet. "Now, if you have nothing else to say, I am busy. We plan to leave in the next couple of days, when the winds are good, and I must supervise the packing."

"Is that a baby I hear?" He pointed to the bedroom door.

I ignored his question and motioned the way out. But he stood, head to one side, listening. "It certainly sounds to me like a bawling bairn." His eyes widened as if he suddenly realised something. Then there was a crash as the door flung open and Catriona ran straight past us and into the bedroom, where the crescendo of wails suddenly stopped and there was silence.

I pointed once more to the door.

His eyes screwed up and the glimmer of a smile spread over his face. "The baby. So…"

"So, nothing. You have overstayed your welcome, Mr Macdonald. It is time to take your leave. Goodbye."

I raised my head and returned to my seat by the window, trying to stop the tremor in my hands as I placed them on my lap. He headed outside and I heaved a sigh of relief as I watched him leave. But then I noticed a small figure hurrying along the path towards us. Oh, dear God, what bad timing; it was Jean arriving to feed the baby. Hopefully she would just walk straight past him.

But no, I watched as he reached out to grab her arm and bent down to speak to her. What an interfering man he was. The sooner we left here the better.

I stepped off the boat onto our jetty and looked around at the sea loch with the backdrop of craggy, cloud-capped mountains and was surprised by how good it felt to be home. Ahead I saw the solid stone edifice of Kintore Castle among the trees and realised I was looking forward to being back after three eventful months.

Meg hopped off the boat after me with a couple of the bags. And then behind, there was Jean with little Rachel, all swaddled up against the chill wind. I felt a pang of emotion as I saw her adorable, plump little face; how my husband would react to her I could not possibly imagine.

Jean handed the baby over to Meg and then jumped ashore herself. She looked up at me and smiled. I knew Jean was grateful to me for allowing her to come and live with us on a generous wage until Rachel was weaned.

After much discussion on the day of her own baby boy's funeral, her husband had agreed that she could travel with us and return in some six months' time, certainly before the winter set in and he needed her to help his mother with the weaving. She understood that I was the only one who was entitled to keep Rachel; there was never any question of allowing the baby to be handed over to her. But for now, I needed her.

As I stepped along the path to the castle, I could see the servants lined up at the door and soon I noticed my husband the Earl appear at the top of the steps. He ran down them and strode towards us, a wide smile on his wrinkled face. I had not seen him for so long, but, good God, today he looked almost attractive, not the plain old man I recalled. His cheeks had a spot of colour and his eyes seemed to flash with joy. Was he really so pleased that I, his barren wife, was returning? Well, I could not wait to reveal my news to him.

He stopped in front of me, beamed and took my hand. He kissed my fingers and then gave me a peck on my cheek, which was really quite unexpected. Was it possible he had been pining for me?

"Mary, my sweet, darling girl, how I have missed you. You look well." He stopped to acknowledge Meg's curtsey and then stared at Jean, who had been taught to bow low before a lord.

"Mary, whose child is that?" He pointed at Rachel, who gurgled and smiled, revealing the Erskine family dimples.

I took his arm and walked with him towards the castle, nodding at the servants as we entered the great hall, where I greeted his mother and sister and the strange, silent twins.

"Let us have some tea and I shall tell you all about our stay on the Monach Islands, my dear." I leant in to whisper in his ear. "Might we have a few minutes together, just you and I first?"

"Of course," he said, flicking his hand at his relatives as if swatting away flies, while gesturing for us to go into the drawing room.

"We shall not be long," I said, seeing the look of surprise

on the faces of his mother and sister as I plucked Rachel from Jean's arms.

Once the door was shut, I told my husband to sit down.

I placed the baby in his arms and realised this must be the first time he had held a child. He was stiff, immobile, obviously scared of dropping her. I knelt beside him as he stared at her pink cheeks and rosebud lips.

"Mary, I don't understand. Who is…?"

"This is our baby girl. Can you not see how she bears the family resemblance? Is she not the most beautiful little thing you have ever seen?"

His mouth hung open as he turned to me. "But, Mary, I don't understand. Were you with child when you left for the Monach Islands?"

I blinked as I prepared to utter my much-rehearsed lines. "Yes, I did not want to tell you in case it was a false alarm, but then she came very early and that is why we stayed there longer than had been anticipated." I shrugged, feigning a casual air. "Is she not perfect?"

Tears began to trickle down his lined cheeks and he kept glancing from the baby's face to mine. "She has your nose and your lips." He sat forward as she began to girn a little. "Please take her, my dear. We must tell Mother. We have much to celebrate." He handed me the baby and stood up to ring the bell. Soon a servant ran in and I could see out of the corner of my eye his mother and sister crouching by the door.

"Mama! Jane! Come in here. We have such news. Great joy has visited us…" He turned to me. "I presume she hasn't been baptised? She will take my mother's name. Arabella is so becoming for a…"

"She's already been baptised by the Reverend Fleming on the Monach Islands. Her name is Rachel." I quickly added, "What has been blessed before God, cannot be changed."

As his mother crossed the floor towards us, her gown

swishing, she glowered at me with steely eyes, then stared at the baby in my arms. I smiled then stretched out my arms as I passed little Rachel over to my husband's mother. I have never felt such a sense of triumph.

She sat down on the chaise longue with a thump, as if not trusting herself upright with the precious bundle.

"Look at this little lady, Mama. Is she not the spitting image of her mother?" My husband was now weeping openly, much to his mother's obvious disgust.

I looked at my mother-in-law's incredulous face gazing at the baby and I thought that it should not be her, but my own mother holding the baby, for it was she the little one resembled, not me.

It took some time before she was able to speak. "But I do not understand, Mary. Why did you not tell us you were with child before you left for those remote islands?" She frowned.

"Yes, why would you do that, if you knew you were carrying a child?" Jane had knelt down beside her mother and was gawking at the baby. "Why did you not feel you could confide in me, at least," she asked, leaning in to look more closely.

"I wanted to be sure; I did not want any of you to be disappointed." How could I tell her it was probably my last chance to find my mother?

"She does look like you, Mary, there's no escaping that." She stroked Rachel's soft, plump cheek. "Was the lying-in dreadful? How did you manage in that barbaric place? I suppose your maid was able to find enough in the way of medical assistance?"

I leant my head on my side and sighed as I recalled my lines.

"Meg has been a stalwart. And as for the accouchement – it was, I am sure, no better or worse than any other woman's. You're both aware how a mother must suffer for her young."

And I shut my eyes as I thought of my own mother and the suffering she was undoubtedly still enduring.

Chapter 54

James

Tomorrow is the day I shall ask Mrs Lindsay to be my wife. The title Lady Grange shall suit her very well and I know she will be so grateful. The sooner she sells the coffee house the better. It would not do for my wife to be employed in any way; certainly not in commerce. I met Lovat last night and he told me of Rachel's plight and now I know I am as good as a bachelor once more, for there is no way she can ever be found. No one can speak English on this most remote of British islands so she can't converse with a soul; and there is only one boat a year to St Kilda and that takes days to arrive. There is no minister, no teacher, indeed no one with any education at all and so presumably no ink nor paper to write.

Lovat had assured me she was still unharmed, healthy even. And that comforted me; she is still, after all, the mother of my children. I would not want her to suffer too much. But of paramount importance is the fact that I am free. I cannot wait to see Mrs Lindsay's face tomorrow in London.

I had just sent Old Peter off down the High Street to buy my passage on the coach to London the following day when there was a knock on the door.

"Your daughter Frances is here to see you, My Lord," muttered Mistress Wilson, as sullen as usual. I used to wonder if she was constantly suffering bereavements, her mien was always so grim, but no, it is just her way, I now realise.

I sighed and took a swig from my brandy. "Show her in."

And in she bounded like a foal, all angular and awkward. I rearranged my glass and decanter by my side. She was so clumsy, she was likely to knock things over.

"Good morning, Fannie. What can I do for you?"

"Papa, I had a letter from Mary yesterday and it contains such news, I had to come and tell you myself, although the journey was unbearable. My coach left Preston Houses a long time ago; the road was blocked near Inveresk because of the mud after all that rain and it took hours. I'm exhausted and quite out of sorts."

"Sit down, my dear. Would you like to join me in a brandy?" I had no idea if this was suitable for her delicate nature, but she was so pale.

She shook her head while delving into her bag. She plucked out a letter and slowly unfolded it. "Shall I read it to you, Papa?"

"Very well," I snapped, wishing she would hurry up. I had much to do before I left the following day.

> *My dear Fannie,*
>   *I am sorry for the tardiness of my reply. I have been away*
> *from Kintore House for some months now.*

"Away from Kintore, Papa! Do you remember, I was frantic with worry when my letters were all unanswered?"

I nodded and waited.

> *I went to see Mama on the Monach Islands — remember*
> *that was where I got that letter from the time you were staying*
> *here? We located the place on the map.*

I leant forward and stared at my daughter. Dear God, that eldest daughter of mine needed to be taken in hand; why was her husband not stricter with her?

Fannie, I found her! She was in a sorry state, not at all her old self. And she looked more like a peasant than a lady – her pallor grey, her complexion rough and her dress loose and shapeless. I was shocked. Indeed, there were many things that surprised me during that visit, but the most awful was that, about a week after I had arrived, she was removed forcibly – in the middle of the night – and I now have no idea where she is.

My heart was thumping against my chest. I could not speak.

"Do you remember, Papa, I told you that Mama was on some remote island and you did not believe me? Well, Mary has been to see her, so you must believe her now."

"It is all a nonsense, Fanny, I told you before, I have no idea why Mary is writing to you with such lies. Hand the letter to me to read myself."

She seemed to be feigning deafness for she stared once more at it. "I'm going to miss out a few paragraphs, Papa, and get to the good news. It's so exciting!"

I could hardly wait.

Once I got home to Kintore Castle last week I was able to introduce my husband the Earl to our beautiful little daughter.

"What? Why are you mumbling, child? I thought you said 'daughter'."

Fannie nodded and continued.

I had her baptised on the Monach Islands and she is called Rachel, in honour of Mama, as I have to say she looks very much like her, with those dimples that she and I both have. The baby is now three months old and my husband is beside himself with joy and...

I raised my hand. "Wait, wait, Fannie. You mean to say

Mary is now a mother? Why are we only hearing of this now, after three months? Word ought to have been sent at once. At this time of year letters should take no longer than a week." I gulped down my brandy. "Also, surely my sister ought to have been informed some time ago and your Aunt Jean could have been with her for her lying-in. I don't understand this at all. None of it makes sense." I stretched out my arm. "Here, give me the letter. I must see if it is in fact Mary's hand."

She clutched the letter to her scrawny chest, but I stood up and grabbed it from her while she slid down her chair, squirming as if I had hit her.

"Mary said not to show it to you, just to tell you about the baby." She began to sniffle in the most inelegant way. Jean was right; it was going to be well-nigh impossible to find a suitable man to take her on.

I sat reading the entire letter and sighed. So, Mary had indeed seen Rachel on the Monach Islands. And unfortunately, my daughter was there when Lovat's men had taken her mother captive for a second time. Ah well, at least she is out of harm's way. But what of this baby? Admittedly, because it was not a male child, the Earl probably presumed I would not be interested; but it is, however, my daughter's baby. My sister is not going to be pleased when I tell her about this, no, not at all. I rang the bell.

"Yes, My Lord?"

Thankfully it was Old Peter, back from the coach house.

"Send someone to Lady Paterson's house at once. Tell her that her brother requires her presence as soon as possible."

He nodded and headed off towards the stairs, hirpling. He walked more like a cripple these days, but I suppose he is over fifty years old. As he passed through the doorway, I had a thought and shouted after him.

"Peter, can you perhaps also send Bobbie to the coach house. It appears I may have to delay my trip to London."

He nodded and I swatted my hand at Fannie, who had approached my chair, attempting feebly to snatch the letter back. She slunk away and I read it thoroughly again.

When I reached the part where Mary described her mother looking more like a peasant than a lady, and later, describing how she looked haggard – her pallor grey, her dress loose and her complexion poor – I stopped reading. I let out a gasp as a vivid recollection came to me of how Rachel used to look in the days drawing near her many accouchements. Dear God, was this baby actually Rachel's?

Chapter 55

Rachel

I sat as usual on the little stool by my low doorway, looking out at the other hovels and at the men murmuring to each other as they walked along towards the cliffs, sturdy ropes slung over their shoulders, in quest of their quarry. I have become used to both the taste and the lingering smell of the seabirds Seonaid cooks for me. I have no choice, for there is little else. Even the breakfast bannocks taste of the sea, for her hands, which are never to my knowledge washed, always glisten with the oil from the birds after plucking and cooking. The fulmars, guille-mots and solan geese are all caught by the men climbing down the cliffs, but I now know that the puffins are often caught by the women and girls.

I was out a few days ago for a walk on the grassy slopes and noticed Seonaid and some of her friends lying around some puffin burrows, whispering. I stopped and crouched down to see what they were doing. Soon, one of them plunged her hand into a hole and dragged out a bird, which was flapping its wings madly and making frantic screeching noises. I then watched, horrified yet fascinated, as the girl – none of them looked older than sixteen – twisted its neck with such dexterity, it was obvious she had done this before.

They all continued at this sport till they had a handful of puffins, then returned to the village, where they would no doubt pluck them, split the carcasses down the middle then hang them up outside their homes. Then the women in the village, including Seonaid, would boil them, usually for hours, perhaps with some oats stirred in to make a thin porridge.

And now, these many months after my arrival, I am resigned to the fact that I am here, as a prisoner; and yet I am still alive. And at least now I have become accepted for what I am – as an oddity, for sure among these barbaric natives, but also as someone who has a heart.

After I had given those herbal remedies to that tiny baby, I heard nothing and indeed found myself avoiding passing the house. Then about two weeks later, the young mother, the baby strapped to her chest, arrived at my door with her mother. The women were smiling and I took that to mean the baby was better. It certainly had lost some of its grey pallor. I asked to see the infected area and so they came inside and laid him on the floor, unwrapping his swaddling cloths. The wound was by no means healed, but it was less sore-looking. I happened to have some dried St John's wort hanging above the fire and I handed it to them. After they had gone, I went up onto the hillside and collected more plants, the ones William had taught me about, just in case.

Another woman came to the door a few days ago and beckoned for me to go with her. I grabbed my shawl and followed her along the feather-strewn path. Inside her home, with the pervasive smell of rank fulmar oil and the peat smoke billowing from the open fire, I could just make out a man lying by the hearth, wincing in pain. I tried to find out what was wrong with him but all I got was that it was sore when he stretched out either his legs or his arms. This was a disaster for a man who needed his hands and feet to crawl along a ledge in the cliffs to catch sea fowl. As I tried to move his leg up a little, I noticed, not for the first time, that the men on this island had very thick ankles, perhaps because they climb so much.

I tried to think about what sort of flowers or herbs might

help rheumatic pains, in case this was what he was suffering. But then I recalled that it was not from the hills or the burns, but from the shore that I needed to find a remedy. I motioned that I would be back and rushed down to the beach, where fortunately the tide was out. In the past, the shingle would have hurt my delicate bare feet, but the soles of my feet were now so hard and gnarled, it was not sore at all. Soon I had what I wanted, a couple of large handfuls of dulse.

I headed back up to the hovel, gave it to the woman and communicated to her that she must make a soup with it and left, smiling as I recalled William telling me about the rheumatic-easing properties of the seaweed one day as we'd strolled along the beach then up through the dunes. And then I suddenly felt a pang of sadness as I thought of his deception. Well, I was glad he'd disappeared. In fact, I hoped he was dead; it was what he deserved. He had given me a baby, which now Mary, My Angel, was surely looking after with love and adoration back home in her grand castle. For that, I must be forever grateful to the minister.

Sitting on the stool by the door, I was awakened from my reverie by the arrival of the young mother and the woman whose husband I had given the dulse to. They held something behind their backs and I stood up, waiting to see what they hid. One brought out a small bottle containing dark liquid and the other a feather. I shook the bottle and gasped! How was this possible? It was ink and a quill. I gesticulated to them, trying to find out where they had found them and they laid them on my doorstep then beckoned for me to follow.

Up the hill from the village, there were the ruins of what used to be a church, not that long ago. I couldn't find out why it was deserted now. The crumbling walls were made of dry-stone and the thatch was badly in need of repair: the roof was half off and, as we entered the small building, I looked up at the sky. I had never thought about going inside, since there was now no minister on the island and I presumed it was derelict. At the far end was a tiny pulpit and the women showed me that underneath was a small cupboard, the door hanging off its hinges. One of the girls tugged it open and pulled out two bottles of ink and some dried-up parchment. I looked up at them and beamed. I had paper to write on; what an unexpected joy.

I skipped back to my hovel with the paper and the ink, sat down and laid the parchment on my knee. I pulled out the cork from one of the bottles and dipped in my quill. I lifted it up and breathed a sigh of relief when I saw that the tip was indeed coated with thick ink. Someone – the previous minister? – had obviously mixed the powdered ink with some water and filled these bottles then stoppered them up. I never found out why there was now no minister here. Perhaps all island minsters were as bad as William; or perhaps the Church simply could not find anyone willing to spend his time out here on this godforsaken lump of rock.

As I held the feather, hovering above the paper, I wondered to whom I would write. I could feel the excitement grow inside as I thought once more of the possibilities of rescue. Then, as my shoulders drooped, I realised there was no point writing to anyone. The annual boat arriving on the island would not be here till next summer, some eight or nine months away, and besides, why would I upset Mary again.

She had her baby and was surely as happy as any mother could hope to be, taking care of my beautiful little Rachel in her splendid home, where the little one would want for nothing. And James obviously did not ever want me back. Good God, he had probably married that strumpet in London by now, so fickle and needy was he.

I decided instead that I would write a list of herbs and flowers
that might be useful for remedies, since the islanders seemed
to have no idea about their medicinal properties. Perhaps, one
day, I might even learn the Gaelic words for them.

A is for Angelica

B is for Butterwort.

C is for Carragheen

D is for Dulse......

Chapter 56

Mary, Countess of Kintore

It was Jean's last day at Kintore Castle and I sat in the nursery watching her feed Rachel. I never thought I might miss the girl to whom I had taken such an aversion initially, but little had I known her own little baby was so gravely ill. At the start, though, just after Mama was abducted, everything had been so strange and so desperate and my critical faculties were not functioning as usual.

But after these wonderful six months back home, while Jean has been feeding my beautiful baby, I have come to appreciate her kind heart. And tomorrow she will go back to her husband and her lowly cottage and to the lack of comforts she has become accustomed to here. But she must be desperate to be back on the Monach Islands once more, if only to be able to speak her own language. Only a couple of the footmen here speak Gaelic, I discovered, so sadly she has been very silent, but she still sings Rachel lullabies in her own tongue.

My husband the Earl is besotted with his daughter. He even comes into the nursery during the daytime, which is quite unheard of for any man – let alone an Earl. His mother, of course, thoroughly disapproves. She and Jane were wary, almost suspicious, after I returned home with Rachel. On the second day, I heard one of the twins say to a maid that their aunt had come home with a foundling baby as they'd obviously overheard their mother say I could not have babies.

The insolence of those strange creatures. Neither has spoken to me since, for I told them off soundly and even apologised to the maid that she'd heard such slander. I cannot believe what a joy it is not to have to try to converse with them, with their sulky, sullen ways.

On the rare occasion that my mother-in-law visits the nursery and sits in the chair with Rachel in her arms, it is as if she had never borne children, for she does not know what to do when she squirms and wriggles. She presumes all babies must only either sleep or feed. Well, not so my Rachel. She is now crawling and laughing and gurgling and... Oh, but sometimes when I watch her determined little frown as she tries to grab something out of reach, I see Mama in her. Her dimples are now even more pronounced, but thankfully my husband was never in Mama's company long enough to notice hers; he sees only how like mine they are.

And when I think of Mama, I am still so sorrowful. She had, I believe, a happy marriage at first, during which she had all of us, her five children; to my knowledge, she was much loved early on. Then, with her increasing anxieties caused presumably by the memories of her father's fate, she began to have her turns. Her temper could be violent and unpleasant; at times claret seemed to be her only redemption. But she was kind underneath the exterior. And then for her to have been abducted with such violence from Edinburgh that night must have been simply the most dreadful thing to have happened to a lady.

There was not time to hear more about it during our short stay together over on the Monachs, for the baby arrived quickly and then, so soon afterwards, when she should have been lying in, she was removed again and with such violence. It distresses me every time I recall Catriona describing the brutality of those thugs that night.

I admit now, I was shocked when I saw her in bed on the first day of our arrival to the Monach Islands; she looked so wretched, hopeless and also filthy. And yet her face transformed when she saw me arrive; she beamed and her lined features assumed a look of pure joy. I now know this was not simply because, with my arrival, she saw an end to her imprisonment, but it was because I am her daughter. Only now that I have my own little Rachel do I realise the immutable love that exists in a mother for her child.

I am awakened from my doleful reverie by Rachel hiccuping happily and I go to take her from Jean. After I have cuddled her awhile and stroked her beautiful face and soft downy head, I lay her down in her crib, swaddle her in her blankets and sit in the chair. I nod to Jean to extinguish the lamp and ask her to sing my baby to sleep in her own language for one last time.

> *I left my baby lying here,*
> *Lying here, lying here,*
> *I left my baby lying here,*
> *To go and gather blaeberries.*
>
> *Hovan, hovan gorry og o,*
> *Gorry og o, gorry og o,*
> *Hovan, hovan gorry og o,*
> *I never found my baby, O!*
>
> *I heard the curlew crying far,*
> *Crying far, crying far,*
> *I heard the curlew crying far,*
> *But never heard my baby, O!*
>
> *Hovan, hovan gorry og o,*
> *Gorry og o, gorry og o,*
> *Hovan, hovan gorry og o,*
> *I never found my baby, O!*

Chapter 57

Johnnie and James

1747

Johnnie

He did not want me to be here. What son, he said, should have to witness his father's demise, and especially in such a horrific and public manner; I had heard rumours there would be hundreds of spectators. But I went down to London anyway, leaving my wife and bairns for what I deemed an inescapable duty. As I journeyed south, I thought of Father and the kindness he had shown me from when I was only a child.

The more I think of it, the more I realise my mother was his only love. His second wife produced his legitimate heirs, of course, but there seemed no genuine love between them. And yet with Maman, he obviously cared for her. When he sent her back to France it was for her own safety; he feared for her life. As a papist and clandestine Jacobite supporter, she might have been vulnerable.

And then when she died so young, he brought her body back and had her buried in the family crypt near his Highland castle, at Wardlaw. The rest of his family were furious, a mere housekeeper – and French at that – to be treated as if she were a lady.

But he was the laird and they could not defy him. That's how he lived his life, provoking and resisting enemies. And now, sadly, this is why I am here, at Tower Hill, to witness his execution.

The trial had been swift; in less than a week Simon Fraser, Lord Lovat, had been convicted of high treason and sentenced to be hung, drawn and quartered. Thank God the king had commuted the sentence to beheading.

He is now so old and infirm I have no idea whether he will even make it unassisted up the steps to the scaffold. How he has managed to live until nearly eighty is a mystery. But still, I shiver as I think of him, riddled with gout and now so blind I doubt he will even be able to see the block on which to lay his head.

How did it come to this? He was, admittedly, a wily old fox, everyone says so. He'd managed to evade the anti-Jacobite brigade successfully for decades. But it had to end some time. His cunning sometimes overstepped the mark and I didn't always agree with him, but who was I, a mere illegitimate son of his, to challenge him. The incident with Annie I still find hard to forgive, even fifteen years later. He had promised me she would come to no harm if I got her involved in the plot to kidnap her mistress. I did not care for her by then, even though she obviously still had feelings for me, but I was aware she was a necessary part in the ploy to rid poor Lord Grange of his shrew of a wife, who was about to betray him to the government.

But father told me that, even though his plan was to have her sent to the Plantations to marry one of his friends there, she had to be disposed of on that very night in Edinburgh. I didn't ask how this happened nor who had the unfortunate task, but he simply told me it was essential for other reasons; reasons that the Cause required. And so, I asked no further questions; she was a means to assist my father's quest and she had served her purpose.

"Move along there. You'll see better over yonder," said a young lad passing. He pointed to a timber stand built up high behind the execution platform. Well, if I had come to see my father meet his Maker, I had better watch the event from a good vantage point, rather than from down here with the milling crowds.

"Thank you," I mumbled and followed the boy. And as I climbed onto the overcrowded stand, I could soon see movement at the other side, as the crowds parted. Dear God, there he was, his body still as portly as ever, his face ruddy from decades of overindulgence and as yet with his silvery grey wig on his head. He was being guided along by two warders.

I felt a sob rise in my throat, but forced myself to suppress it as I watched him ascend the first step up to the platform, with great difficulty. As everyone beside me raised their heads to see him, I could feel bodies jostle and shove, then all at once, I heard timbers creak and the entire makeshift stand on which I stood began to shudder. And suddenly I felt myself hurtling down, amid a flurry of bodies, towards the ground.

James

There was a terrible commotion over at the other side of the execution platform, a sudden crashing as wooden planks smashed down from the stand opposite me. Amid great clouds of dust, bodies and planks of wood were flung down to the ground. Unless one fell on top of another body, those involved must have been badly injured, or perhaps died, I imagined. There was a break in the proceedings as the guards went over and pulled out the injured and the dead.

I turned to see Lovat reach the top step and I then watched as he sank into the chair up on the scaffold. A man who had also climbed the stairs behind him whispered in his ear and I saw Lovat's fleshy body begin to wobble. Was it emotion at the sadness of the deaths of those come to witness his own execution? No, it was not. One by one we spectators realised he was shaking with mirth. He had always had an idiosyncratic and warped sense of humour. It certainly did seem ironic that people who had lined up to watch his execution should die shortly before he did.

I was near enough the scaffold – though thank God not as close as those poor souls who had been at the other side – and was able to recognise the man behind him as William Fraser, his solicitor from Edinburgh. I was so relieved he'd asked Old Willie and not me to be up there with him. It made sense, as he was a distant cousin and handled all of his affairs. Since I had remarried, I had not seen my old friend as much, as I spent more time in London these days.

Lovat removed his hat and handed it to Willie. He then used two hands to pull off his wig and also gave that to him. Finally, he pulled a purse from his pocket and gestured to the executioner to approach. He handed this to the man, who opened it and peered inside. The coins in there were obviously substantial enough to persuade him to go for a clean chop, as he bowed in acknowledgment. Lovat then pointed to the axe in his hand and the man brought it before Lovat who reached out an arthritic hand to feel the edge, before nodding.

He then lifted his bald head, shut his eyes and intoned a prayer, which I could hear over the sudden hush of the crowd. It ended with the words: "Forgive me, Father, for I have sinned."

Then he loosened his necktie and the collar of his shirt and laid his head on the block. He pulled out a handkerchief from his pocket and raised it, a sign for the executioner, presumably, to wait. After what seemed like hours, but was probably no more than a minute, he threw his handkerchief on the floor and the executioner swung his axe. With one clean blow, Lovat's head was off and the crowd began to cheer.

I swallowed and looked at the scaffold, where my friend's body lay prone, his bloodied head on a cloth in front of the block. I muttered a prayer for his soul and began to turn towards home. The crowds were all jostling towards the scaffold for a closer look, so I had no choice but to pass by those dead spectators – nine of them, I now saw, all laid out in a row behind the collapsed platform.

I peered down through the dust and broken wooden planks at one man in particular. How come he looked familiar. Was it possible that I recognised him? I looked more closely at his face and then it dawned on me: he was one of the men who had worked in The Sheep Heid, often serving us drinks when Lovat and I sat during those many winter evenings, planning and scheming. Lovat seemed to have had a warm rapport with him, even though he was only a servant. Well, what a terrible end to the life of a man who had presumably made the long journey just to pay his respects to someone to whom he'd served refreshments over the years.

I set off for home, thinking about how my Lady Grange would be waiting for me, ready to complain as usual about the inadequacy of some poor servant. She'd no doubt be attired in yet another fine frock and have a glass of claret in her hand as her tirade of moans and grumbles ensued.

I had had no idea that she would spend so much of my money once we were finally married. Her character seems to have altered so much since that day of our nuptials and I find she is seldom seen without a flask of wine nearby. She is also becoming crabbier by the day. I sighed and plodded on, with weary steps, towards my home.

As I turned towards Pudding Lane, I came to Old Bessie's Tavern, where the door was wide open this warm April day. The noise inside was raucous and alluring and the smell of stale ale enveloped me as I entered and headed for a quiet table in the corner, before ordering a glass of brandy with which to toast my old friend Lovat.

The sight of his head dropping onto that cloth and the blood gushing forth had been horrific, but the thought uppermost in my mind was that it could so easily have been me. Had he not formulated the plan to remove Rachel from my life before she was able to denounce me as a Jacobite, that might have been my own execution – but years earlier, as I was never as wily as Lovat;

I would not have evaded capture as often as he did. The man brought my brandy and I raised my glass to toast Simon Fraser, Lord Lovat, and thanked God once more for sparing me.

And as I sat there, anonymous in the gloom, I also thought, as I had done on many occasions since I had married my new Lady Grange, of Rachel and wondered how she fared. Was she still stuck on that far-flung rock with no civilisation? Was she in fact still alive? I hadn't wanted her to suffer too much, that was never my intention; her banishment was for her own good, as well as mine.

With Lovat's death, I now had no way of knowing anything about her circumstances. And she had no means of knowing that she was now a grandmother to young Rachel, who has grown to look so much like her that everyone remarks upon it; it really is uncanny. I just have to hope that her temperament remains gentle and kind and she does not turn into the strong-willed, cantankerous woman whose name she bears.

I called over the man to bring me another brandy while contemplating my blessed life. Then I raised the glass up before me, gazed at the amber liquid and made my next toast. To Rachel.

Epilogue

A group of young girls were dancing a reel up on the hill, their bare feet skipping over the clover and grass. An elderly woman in island dress, her long white hair tied up in a straggly bun, sat on a rickety stool, clapping and dipping her head in time to the tune played by the fiddler boy beside her. She laughed as one girl fell backwards onto the grass after a violent spin and beckoned to them to draw near. She spoke softly to the girls, demonstrated how to hold their hands in the air and then told them to start the dance again.

The old lady's posture was perfect, her back straight, even perched on the low stool. She held some yellow and purple flowers in her hand and she waved these at them as she urged them to try the dance one more time. Once it was done, successfully at last, she stood up and spoke to the girls as the fiddler picked up her stool. Together they walked, picking herbs and flowers from all over the hillside and filled the lady's basket. They looked up to greet some men who were passing by, heavy ropes swung round their shoulders. They were heading towards the cliffs where they would work all day before returning home with their quarry.

The woman and the girls and boy continued on towards the village, where the girls hugged the lady, who smiled and waved them off towards their own homes. The boy took the stool to her door then scampered off with his fiddle.

The elderly lady entered the little house, where a woman took the basket from her and handed her a goblet of meadowsweet cordial. She took it outside and stood looking down onto the bay, where the tide was coming in. She smiled as she gazed out to sea, the water shimmering in the bright summer sun.

Tilting her head, she could hear the waves lapping onto the shingle beach, and she looked above her at the soaring seabirds, listening to their plaintive screeches high up in a cloudless sky. She strained her ears to catch the rhythmic sound of the waulking songs as the village women worked their woven wool in time to the beat. It was all music to her ears.

And then she smiled again.

Author's Notes

I first heard of Lady Grange when I was writing my cookbook on Scotland's islands. In the mighty tome *The Scottish Islands*, by Hamish Haswell-Smith, I was looking at the entry for the Monach Islands, since one of my contacts on Harris, Hamish Taylor, had been a lobster fisherman in the waters near there. From here, I turned the pages to an entry about her in the St Kilda section, where she was also mentioned, and then finally to Skye, where she is allegedly buried.

Lady Grange's life was so full of mystery and intrigue that I was fascinated and began to research much about the subject before starting to write this book, which is a fictionalised account of her life, with probably a happier ending than she in fact had.

Her life was recorded in the eighteenth and nineteenth centuries by male authors who were very much on Lord Grange's "side"; she was a woman after all, with no rights – and unbiddable at that. Yes, everyone said she drank a lot and she had a violent temper, but if she had lived in more enlightened times, would she not have been allowed to rail against the iniquities of a husband with a mistress and the inability to do anything outside her role as mother of nine children? (I have changed some of the historical facts, including her age and the number of children she had.)

History tells us nothing, of course, from her own point of view, so I soon realised I wanted to try to explore how she might have felt, given the awful trauma in her life, both as a child and later as a wife. Her life was initially one of luxury and privilege, then of poverty and destitution.

But this is what we do know about her life, from the records: Rachel Chiesley was born in 1679, one of ten siblings, daughter of Margaret Nicholson and John Chiesley of Dalry. Her father murdered Sir George Lockhart of Carnwath, the Lord President of the Court of Session, after this leading advocate had awarded substantial alimony to be paid to Rachel's mother in a separation settlement. Chiesley confessed to the murder and a mere four days later was hanged at the Mercat Cross in Edinburgh in 1689. Rachel was only ten years old.

In or around 1707, Rachel married James Erskine, Lord Grange, who was soon to become Lord Justice Clerk of Scotland. She has been described variously as sharp-tongued and high-tempered, shrewish, embarrassing, headstrong, inebriated, but also as strikingly handsome, having been beautiful in her youth. There is a portrait painted by Sir John Baptiste de Medina in 1710, which is in the possession of the National Galleries of Scotland.

Samuel Johnson wrote of her confinement on St Kilda that: "If (M'Leod) would let it be known that he had such a place for naughty ladies, he might make it a very profitable island." I do believe this was meant to be humorous.

Between 1709 and 1717, she bore Lord Grange nine children, two – or possibly three – of whom died very young; she also suffered at least two miscarriages. Lord and Lady Grange lived in Niddry's Wynd in Edinburgh and also at Preston House, in East Lothian, whose gardens were so remarkable that visitors flocked to see them from Edinburgh each summer. In 1730, after many marital difficulties, they separated. All of these problems, according to the aforementioned eighteenth- and nineteenth-century authors, were caused by her deficiencies – even though Lord Grange himself was recorded as a womaniser, a drunkard and debauched. James' sister, Lady Jean Paterson, helped bring up the younger children after the separation.

Rachel, unwilling to agree to go quietly, was now also threatening to expose her husband as a Jacobite, which, given his high position within the law and the government, would have been a disaster. He therefore had her abducted, in 1732, first via Stirlingshire to the Monach Islands (called Heskeir) to the west of North Uist in the Outer Hebrides, where she remained for two years. The abduction was both violent and inhumane, and even more so for a lady accustomed to the sophistication of Edinburgh society. From 1734 to 1740 or 1741, she lived, again as a prisoner, on the even more remote island of St Kilda. Then in 1740 or 1741, she was taken to Skye, where she died only a couple of years later.

It was reported on February 14, 2022, by the National Trust for Scotland that ferocious storms had damaged many buildings on St Kilda, in particular a cleit (a circular stone bothy or storage building found only on St Kilda) that was named "Lady Grange's House". Though she lived on these most remote Outer Hebridean islands during the 1730s, the damaged cleit, with its unique turf roof, dates probably from the mid-nineteenth century and was used for storage or as a place of shelter for islanders.

It is worth noting that, though by 1930 when the islands were evacuated for good, there were only thirty-six islanders, in the first half of the nineteenth century there were as many as 200 inhabitants of St Kilda. There are more than 1,200 similar cleits on the main island of Hirta now. It is thought that the damaged cleit incorporated stones from the original house Lady Grange was held in, and the cleit is believed to have been built on the site of her former house. The cleit is being rebuilt using traditional St Kildan methods. A dual Unesco World Heritage site, the tiny archipelago still holds a mystique more than 300 years after her imprisonment there.

There is little documented information about Lady Grange's life after her abuction, but she had managed to write some letters towards the end of her captivity on St Kilda, two of which eventually arrived in Edinburgh. In these, she wrote that she hoped to make peace with her husband and begged to be removed from the island.

Her husband heard about the letters, and so the rescue ship, commissioned by an eminent Scottish lawyer on reading them, arrived too late to St Kilda – Lord Grange had already had her removed to her final place of imprisonment on Skye.

Lord Grange married his long-time mistress Fanny Lindsay in 1745 on hearing of his wife's death. He had managed to evade prosecution for his part in supporting the Jacobite movement and the restoration of the House of Stuart to the throne.

Lord Grange's friend Simon Fraser, Lord Lovat, who was behind the plan to have Rachel kidnapped, was also lucky, evading punishment for being an active Jacobite – until his eightieth year. He was then the last man in Britain to be beheaded. At his execution, a timber stand collapsed, killing nine onlookers and injuring many more – and Lovat was indeed seen to laugh out loud.

Even after his death, rumours grew about the whereabouts of his body. Instead of being laid to rest in the chapel within the Tower of London, his family insisted that he had in fact been taken north and buried in the family crypt at Wardlaw. In 2018, the coffin was opened up by the forensic team from my alma mater, Dundee University, and it was discovered that instead of an elderly man, the body was that of a young woman in her thirties.

I have made much of the part played by Lady Grange's eldest daughter Mary, whom she called "My Angel". She became Countess of Kintore at a young age, but there are no records of whether she or any of her siblings tried to find their mother. I have removed the seat of the Earl of Kintore from Aberdeenshire to the west coast of Scotland, for relative ease of access to the Monach Islands. Some authors write of a "mock funeral" for Rachel just after her abduction and so possibly the children presumed their mother was dead.

I found it interesting that when Skye-born writer Martin Martin was visiting St Kilda in 1698, he wrote of the plants there, including sage, silverweed, sorrel, sea-pink and chicken-weed. He mentioned the "drying and healing quality" of many flowers and herbs and wrote: "The inhabitants are ignorant of the virtues of these herbs; they never had a potion of physic given them in their lives." On other Hebridean islands, there are many herbal remedies recorded, from the flowers and herbs on the machair; but for some reason, there seemed to be little use for herbal remedies on St Kilda at that time.

Mine is a story based on historical fact; but it is written with the freedom that fiction accords. It is a story that tries to imagine the plight of a woman who had no say whatsoever over her destiny. But she was feisty and strong. I like to think, therefore, that, despite the traumatic abductions and loneliness she must have suffered on both the Monach Islands and then St Kilda, she also found happiness, perhaps even love.

The portrait painted of her in 1710 shows a woman not only of striking beauty but one with a steely look that suggests an indomitable character. A flicker of a smile plays around her mouth. Her life may have been tragic, but her story need not have been.

Bibliography

– Barker, Anne: *Remembered Remedies, Scottish Traditional Plant Lore* (Birlinn 2011)
– Burt, Edmund: *Burt's Letters* (Birlinn 2012)
– Chambers, Robert: *Traditions of Edinburgh* (W & R Chambers 1868 edition; first published in 1824)
– Cheape, Jane: *Hand to Mouth, the Traditional Food of the Scottish Islands* (Acair Ltd 2002)
– Foyster, Elizabeth & Whatley, Christopher: *A History of Everyday Life in Scotland 1600–1800* (Edinburgh University Press 2010)
– Glover, Sue: *The Straw Chair* (Methuen Publishing 1997)
– Harrower-Gray, Annie: *Scotland's Hidden Harlots and Heroines* (Pen & Sword Books Ltd 2014)
– Haswell-Smith, Hamish: *The Scottish Islands* (Canongate 2004)
– Johnson, Samuel & Bosworth, James: *The Journal of a Tour to the Hebrides* (1773) (Penguin Classics 1984)
– Kay, Billy & Maclean, Cailean: *Knee Deep in Claret* (Auld Alliance Publishing 1983)
– Macaulay, Margaret: *The Prisoner of St Kilda* (Luath Press 2010)
– Maclean, Charles: *St Kilda: Island on the Edge of the World* (Canongate 1972)
– Martin, Martin: *A Description of the Western Islands of Scotland circa 1695 & A late Voyage to St Kilda 1698* (Birlinn 1999)

– Nenadic, Stana: *Lairds and Luxury* (Birlinn 2007)
– Shand, Alexander: *The Lady Grange* (Smith, Elder & Co 1897)
– Steel, Tom: *The Life and Death of St Kilda* (Harper Collins 1994)
– Stephen, Ian: *Waypoints* (Adlard Coles Nautical 2017)

Glossary

bannock: a round, scone-like bread of barley (beremeal), oatmeal, peasemeal or wheat, baked on the girdle (Scots for griddle)

birlinn: wooden boat used in the Hebrides and western Scotland

boorach: word of Gaelic origin meaning a mess or muddle

clarty: dirty, filthy

close: a passageway, used especially in Old Town Edinburgh

collops: thin slice of meat (beef, veal, venison) usually fried in butter

cottar: a tenant farmer

douce: sweet, pleasant

gawk: to stare idly or vacantly

girn: to whimper or whinge, especially in pain

glaikit: stupid, not very bright

guddle: a mess

hirple: walk with a limp, hobble

hoik: to lift or pull up abruptly

perjink: fastidious or obsessively neat person

powsowdie: sheep's head broth

skelp: a slap or smack

stoup: a flagon or decanter

twilted: archaic version of quilted

wynd: similar to close – an alleyway, used in Old Town Edinburgh

Acknowledgements

Thanks to staff at the National Library of Scotland for their assistance during the long, yet fascinating researching process.

My thanks also go to Maureen Kelly, Heather McHaffie, Donald Maclennan, Judi and John Matheson and Hamish Taylor for their expertise and knowledge.

Thanks as always to my assiduous readers – Anne Dow, Elisabeth Hadden and Isabelle Plews.

And, as ever, my gratitude to agent extraordinaire Jenny Brown, whose guidance is always invaluable and whose patience merits sainthood.

I am also hugely grateful to Sara Hunt for all her support and commitment; to Ali Moore for her diligent and insightful editing; and to Hamzah Hussain for proofreading.